*For my father*

# A

'"A", the noblest, most primordial of all sounds, resonant in the chest and throat; children learn to produce it first and most easily; it is justly placed at the head of the alphabet in most languages.'

The Grimms' Dictionary

# THE ALPHA BET MURDERS

## LARS SCHÜTZ

MANILLA

First published in Germany in 2018 by Ullstein Buchverlage GmbH, Berlin

First published in Great Britain in 2019 by Manilla
80–81 Wimpole St, London W1G 9RE

A CIP catalogue record for this book is
available from the British Library.

ISBN: 978–1–78576–863–7

*Also available as an ebook*

1 3 5 7 9 10 8 6 4 2

Typeset by IDSUK (Data Connection) Ltd
Printed and bound in Great Britain by Clays Ltd, Elcograf S.p.A.

Manilla is an imprint of Bonnier Books UK
www.bonnierbooks.co.uk

# 1

*2ⁿᵈ December, morning*

*Whirring.*

*A burning pain ran down Tugba's back.*

*She knew that sting. Two years ago, she'd had her philosophy of life tattooed on her left arm:* There's no shame in not knowing, only in not learning.

*In Turkish. To commemorate her father.*

*But the man at the studio was trained.*

*He knew what he was doing.*

*Not like her torturer.*

*Again, he drew down the tattoo gun. The needle scraped across her skin. The whirring died away, and something warm trickled down her ribs.*

*She wrenched at the cable ties holding her to the heating pipe. No use. The nylon merely bit deeper into her wrists.*

*The man behind her snorted, giving her a kick in the kidneys. She screamed into the gag: her own underwear, which he'd stuffed into her mouth. She swallowed. Coughed. Choked.*

*Abruptly he rammed a hunting knife into the ground right in front of her eyes.*

*He was going to end it.*

*The certainty sent her mind spiralling back into the past, to memories of her father.*

*Not to the emaciated ghost the cancer had made of him, at the last – but to the man she'd always idolised.*

*It was he who'd persuaded her to become a teacher.*

*How proud he would have been to see her pass her exams with flying colours and earn a place at Montabaur.*

*She stretched and craned her neck back, trying to catch a glimpse out of the window above the radiator. The first light of morning was filtering through the blinds in her apartment. How many hours had he kept her prisoner?*

*The whirring again.*

*Tugba closed her yes. Friday night had started quietly. Putting off checking through her coursework until the next day, she'd made pasta and settled down in front of the TV. The movie, The Notebook, now lay a few feet away on the coffee table. The aroma of spaghetti bolognaise still hung in the air. Innocent reminders of the normality this stranger had so abruptly torn from her.*

*The whirring faded. Her back was on fire. A wave of nausea. She controlled herself, using all her willpower. If she vomited into her gagged mouth, she'd probably choke.*

*Why hadn't she been more cautious? Why had she opened the door?*

*All night long she'd been asking herself those questions. As he tore the clothes from her body. As he hit her again and again. As he drew the tattoo gun across her back.*

*Her skin itched, as though the pain were forcing sweat from every pore. She bit down on the gag, which had long since become soaked with saliva.*

*Her torturer jerked the knife out of the linoleum and wrenched her head back by the hair so hard it felt like he was trying to scalp her.*

*Tugba's breath came in spasms. She expected him to cut her throat. She expected pain. Darkness.*

*Nothing like that.*

*He didn't draw the knife across her exposed throat – instead he cut the cable ties, unbinding her wrists.*

*What was he thinking?*

*She wanted to turn her head. To see him. To look into his face. But he bored his fingers into her neck, pressing her to the ground.*

*He lowered his mouth to her ear. His heavy breath smelled of peppermint chewing gum, and something else. Something barely perceptible. It made her think of cemeteries. Of decay.*

*'The alphabet hasn't got to you yet.'*

*His hoarse voice. Trembling with excitement.*

*What alphabet?*

*She screamed into the gag, but all that came out were inarticulate noises. She writhed.*

*Something hard struck her in the back of the head. The pain was eating into her brain.*

'A!'

*The next blow.*

'B!'

*He sounded like an obsessive priest, the letters like a prayer. Like the pain, they echoed for several seconds inside Tugba's head.*

'C!'

*A dull throbbing clouded her thoughts.*

*Her father's words flashed across her mind:* There's no shame in not knowing, only in not learning.

# 2

*3rd December, morning*

'The bison are going crazy!' The ranger came running up to the window of Enno Buck's jeep before he could even switch off the engine.

'Calm down, Mirco—' Buck knocked back the last gulp of black tea from his thermos.

When he got out, his wellington boots sank up to the ankles in the fresh snow. The icy wind drove thick flakes into his face, which melted on his cheeks.

He never got to the park on time in weather like this. Work started at half seven. By that time the council had barely cleared a fraction of the Westerwald roads.

Picking up his broad-brimmed leather hat from the dashboard, he pulled it down over his forehead. A habit from his year in Canberra. It was the only item of fashion he really cared about.

'Okay, let's take a look. Did you see anything?'

The young ranger shook his head.

Switching on their torches, they tramped off towards the bison enclosure, which was near the car park. Only gradually was the darkness receding, dragging itself through the forest like a dying animal.

Even from a distance they could hear the lowing and stamping of the bison. The torch beams flitted across muted brown hides, making the animals' small eyes glitter. Most of the herd was clustered towards the back of the enclosure.

Buck's heart began to beat faster. Despite the subzero temperatures, he was sweating. The European bison – as tall as a man and weighing up to a tonne, related to the American bison – always filled him with respect. Not fear, respect. He drew a clear distinction.

'Can you see anything?' asked Mirco.

'No.' Buck leant against the fence. 'Unlock it, we're going in. Me first.'

'Shouldn't we wait until they've calmed down?'

Buck ran both hands through his beard, which was turning increasingly grey year by year. 'No time. I want to know right now what's wrong in there.'

His took his keepering job seriously. His job was to protect the animals. From sickness and weather. From greed. From visitors. Sometimes even from each other.

And from whatever was happening in the enclosure.

Clamping the torch between his teeth, Mirco unlocked the gate. It squeaked as he pushed it ajar.

'After you then, boss!'

Buck clapped him on the shoulder and stepped into the enclosure. The snow crunched under his heels with every step.

He stretched out his arm as far as he could, holding the torch fixed on the group of bison.

'Make yourself look big! Don't make any sudden movements!' called Mirco behind him.

One of the bison trotted in their direction, planting itself in front of the herd. It gave off a powerful reek of musk, and it stank of dung. The creature stamped its hooves, lowering its head. It snorted. Thick clouds poured from its nostrils.

'Eeeeasy now!'

Buck raised his palms soothingly and slowly edged around the animal, as though in slow motion.

'Boss, over there!'

Mirco was pointing his torch at the fence to the left. Buck peered over.'

'Bloody hell!'

A hip-height, semi-circular hole. Probably done with a bolt-cutter. Somebody'd been inside – was there still, perhaps.

The bison kept its eye on him; but let them both pass. As they approached the herd, the animals scattered, fleeing into the corners of the enclosure.

Something was lying in the middle of the churned earth where the European bison had gathered. Their torches bathed it in white light.

'Is that a miscarriage?' stammered Mirco.

The bundle of blood- and dirt-spattered skin fragments, exposed flesh and organs had made Buck wonder the same thing.

Until he looked more closely.

Until the metallic, slightly sweet stench of fresh blood eclipsed even the bison's musk.

His stomach turned. The black tea surged back up his gullet. Choking, he forced it back down. He was a keeper; he knew the interplay between life and death. The stinking, bloody reality of existence. Yet he'd never seen anything like this.

What lay before him had once been a human being.

# 3

*3rd December, afternoon*

'Where are you?' asked Miriam down the phone. 'I've been standing outside your door for half an hour!'

'In the car.' Jan sighed. 'Work rang.'

'On a Sunday?'

He didn't answer straight away; he was concentrating on moving into the outside lane. In half an hour he was expected at the police headquarters in Montabaur, where he had a meeting with the Superintendent. Lucky for him the A3 was so empty today.

'My deepest apologies for not informing you,' he said ironically. 'I didn't imagine my day turning out like this either.'

'Is it a murder?' The sixteen-year-old rarely sounded so euphoric.

Jan didn't reply.

'That's a yes, then,' said Miriam. 'But what do they want with *you*?'

'That, dear Anarchist, is what I'd like to know.'

'Stop calling me Anarchist.'

'Then stop acting like one.'

He squinted. He could almost see the outline of Montabaur Castle on the horizon. The exit couldn't be far.

'To what do I owe the honour of your abortive visit?' he asked.

'I'm in trouble,' she said, sounding extremely sheepish, by her standards.

'I expected nothing else.'

Miriam was a runaway who'd been eking out an existence on the streets of Mainz for two years. He'd questioned her once as a witness in a missing persons case. During his career as a behavioural investigative advisor – or profiler, as most people called his job – he'd only been called in on a few murder investigations. Until today, at least.

At first, he'd tried to make Miriam go back to her parents, but she'd given him very plausible reasons – mainly because of her dad – why that was impossible. She still baulked at the idea of a home or a foster family.

Yet Jan had won her trust, and ever since she would occasionally drop by to sleep on his sofa, work through his film collection or empty his fridge – complaining about his all-vegan selection.

He wasn't a father figure, and he didn't want to be. He was simply a friend who looked out for her.

As they talked, he had taken his foot off the accelerator slightly: not a good idea in the outside lane. An Audi was tailgating him, flashing its headlights to indicate that the driver thought he was going too slowly.

Jan rolled his eyes and pulled back into the inside lane. He had to take the next exit anyway.

'What's happened this time?' he asked.

'There's these two guys I owe money to,' she said, pausing. Evidently, she was waiting for a reproof.

His silence was enough. She knew exactly what he was thinking.

'I can pay them back next month, just not right now. And I spent it on something decent, by the way . . .'

'I don't want to know what you spent it on, okay?'

A year ago, he'd found a bag of magic mushrooms in her leather jacket. He'd never been so furious with her as at that moment. So furious and so disappointed. Although he couldn't tell whether he was more disappointed in her or in his abilities as a psychologist.

'Anyway, they're after me,' continued Miriam. 'They don't know I stay at your place sometimes. I just have to keep my head down for a couple of days. Please!'

He steered around the roundabout at the train station. The last time he'd been here, it hadn't existed. He didn't even want to know how much had happened elsewhere in the Westerwald.

You always thought home wouldn't change. That it would stay like it was in your memory. But sometimes it changed more than you did yourself.

'So?' Miriam jolted him back from his reverie.

Jan jumped, almost taking his hands off the wheel. Driving always tired him. He put *Get coffee!* at the top of his mental to-do list. 'Sure' he said. 'Key's under one of the big white stones to the right of the path.'

'Not exactly burglar-proof,' replied Miriam. He heard stones clattering in the background. 'Aha, got it!'

'Don't complain. You wouldn't be able to get in without it.' He'd been planning to invite her over for Christmas anyway – who else could he spend the holidays with? He liked it when she came to stay. She drove away the silence. 'But don't let anybody in. Put the blinds down at night. And don't turn up the stereo again! The neighbours—'

'Oh, the line's getting bad,' she fobbed him off. 'Talk to you later. Byeeee!'

'Miri—'

All he could hear was the dialling tone. She'd hung up. He smiled and removed the phone from between his shoulder and ear. 'You little beast—'

Both hands back on the steering wheel, he turned into the train station car park. It was so big it could have belonged to a stadium for a second-division football club. During the week, commuters left their cars there before taking the express trains to work in Frankfurt or Mainz. Now, it was yawningly empty.

Sighing, Jan looked at the radio clock. 3.26 p.m.

Rabea would have arrived on the train from Basel twelve minutes ago.

When he thought about the awful mood she must be in right now, that was definitely twelve minutes too long.

# 4

Delayed. Obviously.

Goddammit, what else had she expected?

The train had been in the tunnel for half an hour.

Rabea puffed the air out of her cheeks and sank deeper into her seat. For the umpteenth time she flicked through her newspaper, so bored by now that she was reading the financial pages.

That weekend, she had been to visit her family in Switzerland, for the first time in six months.

As if some higher power were pranking her, the Rheinland-Pfalz State Office of Criminal Investigations had ordered her and Jan to Westerwald today of all days.

Accordingly, Jan had sounded apologetic when he'd phoned and woken her that morning. 'I'd be happy to do it by myself,' he'd muttered, 'but I can't manage without your gift for observation. You're the best assistant out there.'

Despite the flattery, she'd chucked her phone into the corner of the room.

Maybe she should have flipped Jan and the department the bird and simply continued her long weekend in the Emmental. Yet something about this case had caught her attention. Something she couldn't explain to her mother as she dashed pell-mell out of the house.

A jolt. The train was back in motion. In her second-class compartment there was a murmur of surprise. The bald man in the pinstripe suit, who'd been asleep since Freiburg and had a thread of spittle dangling from his mouth, gave an indignant snort.

'About time,' muttered Rabea, putting the paper down.

She really needed her own car.

Rabea stood up, although after the long journey she'd practically fused with the seat. Balancing on her tip-toes, she reached for her suitcase on the luggage rack.

A wiry man, a classic wannabe alpha type, came over and stood in front of her. 'Pretty lady like you doesn't have to do that by herself,' he cooed.

Rabea demurred, pulled out the handle of her suitcase and fled towards the exit.

She'd been on a diet since the beginning of the year – which for her basically meant drastically reducing her consumption of chocolate. Men had been approaching her more and more recently, including ones like that guy – easily twenty years older than her – whom she could have done without.

The train drew into the station with a squeal of brakes.

Montabaur. Before this case, Rabea had only known the place from motorway signs.

The wind whipped snowflakes into her face as she stepped out onto the icy surface of the platform. Only a few people were getting on and off here, and a single scan of the platform revealed Jan Grall. Visibly freezing, he was leaning against an advertising billboard, his hands buried in the pockets of his black pea coat.

As she walked towards him, it struck her afresh how tall he was. Well over six foot six; he might be the tallest man she knew. At the same time, he was so lean he reminded her of a stick insect. At thirty-eight, he was seven years older than her, but it could have been decades. As ever, his sharply chiselled face was so pale that he looked ill.

'Glad you came,' he said as she approached. 'It was far from a given.'

'I'd hope not. First off, I need a coffee.'

'I got you one already, it's waiting for you in the car.' He smiled cautiously.

They shook hands. It was the most they could ever bring themselves to do.

'You can make up for your holiday as soon as we're done here. I'll sort it out.' Without asking, he took her suitcase and carried it up the steps to the main concourse.

Something stirred in Rabea's memory. A fleeting remark he'd once made. 'Westerwald. You're from around here, aren't you?'

'Yep.' It was unmistakeably clear from his gaze he didn't want to discuss it.

She wasn't that easily fobbed off. 'Is that why we were the ones they dragged out here?'

Jan was silent. Their steps echoed through the vaulted concourse; its modern architecture seemed out of place in the rugged landscape.

'There was one thing I didn't miss in Switzerland,' said Rabea. 'Having to drag every ounce of information out of you bit by bit.'

'Fine,' sighed Jan. He stopped short just before the swing doors to the car park. 'A man has been killed in a particularly sadistic manner. There's an anomaly. That's why the police need a behavioural analysis team.'

'The "A" on his chest,' said Rabea tonelessly.

Jan nodded. 'And we're that team. Those are the facts. Don't think there's any more to it than that.'

He hurried out through the door.

Rabea shook her head and smiled wearily. Jan was a good judge of character, but he'd always been a terrible liar.

She followed him out into the cold. He'd stopped a few yards away and was on his antiquated mobile phone.

'Got it. Be there in two ticks.' He hung up and turned to Rabea. All the shine had drained from his dark eyes.

'That was Detective Chief Superintendent Stüter,' he said. 'There's a second body – "B".'

# 5

If Jan Grall had been pressed to say what he missed most about Westerwald, it would be the expansive landscape. Mainz had plenty to see, but not this miles-wide view of fog-shrouded hills.

Rabea drew his attention away from the valley. 'Could you please stop staring out of the window when you're driving?'

'Don't worry, I've driven down here a thousand times,' said Jan. Still, he did as she asked and fixed his gaze back on the road to Marienberg.

'Including on ice like this?' Usually, Rabea Wyler was careful to suppress her Swiss-German accent, but when she got as agitated as she was now, Jan could hear it clearly.

'Absolutely on ice like this,' he replied, grinning. 'That was always the most fun ... but let's run through what we know so far quickly. Maybe the whole thing will make more sense once we've talked it over.'

That wasn't the real reason – he had to distract himself.

'I read through the scraps of information they sent me from the department in Koblenz on the train; that's all I've got.'

'Doesn't matter.' He switched off the radio. It was only playing some Lady Gaga plastic pop anyway.

Rabea grabbed her shoulder bag from the back seat, rummaged around inside it and took out her iPad. 'The letter "A",' she said. 'Apparently it was tattooed onto the skin. Right now, we don't know whether it was done post mortem. And now there's another body with the letter "B". A serial killer?'

'Could also be a double murder with two different dump sites,' interjected Jan.

Still, he'd asked himself the same question, and many others besides. Why did it have to happen here? Why in his home town, a place he'd never wanted to return to?

As he mused, he navigated the roads unconsciously. Although he hadn't been here for years, he knew every turning and every pothole.

Rabea ran a hand through her short blonde hair and took a big gulp of coffee. Jan noted her smile of pleasure with satisfaction. Two sugars and far too much milk; he'd dosed it perfectly.

'The site where the body was found is unusual. A wildlife reserve. Why go to such effort and risk? Then the letters,' said Jan. 'But first let's look at the site. As you know, we're not interested in what the killer had to do—'

'—but what he *didn't* have to do,' she completed one of his behavioural-analysis watchwords.

'Aren't you glad to be back at last?' Rabea brought the conversation back to her new favourite subject.

Jan growled, squinting as though he was concentrating solely on the drive through Bad Marienberg.

'Still don't want to talk about it, eh?'

'Imagine that.'

Rabea shrugged and wolfed down an energy bar. They seemed to be her sole source of nutrition these days. Unlike her, Jan had never had to think much about what he ate. Since he'd become a vegan, he looked almost anorexic.

They drove into town via Langenbacher Strasse. To their right, on the slope of Schorrberg Mountain, stretched Bad Marienberg Cemetery. This deliberate positioning of the graves above the valley gave the impression that the dead could oversee the activities of the living.

Jan's hands closed convulsively over the wheel. He knew some of the names engraved on the stones up there. Names he'd been trying to forget for years.

Taking narrow side roads, they drove up out of the valley. The higher they climbed, the thicker the fog. Detached houses with carefully tended front gardens were arrayed cheek-by-jowl. The only person Jan saw was a stooped old man being dragged limply along the pavement by his Labrador.

'Is it always this bustling?' asked Rabea.

'It's Sunday. Not like there's much going on in Mainz right now either.'

On Westendstrasse, Jan threw a glance back towards the valley. Only the evangelical church was visible, rising out of the sea of fog like a lighthouse.

They made for the wildlife park. Even from a distance, Jan could see the outline of the park's hotel, situated majestically above the surrounding fields and woods like the seat of some landed aristocrat.

'Is that the place they've put us up?' Rabea pressed her nose to the glass.

'That's right. The first house on the square.'

'I'm honoured – hang on, is that a panoramic restaurant up there?'

Again, Jan nodded. He could already sense his reluctance to eat there. The idyllic view would awaken memories he'd put to bed years before.

They turned into the wildlife reserve car park, just behind the hotel complex. There were already several police cars and a forensics van parked on the gravel.

Jan's parents had often brought him here as a child. As he climbed out of the car, he noticed the familiar smell of damp hide and dung overlaying the fresh scent of the nearby forest.

'Cold here,' shivered Rabea, zipping her fleece up to her chin.

Jan didn't even nod agreement; he merely turned up the collar of his coat. Even after all these years, he'd not forgotten the polar climate.

They set off towards the enclosure in silence, accompanied only by the sound of their footsteps crunching along the snowy gravel path.

The bison's large enclosure was immediately adjacent to the car park. At least a dozen forensics technicians in white overalls were trampling through the slush beyond the wire fence. A large white plastic tent had been erected above an area towards the back of the enclosure. It protected the site both from the weather and, mainly, from curious onlookers.

Only now did Jan notice the bison being held back by three rangers. Hopefully the men knew what they were doing. He didn't fancy getting better acquainted with the creatures' horns.

A group of people had already gathered outside the fence, mainly pensioners with their dogs and young families. The usual park visitors. Some were probably also guests at the Steigalm, the café directly opposite the enclosure.

With an audience like that, it wouldn't be long before the media got wind of the case.

Just as they reached the enclosure, a portly uniformed officer emerged through a small gate in the fence.

'Nothing for you to see here,' he announced to the gawkers, waving his arms. 'Move along, please!'

'It's a free country! I'm allowed to stand where I want!' came the croaky response from one silver-haired senior.

The officer's face went scarlet, but before he could come up with a reply, he saw Jan and Rabea approaching. 'You're the profilers, aren't you?' he called. His expression brightened. 'Then we'll be able to move the body soon. The bison are getting restless.'

Jan gulped. Great. He even forgot to correct the officer – they were called behavioural investigative advisors, not profilers. The term gave people the wrong idea.

As soon as they were inside the enclosure, the officer bolted the gate and relocked the padlock. 'Better safe than sorry,' he grunted. 'Don't want the hacks showing up in here.'

They marched across to the crime scene. The closer they got, the more Jan was gripped with a creeping sense of apprehension. The forensics technicians, looking like ghosts in their overalls, spoke only in whispers.

The tent opened. A tall man emerged and strode towards them. As he unzipped his disposable overalls, he revealed a tailored black suit.

'So, you're the psycho experts, eh?' said the bald-headed man. He shook their hands. 'Stüter. We spoke on the phone.'

His handshake was so firm that Jan's fingers almost felt like they were broken.

Stüter was so hairless, he looked as though he were seriously ill. There wasn't a single hair on his head. That, and his rotund build, made him look like a white billiard ball.

Jan knew plenty of policemen like Stüter. Experienced officers over fifty, who took a dim view of new investigative methods. Especially of people like Jan, who drew up psychological profiles of the criminals instead of looking for what they considered tangible evidence.

'Frau Ichigawa from the department at Koblenz suggested we call you in,' explained Stüter, as if some apology were necessary. 'There's a media scrum in store for us, and she probably thinks we'd make a bad impression without outside help.'

'Ichigawa?' Jan's pulse raced. 'Anita Ichigawa?'

'That's the one. Not many people with names like that round here. Do you know each other?' asked Stüter. 'The lady made Senior Chief Superintendent in the Major Crimes Department at lightning speed. Of course, that's why they named her head of the special investigation team.'

'We can argue about wounded pride later,' replied Jan. 'We're here to advise and support you and your people. I have no intention of muscling in on your investigation.'

Stüter raised his eyebrows, the only remaining hair on his head. 'You didn't say whether you knew Frau Ichigawa.'

Rabea, too, was gazing at him with interest, one eyebrow raised.

'Not well. Now, I'd like you to tell me about the body.' Jan groaned inwardly; he missed Anita.

Stüter ran a hand over his shiny scalp. 'There's astonishingly little to tell about our first corpse. We've got no idea who the guy is.'

The Chief Superintendent turned around and strode back to the tent. Outside, he handed each of them shrink-wrapped overalls, gloves and plastic overshoes. 'You know the drill. Wrap yourselves up first.'

His arms folded across his chest, the Chief Superintendent watched as they wriggled into the cumbersome white suits. By the time Jan was pulling on his overshoes, Rabea was ready and waiting. His back cracked alarmingly as he did so.

'Always an undignified spectacle,' said Stüter after they were done, holding the tent flap aside. 'After you.'

So far, Jan had only seen a few bodies and he wasn't eager to see more. No matter how much you compartmentalised, being confronted with blood and death never left you unscathed. His last visit to the scene of a murder had been a robbery-homicide at a petrol station. A clean gunshot wound to the chest from close proximity. Lots of blood, but no gore.

This – this was different.

The naked man lay on his back, his arms and legs stretched out at awkward angles. Dried blood and muck were sticking to his pale, hairy body, and it took Jan a few moments to see the tattooed 'A' on his sternum.

'We assume that the body's been lying in the reserve for several hours,' said Stüter. 'So long that the bison have trampled it a few times.'

Rabea audibly suppressed a retch. Queasiness was building in the pit of Jan's stomach, too. He found it hard to breathe the stuffy, exhausted air of the tent.

Bloody hoof prints criss-crossed the man's body. His genitals were crushed, dozens of bones were shattered, and his belly had been slit open by a sharp-edged hoof or object. All the head lacerations and dirt made it difficult to judge his age.

'Fifty-ish,' he said. 'Cautious estimate.'

'The cause of death,' said Rabea, swallowing, 'the cause of death is the wound on his head, right?'

Stüter, who was kneeling in the mud next to the body, confirmed it. 'At least, that's our working hypothesis. Only the coroner will be able to say for sure. Ichigawa is arranging an immediate autopsy.'

Stüter looked up at them. His complexion was the same colour as the corpse's. 'Blunt force trauma. Maybe a hammer. Somebody hit him on the head until his skull shattered.'

'It couldn't have happened without a fight,' said Jan. 'Did you find anything? Skin fragments under the fingernails? Scratches?'

Stüter gingerly raised the dead man's right hand towards his face. 'I can't say, as yet. But it's possible.' He turned to Jan. 'My people are checking the missing persons register and making inquiries in the area. I don't think it will be long before we identify the victim.'

'Definitely. All the neighbours know each other round here.' Jan knew that all too well. He must have provided fodder for whispered conversations over coffee tables for years.

Stüter took it as an opening to ask about his origins. 'The way you talk. You come from around here. Where, exactly?'

Jan's heart jolted. The tent seemed to be getting smaller by the minute. He'd hidden his Westerwald dialect as well as he could – what had given him away?

'I come from Hardt,' he replied.

'That's just around the corner!' For the first time, the Chief Superintendent's expression brightened. 'What a coincidence they sent you here.'

Yeah, thought Jan. What a coincidence. He crouched down beside the dead man, noting the whitish livor mortis on the knees, lower abdomen and wrists. After he was killed, the victim had initially been lying on his stomach. 'He was already dead when he was dragged into the enclosure.'

Stüter nodded. 'He's definitely been moved. No surprises there. The rangers found a hole in the fence, and we identified drag marks from that point to here.'

'Any footprints?' asked Jan.

'Wiped away somehow and covered with new snow. He didn't want to make it easy for us.'

'Even so, we've got to see everything. The dump site and murder site are both at the heart of behavioural analysis,' added Rabea. 'Everything the killer did here, every decision, says something about him. About his impulses. His planning. Whether his violence is functional or compulsive.'

'Don't explain your job, just do it,' grunted Stüter.

Ignoring him, Rabea gazed closely at the tattooed letter 'A'. Jan followed her eyes. He didn't know much about this form of body art. He'd never even seen the inside of a tattoo parlour, let alone ever considered getting one. Still, even he could tell the tattoo was amateurishly done, the lines shaky and blurred, the ink already faded in several places.

'Looks like an amateur,' he said.

Rabea looked up. 'Or he wants to make it look that way.'

'Good point.' He smiled at her.

'A tattoo is like thousands of tiny stab wounds,' continued Rabea. 'This is still damp, no healing. We'll wait for the autopsy, but this looks post mortem.'

'Much easier to work on a corpse, too,' mused Jan. Was that the only reason? Or was the tattoo the final act in his process? A kind of signature?'

Shouts reached them from the back of the enclosure. Rabea pulled the tent flap aside. One of the bison was trotting towards a ranger, snorting, and only stopped at the last moment.

It was time they left.

Stüter was scratching his neck, stooping over as though hoping the solution to the case would fall out. 'As I said, the dump site doesn't give us much. Next to those beasts over there are the ranger and keeper who found the body. Maybe you'll have more luck with them than we did. After all, you're the psychologists so maybe you know a few tricks. If you'll follow me!'

'As long as we're not going to be trampled to death,' muttered Rabea, glancing at the bison. Then she whispered to Jan, "What does he mean, tricks? We're not circus magicians!'

'Just ignore him.'

With every step they took closer to the animals, the stench of wet hide and dung grew stronger. One of the bison noticed them and began snuffling and scratching with its hooves.

The ranger, who was standing with his back to them, spread his arms wide and said something soothing.

Jan's heart dropped into the pit of his stomach like a lead weight.

'Enno Buck?' asked Stüter.

The man closest to him turned around. Over his checked shirt he wore dirty dark-blue dungarees. Jan estimated his age at around fifty-five. His hair was streaked with grey, and his weather-beaten face was a fine tangle of creases. The broad brim of his leather hat threw a shadow across his face that reached to the tip of his nose. Intelligent eyes flashed from the semi-darkness beneath.

'Gentlemen, lady. What's up?' His Westerwald accent sounded slightly nasal.

'Stüter, Chief Superintendent. An officer asked you to wait for me. These are my colleagues Grall and – and –' He clicked his fingers, trying to recall Rabea's name.

'Wyler,' she prompted.

'Right, Wyler – we'd like to ask you a few questions. Herr Grall, if you would?'

Stüter evidently wanted to test him, but a routine interview didn't offer much opportunity to use psychology. Instead, Jan turned to the classics. 'When did you find the body?'

Buck shrugged. 'This morning. Round half seven. My colleague Mirco checked the enclosure and noticed the bison were very disturbed. Means something had upset them. They're actually a pretty calm lot. So, we went straight in to take a look and found the body.'

'Did you notice anything strange this morning? Did you see anyone? Try to remember even insignificant details.'

'Nope, nope!' He shook his head. 'Everything as per usual. Actually—' he cocked his head. 'Hang on, I do remember something. But that was two, three weeks ago.'

Jan pricked up his ears.

'In the fallow deer enclosure – a young animal, lying a little apart, hidden under leaves and branches. Somebody'd cut its throat. And tattooed a circle on its belly.'

Jan exchanged a glance with Rabea. The same killer. They were dealing with someone unpractised with death. He'd tried it out on animals first.

'Who has access to the enclosures apart from the keepers?' Stüter had a characteristic way of lifting the right corner of his mouth after he'd asked a question.

'Anybody, basically. At night, the park is only protected by one guard. And he didn't notice anything. You don't exactly have to be an athlete to climb over the fences.'

Jan could attest to that. Awkwardly, he thought back to the night when he and a couple of school friends had drunkenly climbed over the fences and ridden a poor goat as though they were in a rodeo. 'Did you document the animal's body at all?' Stüter took a notepad out of his inside pocket. At least he hadn't switched to using a tablet, like Rabea.

'We took photos. We'd have let you lot know if it happened again.'

'You don't seem that upset,' remarked Rabea suddenly.

There was no note of accusation in her voice, but Buck's face reddened. 'What do you think we do here all day? We work with animals. Of course, I was shocked – but it's not the first time I've seen blood and death.'

Rabea nodded and murmured an apology but added another question: 'Deer are quite shy. How could the killer have managed to get close enough to one? Unless—'

'—unless it knew him?' Buck finished the sentence for her. His face was glowing a deep scarlet. 'You really want to throw suspicion on the keepers, eh? Well, let me tell you something. This place makes most of its money from selling boxes of food that visitors can use to coax the animals towards them.'

'So, it could have been anybody,' said Jan.

# 6

They left the enclosure and stepped back onto the path, where the group of onlookers was growing. A man with a crewcut was even carrying his young daughter on his shoulders so that she could see better.

As they elbowed a path through the crowd, a woman wearing black trousers and a denim jacket came towards them. A digital camera hung around her neck.

'That's all we need,' sighed Stüter. 'Nora Schneill from the local rag.'

The reporter was making a beeline for the Chief Superintendent, her phone out and recording. 'Rolf, can you tell me anything about the discovery of the body?'

'No, I can't,' snapped Stüter, barging past her and through the throng. 'There'll be a press conference this evening, and you can ask questions then. Now, if you'll excuse me – I've got an investigation to attend to!'

Nora Schneill pouted, making her pretty, oval face even more attractive. Before Jan had time to wonder why she and Stüter were on first-name terms, she was holding the phone under his nose. 'Are you and your colleague the behavioural investigative advisors from Mainz?'

'I can answer that question with a yes, but your next one – whether I can tell you anything about the body – with a no, and I'd also like to ask you how you knew we were here.'

This time she didn't pout; her eyes widened. Jan grinned. He liked piling as many clauses as possible into his answers, leaving his interlocutor temporarily speechless.

'Well, still – if you change your mind, this is how to reach me.' She flashed a business card and pressed it into his hand, again with a broad smile.

'I'll take you up on that,' he said, tucking the card into his pocket. Then he re-joined Stüter, who was clearing a path through the gawpers like a berserker.

'I'm surprised Lünner from the Marienberg paper hasn't shown up yet,' grunted the Chief Superintendent when they finally emerged from the crowd. 'He's normally first to hear about this stuff. And he's even more unbearable than Schneill.'

'I thought she was very nice,' confessed Jan.

A uniformed officer approached them. 'Shall we go to the next site?' he asked, his walrus moustache bobbing. 'It's only a ten-minute walk to Basalt Park, but hardly anybody wants to risk going down in snow like this. Probably why the body wasn't discovered sooner.'

They crossed the car park, where the coroner's vehicle was just pulling up, and walked down Kurallee. On the right-hand side loomed a spindly steel tower, which caught Rabea's eye. 'What's that? A watchtower?'

Stüter gave a hoarse laugh. 'No, just an observation deck. The Hedwig Tower. Can't see much in this fog, though.'

A lot had changed since Jan had left. 'When did they put that up?' he asked.

'Five, six years ago,' answered Stüter. 'You've been gone a while, eh?'

'Time doesn't stand still anywhere,' remarked Jan laconically.

It seemed to him that the fog had settled not just in the Westerwald peaks but in his mind. Too many memories, too many feelings came pelting down; he couldn't think straight.

Hypersensitivity. A blessing and a curse. A constant source of stress in his life. He urgently needed peace and quiet.

Thankfully Rabea interrupted his thoughts. 'We know a few things already.'

'Yeah? What've we got so far?' Stüter's lips vibrated as he exhaled. 'A slaughtered animal in the wildlife park and an unidentified body!'

'We've got more than that,' Rabea objected. 'Everything our killer does betrays something more about him. Then we can use those pieces to form a picture.'

'Really?' Stüter had rolled down his overalls to his hips, buttoned up his jacket and was strolling beside her, his hands in his trouser pockets. 'Do tell me about these puzzle pieces!'

'He's no tattoo artist. Or he wouldn't have had to practise on animals.'

'We'll still have to ask a tattooist,' said Stüter. 'Expertise, you see. We've got to find out whether you can tell from a tattoo what kind of implement was used. Maybe we can find out where the killer bought it. What else have you got?'

They dodged a delivery van driving up to the hotel. Coughing the exhaust fumes out of her lungs, Rabea continued. 'Most likely he comes from an unobtrusive and stable environment. He's not accustomed to violence – hence the rehearsal with the animals. Maybe there was a trigger in his recent past that awoke his propensity for murder. That made him plan all this.'

There's a beast inside every human being, thought Jan. Only difference, some of them get woken up.

'That's a lot of "maybes" and "likelys",' replied Stüter.

Rolling his eyes, Jan said, 'We're not reading coffee grounds – this is professional police work. We try to understand why a killer might act in a particular way. If we can identify what motivates them, what they need, then we can identify their background, their age, their sex, their level of education.'

Kurallee led to Westendstrasse, on the other side of which was the expanse of Basalt Park.

'The north entrance is a bit overgrown,' said Stüter. 'Watch out, it's steep.'

They walked down the slope. The former basalt quarry yawned like a meteorite crater in the middle of the spruce forest. A lake, now covered in a fragile layer of ice, had formed inside the pit over the decades. A spiral path, sprinkled with white snow, led down to the bank. Barrier tape was stretched between two pines at the entrance to the path. A gangly policeman leant against the right trunk, glued to his smartphone.

Stüter grunted. 'Think the path's going to watch itself, Inspector Köllner?'

The young man jumped and put the phone away. His freckles and tousled, pitch-black curls gave him the air of an absent-minded philosophy student.

'Oh sorry, just looking something up.'

Stüter seemed to have something against the Inspector.

Jan turned to his freckled colleague. 'Could you tell us something about where the body was found? Where was it lying?'

'You're already off the mark. It wasn't lying anywhere. It was hanging.'

# B

'"B" assumes its important position behind "A" in all the alphabets derived from Phoenician Greek. It is of great significance that immediately following "A", the basis of all vowels, are the three media as the basis and foundation of all mute consonants.'

The Grimms' Dictionary

# 7

*3rd December, late afternoon*

A person's reaction to finding a body depends on two factors: their psychological state and the state of the body.

There are people with stable personalities who collapse when they see someone peacefully lying as though asleep, and there are unstable bundles of nerves who can look at a waterlogged corpse without any issues.

Jan had always been among the hardier type, but when he saw the man's body hanging from a beam in the building on the edge of the lake, he swallowed.

The man was smeared all over with blood and it was only on a second glance that Jan realised he was naked. It took a third look before he saw the 'B' tattooed on the corpse's chest.

The body swayed gently to and fro in the wind, its white, rolled-back eyes gazing down watchfully at the activity beneath it.

Investigators, the soles of their shoes covered in plastic wrap, were walking around. Underneath the body, a woman was kneeling and taking photographs with a digital camera.

Stüter stopped abruptly, staring at the dead man open-mouthed. 'Now we know why Lünner from the Marienberg paper didn't show up,' he said. His voice sounded like breaking ice. 'He can't.'

'That's the journalist?' asked Rabea. She eyed the body. 'Then at least we've identified one victim,' she sighed.

The editor of a regional newspaper and an unknown man in the wildlife park. Jan buried his hands in the pockets of his coat. Probably not a sexually motivated crime, then. According to all the typologies he knew, men were rarely the victims of sex crimes. What was the connection between the two men? Had they known the murderer? Had they been in touch with him? Possibly the connection existed solely in the killer's mind. The FBI talked about unspecific motive killings – murders that only held significance for the murderer. A serial killer could latch onto the tiniest details: the same background, the same style of clothing, the same eye colour. They'd have to check everything.

The woman with the camera had come up to them. A Doctor Who T-shirt peeked out around the collar of her pristine white coveralls. Small R2D2 earrings dangled from her earlobes, and her mahogany-red curls were tied back into a ponytail.

Her serious expression didn't seem to fit with the dimples next to her mouth. 'Dr Diana Harreiter, medical examiner,' she introduced herself. 'You're the behavioural investigative advisors, right?'

She was the first one to call them that without a trace of contempt – she was already gathering brownie points.

'Right, Jan Grall. Are you able to—'

Stüter cut him off. 'Just so we're clear, you're here to advise. That means you only jump in when you think you know something about the killer's mental state.'

'Of course.' He preferred not to retort, knowing that a tussle with the Chief Superintendent would get him nowhere.

'Right,' grunted Stüter, visibly content once more with himself and the world, 'are you able to tell us anything yet? Where did all this blood come from?'

Harreiter shook her head. 'To determine time of death I'll have to examine rigor mortis and livor mortis. For that we'll have to get him down, but first the crime-scene technicians have got to finish. And the advisors have to see the site in its original state.'

'Does it help you at all to leave the poor man swinging up there?' Stüter turned to them both.

'Naked and strung up,' said Rabea. 'More like an execution than a murder. A public humiliation. Especially if the cause of death wasn't strangulation.'

'I have nothing to add to that. It's true of the site at the enclosure, too. The deceased had been trampled by animals. A similarly humiliating end,' said Jan. 'Cut the rope.'

Stüter nodded to one of the technicians, who fetched a ladder. Two others spread a white body sheet underneath the hanged man.

The technician climbed the ladder, took out a pocket knife and sawed away at the thick hemp rope.

Jan hopped from one leg to the other to keep himself warm. Didn't they have professional equipment for this sort of thing? Endless minutes passed while the man worked, using his small knife.

'What do you know about Herr Lünner?' Rabea asked the Chief Superintendent. 'As an editor, he must have made enemies.'

Stüter cocked his head and observed the dead man. 'He was a paragon of an investigative journalist. As dedicated as it's possible to be, but somehow he never made it out of the provinces.'

'What exactly do you mean by investigative? Did he find out the beer was being watered down at the village fete?'

Jan threw his assistant a reproving glance, although he had to stifle a laugh.

'Enough joking around there, Heidi.' Stüter's mouth twisted like a wolf's. So, he'd noticed Rabea's accent. 'A few weeks ago, Lünner printed a series of articles about how several town councillors were siphoning money meant for the new bypass into their own pockets.'

Jan looked up at the dead man and clicked his tongue. The technician had nearly cut through the rope. A few more threads tore with a groan and the corpse was hanging from the last one.

'He'd have made a lot of people very angry. Maybe—'

Rabea was about to continue, but Jan put a hand on her shoulder and shook his head. He knew exactly what she was going to say: that somebody had decided to do away with the journalist and only committed the other murder to lay a false trail. It was best she kept that hypothesis to herself for a while.

Understanding, she bit her lip. The red-haired medical examiner looked from one face to another, quietly grinning, until somebody behind them cried, 'Herr Stüter! You need to see this!'

A technician in white overalls stepped out through the doorway of the building, holding a crumpled piece of paper the size of a poster in his gloved fingers.

'Where'd you find that?' Stüter took it gingerly. Köllner, Rabea and Jan drew in around him. There was something on the paper. A few printed letters in various fonts; judging by the colours of the paper, they'd been cut from several different books. They were so small Jan couldn't make them out.

'What does it say?' asked Stüter. 'Couldn't he have used letters from the newspaper? At least we wouldn't need a magnifying glass for that.'

Köllner read aloud: 'Happy families are all alike; every unhappy family is unhappy in its own way.'

'Sounds like a quote from a book of poetry.' Stüter scratched his chin.

'I recognise it!' said Köllner triumphantly. 'It's the first line of *Anna Karenina*, by Tolstoy. One of the most famous openings in world literature.'

'I'm too busy for that sort of nonsense,' retorted Stüter. He turned to the blonde technician who'd brought over the piece of paper. 'Where did you find this?'

'It was nailed to the wall on the left when we went inside,' said the man, with a high voice that didn't seem to fit his burly exterior. 'Take a look at the paper. It's not yellowed, and there are no sizeable water stains or patches of dirt. I'd say it's only been there a few hours.'

'Then it was probably left by the killer,' concluded Stüter. He turned to Jan again. 'An educated serial killer, then. Should be able to make something of that, eh?'

'We'll have to check whether he left a similar message at the other dump site. Then maybe we could deduce a pattern.'

Since writing his thesis on what motivated killers like Jeffrey Dahmer or Harold Shipman, who'd killed at least 218 people, Jan had absorbed the profiles of hundreds of serial killers, regardless of nationality or era. As he ran through this archive in his head, he found nothing comparable to this interest in literary symbolism.

Many serial killers came from low-education environments, with exceptions like the co-ed killer, Ed Kemper, who had an IQ of 145. Still, that didn't necessarily mean anything – and it wasn't even clear they were dealing with a serial killer. Perhaps this was simply a double murderer who'd chosen two different dump sites. But then, why the letters?

'Our killer was certainly busy last night,' remarked Jan. 'Both sites are nearby, true, but it would have taken great strength and been a huge risk to kill and arrange both of them in one night. Whatever it is, he values his goal more highly than anything else.'

'His goal?' asked Köllner. 'He's not finished yet?'

'"A", "B" . . . what's next?'

The Inspector's voice was toneless. '"C".'

The rope broke and the corpse hit the sheet with a dull thud. The sound made Jan retch, but he suppressed it with a gulp.

He'd already been feeling nauseous.

Only now did he realise how much he was shivering. The overalls were squeezing the air out of him. The world pelted him, raining symbols. Signals and questions. Tiny nuances that wouldn't let him go. The way somebody had stressed a word. The oppressive rhythm of the hanged man swinging back and forth. The snapping branches. The technicians whispering instructions.

All these puzzles. The labyrinth of hypotheses.

He tried to control his breath. Not now, not now.

For years he'd wondered why he was so sensitive. Why he perceived more than others did. It wasn't until he'd met his mentor at Bochum University that he'd been diagnosed with hypersensitivity, a psychological phenomenon that constantly threatened him with sensory overload.

It had taken him all his student years and great effort to control it, but now it was among his most important tools.

'Everything all right? You're very pale.' Rabea carefully stroked his back. The others stared.

'I'll explain later,' he simply whispered, telling the others, 'It's fine. Just the corpse.'

Another lie.

## 8

'You want to know why I shave myself bald?'

They were driving past the mossy wall of the castle gardens, just entering Hachenburg, when Stüter asked the question. He was sitting next to Jan in the passenger seat of the Mercedes, while Rabea typed information into her iPad on the back seat.

'I'm sure you have your reasons.'

Jan frowned. Why was the Superintendent bringing this up all of a sudden?

He turned onto Alexanderring, the road that ran underneath Hachenburg Castle. That way he'd avoid the narrow streets of the old town centre, where he'd never liked driving.

Although Jan and Rabea had wanted to stay longer at the sites, Stüter had ordered them to the car. Anita Ichigawa had arranged a meeting for the investigation team at the police station in Hachenburg.

It was a good idea to keep appointments with Anita – Jan knew that all too well.

'My father has dementia. It's so advanced that he only recognises me on good days,' said Stüter, answering his own question. He huddled in his seat, bracing his knees against the glove compartment.

'Listen, this is a bit too personal for——'

'No, no!' Stüter waved his hands. 'I prefer it this way. I like to play with my cards on the table. I've got nothing to hide. If you're working with people on a case like this, you've got to trust each other. And this is part of that.'

They joined Saynstrasse. Only a few yards to the police station now. Stüter was beginning to confound Jan's judgement of him. What was this man getting at? In such cases it was most advisable to simply listen.

'The illness, the dementia, began around the same time my father started going grey. It felt to me like that was a sign of mental decline.'

Stüter fell silent, kneading his hands.

'So, you took action? You were afraid of your own decline.'

'Yes. I was afraid of getting older, of creeping decline. Of not being master of my brain, or, God forbid, my bladder. I'm being frank with you, so you don't start trying to analyse me.'

Fear of losing control. That sounded about right. Stüter even wanted to control Jan's impression of him. So, it seemed only logical that he was upset by anything external that forced itself into his system.

Like the investigation team, for example.

'We still don't have a name for the team,' he grumbled. 'Although I'm sure Ichigawa will come up with something

PR-friendly. *Investigation Team Letter Murders, Investigation Team Alphabet Killer, Investigation Team ABC*, something along those lines.'

They got out of the car and crossed the car park. The two-storey, bright yellow police station nestled in the shadow of some fir trees. A completely nondescript official building.

'Have you ever heard of the Black Swan theory?' asked Stüter suddenly. 'Totally unforeseeable events are referred to as "black swans". The nuclear disaster at Fukushima, for example, the discovery of penicillin, or nine-eleven. We often find explanations in hindsight, but we can't predict them. Ever. Even though they have a huge impact. The Alphabet Killer is a "black swan". Someone like that can't be predicted. Can't be decoded. We can only react, never act.'

With those words, Stüter turned away from Jan and followed Rabea, who was already walking towards the station.

Jan caught up with him in a few strides. 'That's why you don't think much of behavioural analysis, right?'

'If you can tell me which people are going to become "black swans", I might revise my opinion.' Stüter paused and looked at him, his eyes narrowed to slits. 'I know the name Grall from somewhere. Something happened, years ago.'

Jan felt a twitch in his right thigh, which rapidly became a warm throb. He compressed his lips. The old wound. Sometimes it would turn up like a bad penny, like an unloved old acquaintance, bumping into you on the street with a spiteful grin.

'You must have got me mixed up with someone else. I don't know what you're referring to.' He grabbed the handle of the police-station door. 'Come on, let's not keep Anita waiting.'

Jan opened the door, but Stüter grabbed his shoulder. 'You're on first-name terms with Ichigawa, I see. You know, for someone who deals with human behaviour day after day, you're a bloody awful liar.'

After the Chief Superintendent had let go of his shoulder, Jan could still feel the unforgiving pressure of his fingers.

# 9

Anita Ichigawa.

Japanese father, German mother. Iron will.

Model investigator with the major crimes squad at Koblenz and model person in general. High IQ, former Olympian in judo, expert in Far Eastern poetry.

If she hadn't made a career with the police, she would certainly have been working at CERN or as a professor at some elite university by now.

Even now, Jan couldn't believe it. He wasn't just back in his old neck of the woods – now he had to tussle with her again as well. It had to be some grotesque nightmare. Some particularly cruel instrument of torture generated by his subconscious.

'As you can see,' said the Chief Superintendent as they walked through the station, 'we're quite small and serviceable here in Hachenburg.'

That was putting it diplomatically. In the narrow lobby they were squeezing through, there was just enough room for a counter and a few yucca plants with dusty leaves. The usual posters on drug prevention and traffic safety plastered the egg-yolk-yellow walls.

'Koblenz is only a few miles further down the road,' said Stüter, his hands buried in his trouser pockets. 'There we'd have more options, the forensics departments on site, the whole shebang. But Ichigawa insisted on hosting the team here. As near to where the bodies were found as possible. So, welcome to our little kingdom.'

He ushered them into a meeting room that had been turned into a makeshift centre of operations. A sheet of A4 paper with the words INVESTIGATION TEAM ALPHABET KILLER was stuck to the door. 'Stupid name,' remarked Stüter in passing. Several desks were scattered across the room, in no discernible arrangement. A tangle of cables connecting the computers led across the carpeted floor like roots. Next to a map of the Westerwald area hung a whiteboard and a large screen with a projector aimed at it.

*Serviceable*. Jan remembered the word Stüter had used. It was a joke that the investigation of such a serious case should be coordinated from such a makeshift space.

Although there were more than a dozen officers scurrying around in the divided room, it didn't take Jan long to spot Anita Ichigawa. As usual, she seemed to radiate her own field of gravity – a source of constant attraction.

She was talking to another officer from Major Crimes. Although she was a head shorter and at least fifteen years younger, she seemed to dominate the conversation effortlessly. She'd always been good at holding her ground with men.

As usual, Anita wore a black trouser suit. Maximum professionalism. The colour black was like a fashionable *leitmotif* running through her wardrobe. Her discipline when it came to clothes held true for other areas of her life, too: no parties, no interest in films, no distractions. Only music by classical composers.

When she saw Jan, Rabea and Stüter approaching, she abruptly fell silent. Anita's fine-featured face didn't seem a day older. She was still enveloped in the scent of Chanel and lemon shampoo. Her eyes sparkled at him in a way he couldn't interpret.

'Jan. I'm glad to see you.'

The words turned him ice-cold; she seemed absolutely sincere, not just polite. He had been prepared for anything except her being pleased to see him.

'As soon as I heard about this strange body being found this morning, I knew we needed behavioural investigative advisors. Good ones. Ones like you. I'm glad I could sort out the formalities with the public prosecutor so quickly.'

Anita's gaze flitted to Rabea. 'She's new, isn't she? Your assistant?'

'My partner.'

Rabea, noticing her expression, stepped closer. She and Anita faced each other, trading barbed words of greeting and appraising glances.

'Jan is a – very interesting partner,' said Anita, her undertone impossible to ignore.

Rabea visibly stifled a laugh.

'How do you want to proceed?' asked Jan, trying to bring the conversation onto safer ground.

'The most important thing is this: if the killer goes hunting again, I want to take positive action. I don't want to be constantly on the back foot. Using the profile you provide, we'll institute a large-scale manhunt throughout the region, the likes of which Germany has never seen. A net we'll keep tightening – until our man's wriggling inside it.'

The corner of Jan's mouth twitched. Anita wanted to use their analysis as a springboard.

Rabea and he sat down at their desks, which were placed exactly opposite each other. Rabea switched on her computer and stared at her cathode-ray monitor as though it was a relic from the Bronze Age. 'Thank God I brought my iPad.'

Meanwhile, Anita had climbed onto an office chair to get an overview of the hopelessly overfull room. Silence fell across the confused groups of officers of all ranks, forensics technicians and people from the prosecutor's office. Only Stüter continued pacing to and fro in front of the whiteboard, like a tiger in its cage.

'What are we waiting—'

Rabea didn't get the chance to finish her sentence. The door swung open and Daniel Köllner burst in, completely out of breath.

'We're waiting for him.' Stüter's eyes followed the Inspector until he'd sat down at his workspace.

'Sorry,' muttered the gangly young man. 'But I—'

'Be punctual next time you attend a meeting,' Stüter interrupted him curtly.

Jan rolled his eyes. The young police officer must have a thick skin if he could put up with this torture day in and day out.

'Let the man talk!' said Anita, her arms crossed.

Stüter gave a minute jerk of his head, which could have been interpreted as a nod, and made an elegant gesture in Köllner's direction.

'I know who the dead man in the bison enclosure is,' began Köllner. His voice was trembling, but he grew more sure of himself with every word. 'I thought his face looked familiar from the newspaper. I made a call in the car and confirmed my suspicions: it's Leonard Ziehner. A publisher from Bad Marienberg. His wife was just reporting him missing.' He rubbed the bridge of his crooked nose. 'When she – when she asked me if her husband was all right, I couldn't tell her. All I said was that we'd be in touch, and then I just hung up.'

There was total silence in the operations room. Even Stüter was simply staring disconsolately at the carpet. Eventually, Anita spoke. 'This changes our plans, of course. Excellent work, Herr Köllner. We now know the identity of both victims. Something to show at the press conference.'

'There's still time before this evening,' said Stüter. 'Why not interview the relatives? Might learn some more information.'

Anita nodded in agreement. It was the first time she and the Chief Superintendent had agreed on anything.

'I'll go to see Herr Ziehner's family.' Rabea raised her hand. 'Although I don't know my way around the area at all.'

Anita leant forward. 'Not a problem. I'll go with you.'

'Then I'll take Mark Lünner's family,' said Jan. 'If you've got no objection, Herr Stüter, I'd like to take Herr Köllner.'

'You can't manage it alone?'

'Somewhere out there there's a guy wandering around who's brutally murdered two people,' interjected Anita. 'Who's to say the killer isn't a family member? It would be silly to send someone in alone.'

'In any case, I'm only here to advise,' said Jan, reminding the Chief Superintendent of his own words, and adding sarcastically, 'Your people should do the real investigative work.'

Stüter grumbled something that sounded like assent.

'Right, then.' Anita clapped her hands. 'We've convened the team for less than ten minutes and already we've got results. Excellent!'

Rabea winked at Jan across the desks. 'Anything strike you?'

He thought briefly, then shook his head. 'What are you getting at?'

'The victims' jobs. Editor and publisher.'

'And the literary quotation—' Jan mused for a few seconds. 'Might be something in it, but it's too prem—'

'Too what? Too premature?' She was pulling on her fleece. 'Our killer's murdered two people in a single night, so far as we know. That's bloody quick. And if your supposition is correct, he's only just begun. We might have no choice but to draw premature conclusions if we want to keep up.'

# 10

'You're Swiss, aren't you?'

Ichigawa's first words since leaving Hachenburg. She seemed tense as she steered the Audi along the flat roads, which glittered like rivers in the afternoon sun.

'What gave me away? The name or the accent?'

Silence had suited Rabea just fine. Her body was crying out for sleep. Arms crossed over her chest, she'd dozed off, listening to a radio report on the murders with half an ear.

Shortly after they entered Bad Marienberg, Ichigawa smiled. 'The name. Sounds pretty Alpine.'

'And I suppose my German's a little broken.' Rabea sat up straight. 'How do you and Jan know each other? When he heard your name, he lost control for a moment. That's—'

'—definitely not his style, I know. We go back a long way. We were together. Briefly. Less than three months. We met when he was still a police psychologist in Mainz, and he helped the Koblenz team negotiate during a hostage-taking. But I've already said too much. I don't want it spread around.'

'Understandable.' Jan Grall and Anita Ichigawa. The sensitive psychologist and the hard-as-nails detective. Rabea tried to picture it. How could that particular combination ever have worked?

'It'll already be a struggle for Jan, just being back here.' Ichigawa ran a hand through her bob.

'What do you mean?'

Ichigawa gave a knowing smile. 'No matter what you do here, you can be sure you'll be remembered for decades afterwards.'

'I think that's what always annoyed me about Switzerland.'

'How long have you been in Germany?'

Ichigawa had stopped at a red light. On their right was a pedestrian zone, with a row of restored half-timbered houses either side. They stared down like older brothers at a dozen wooden huts in the middle – a small Christmas market. Rabea thought she could smell mulled wine and roasted almonds. Sometimes, on the hunt, you almost forgot about the beauty the world had to offer.

'Nearly six months. This place reminds me a lot of Switzerland,' she said. 'Everybody knows everybody. That can be nice, no question. But I like time alone. And where I come from – Emmental – I always felt like I was being watched.'

'You don't get that in a city like Mainz, of course.' The light turned green, and the Audi climbed the road that led out of the valley. 'At the moment Koblenz is enough for me, but I don't want to stay there forever. Why did you come to Germany?'

'Jan brought me in. He dealt with the red tape. Stood up for me.'

'Not bad.' Ichigawa puffed through the gap in her front teeth. 'He really must have seen something in you. How did he find you?'

'I was a student at the Bern ViCLAS Centre when I got his call. He was looking for an assistant and heard about me through a friend with the federal police. We always do a few training modules there.' She tucked a lock of hair behind her ear. 'I think my background piqued his interest.'

'Your background?'

Rabea swallowed drily. A film started playing before her mind's eye. A macabre old classic. A horror flick that had premiered twenty years earlier and was still showing in her nightmares.

*You've got to be strong now, little one.* Her parents' words, always just before the credits. Just before she woke up, drenched in sweat.

'My path was predestined, if you want to put it like that,' she said tersely.

Ichigawa sensed that was all she was going to say. She shook her head barely perceptibly. 'A serial killer. We've had our fair share of nastiness, but not like this. Mothers strangling their kids, husbands sticking an axe between their wife's shoulders. But this – this is the stuff you only read about in American crime novels.'

'Not without reason. Serial murders are actually a very rare phenomenon – rarer in Germany than in the USA.

You're more likely to die in a plane crash or get struck by lightning than run into a serial killer.'

'Try telling that to the victims' families—'

She leant her head against the window. 'That's the tricky thing about probabilities. As vanishingly unlikely as they are, they're still possible.'

Ichigawa turned down a side street, parking outside an enormous property. The front garden was so overgrown it looked like it was trying to hide the one-storey building behind it.

'One more thing, Frau Wyler.' As Ichigawa took the key out of the ignition, the blaring radio fell silent, lending her monotone voice additional weight. 'I know Jan better than you do. He's a brilliant analyst. But he's every bit as dangerous as the people he hunts.'

## 11

Jan took a deep breath of cold, clear air.

The evening sun was already shimmering scarlet on the snow-covered rooftops. Lünner's timber house lay in Fehl-Ritzhausen, an area full of new buildings and about fifteen minutes from Bad Marienberg by car. In summer, at least. With all the snow on the roads, Köllner and he had taken nearly twice that long. He hadn't been there many times before. Just for a few football games as a left-winger against the SG Fehl-Ritzhausen youth team, all of them losses.

'Why did you want me to come with you?' asked Köllner.

His coarse-featured face gave him a crass appearance, but his vigilant grey eyes made it obvious he didn't miss much. Vigilance that prompted him to ask questions like that.

'I wanted to discuss something personal,' replied Jan. They were already standing outside the front door.

'Which was?'

'How do you put up with Stüter?'

The Inspector laughed cautiously, almost as though afraid Stüter was eavesdropping.

'I imagine you two have become firm friends over the past couple of hours,' he remarked ironically.

'Everything you tell me stays between us, rest assured.'

'Stüter's not a bad person.' Köllner shrugged. 'He's a policeman through and through. Old school. If it was up to him, he'd decide everything himself. Which makes him a difficult boss.'

'You're observant. Even so, I respect how stoically you put up with him.'

'He's an old friend of my father's,' explained Köllner. 'My father is a police chief in Wiesbaden. I think Stüter just doesn't want to let him down. He wants to make me a good officer. You studied psychology – shouldn't be hard for you to deal with him.'

'I know people, but that doesn't mean I like them.' Jan nodded at the door. 'Shall we?'

Köllner nodded, puffing air into his cheeks. 'You want to do the talking?'

'I'm afraid you can't avoid delivering bad news in this job.'

'I know, it's just—'

'Fine, I understand,' replied Jan good-naturedly, ringing the bell. He prepared himself to deal with a dramatic reaction from Lünner's girlfriend, Viola Backes. A fugue state. Disorientation. Racing pulse, nausea, sweating. He hadn't simply read about it in books – he'd witnessed it first-hand.

The front door was flung open with such force that the wilted wreath on the door rocked.

'He's dead, isn't he?' The blonde woman stared at him, her eyes glittering, thin as a reed and as tall as he was. Her cheeks were stained with running mascara, like war-paint.

Jan stammered. 'Um, I – I wanted to tell you differently, but yes.'

She punched him square in the face.

Not a slap – a perfect right cross.

He yelled and stumbled back, holding his nose, which felt crushed.

Viola Backes buried her face into her hands, sobbing, then turned on her heel and marched back down the corridor.

'Hey, stay where you are!' bellowed Köllner, with more energy than Jan would have expected.

The woman continued walking, undeterred. 'And I know who the fucking killer is!'

Köllner grabbed Jan's shoulders. 'You all right?'

He took his hand from his nose. It was covered in blood. Not the first time someone had clocked him one, unfortunately – not by a long chalk.

The Inspector gave him a tissue. He took it gratefully, tore it in half and stuffed the two pieces into his nostrils. 'Did you hear what she just said?'

'She knows who the killer is—'

## 12

'My sister will be here soon.' Frau Ziehner put the phone back onto the tiled table, nervously dabbing the corners of her eyes with a tissue.

'It's best to have somebody here to look after you. If you like, we can fetch a minister too,' said Rabea, taking the woman's folded hands in hers. She could empathise better than Adelheid Ziehner probably imagined.

'Thank you – thank you for your help. But for the moment my sister is the only minister I want.' The woman, tall and in her mid-fifties, brushed a lock of blonde hair back from her face. 'I had a kind of premonition when Leonard didn't come back to the house last night. And this morning I heard about those two bodies. First, I thought he might have spent the night at the pub. They have a little hostel there, and sometimes, when he's drunk too much – but that doesn't matter any more.'

'Can you tell us where he was going that night?' Ichigawa arched her back. Her body language spoke volumes about how uncomfortable she felt. Rabea could almost hear her professional façade cracking.

'He was at the printer's. He wanted to check everything was in order.' The woman fiddled with the bronze brooch on the collar of her blouse. 'I spoke to the printer. His car's still there.'

Ichigawa and Rabea exchanged a brief glance. So, the killer had overpowered him at the printer's.

'Do have a biscuit, please.' Frau Ziehner pointed at the table, where a pot of tea and some biscuits were laid out. Her smile looked like a grimace.

A gigantic tiled stove dominated the living room. The warmth it radiated had overheated the room so much that Rabea's forehead was beaded with sweat. All the furniture dated from the beginning of the last century. Monstrous, bulky and dark. Books in various stages of disintegration were stacked on the shelves. Their dusty, slightly sweet aroma singed her nose. She felt as if she was in an antique shop.

Occasionally Rabea was astonished by how few gestures and how little information she needed to understand a person. No wonder she'd had so many dates where she dismissed the guy after fifteen minutes.

Frau Ziehner sought refuge in routines, but the moment of collapse would come. It always did. Until then, however, she would try to smile away her loss, as she'd probably smiled away so many over the course of her life.

At least Rabea could use Frau Ziehner's composure to ask her questions calmly.

Ichigawa cleared her throat. 'Did your husband have any enemies? Anybody threatening him recently?'

That question was like a three-pointer in basketball, which Rabea had played at school. Nine times out of ten it was pointless, but if you scored it was a major step towards success. She was keen to see how the woman reacted to Ichigawa's question but wasn't getting her hopes up.

Adelheid Ziehner sipped her tea, her fingers trembling. It was rare for a murderer with a modus operandi like this one to be openly at daggers drawn with his victims. Nonethless she nodded, putting the cup back on the table. 'My husband is a publisher – was – as I'm sure you know,' she said. 'A particular kind of publisher. In the industry they refer to his business model as a vanity press. He had no editorial staff, no quality control. He printed anything authors sent him in their desperation to be published. For accordingly high sums, of course.'

'And one of these authors fell out with him?'

'One? Dozens!' Frau Ziehner made a sound that sounded grotesquely like a sob and a laugh at the same time. 'Leonard got them to sign contracts by making promises he didn't keep. Painted pictures for them of a great literary career and interviews in the cultural section. In reality, their god-awful tomes are mouldering in our basement. Most of them only woke up to reality once they saw the bill for printing and storage.'

Ichigawa knitted her brows. 'Must have made them quite angry, having their dreams burst like a soap bubble.'

'There were complaints, of course, nasty emails, sometimes threats.' Her index finger traced the edge of her teacup before stopping abruptly. 'None of them worried me, though. Only one of them was really unpleasant.'

## 13

'Sorry about your nose.' Frau Backes fidgeted in her chair. 'Is it broken?'

Jan took out one of the crumpled wodges of tissue and stroked the bridge of his nose. 'I don't think so,' he said, although that's exactly what it felt like.

The young woman was clinging to her glass of water as though her life depended on it. 'Marek often used to be away for long periods of time. But he'd always tell me. He'd always call. When I heard the news about the two bodies, I put two and two together.'

She raised her hand as though to run it through her hair but lowered it again halfway through the gesture. She continued, 'And then it was true. I was furious. Not sure with whom. Probably myself, mostly. Because I should have seen it coming.'

'It's fine.' Jan rested his forearm on the dining table, which stood across the dead journalist's living room.

If he hadn't already known Marek Lünner was a reporter, he'd have realised by now. Overflowing bookshelves, half an archive's worth of newspapers, the desk piled high with documents, and countless maps on the walls.

'So, you know somebody who threatened Marek, then?'

'Just a minute.' Frau Backes stood up, shakily supporting herself on the table and chair. She went over to the desk and leafed through some sheaves of paper, finally taking out a sheet and returning.

She slapped it down onto the table. 'If this isn't a threat, then I don't know what is.'

Jan slid the piece of paper across to him and Köllner. Somebody had scribbled all over it in black ballpoint pen. It took some effort to decipher the florid, sprawling writing.

*Herr Lünner,*

*I won't be suppressed! The truth won't be suppressed!*

*If you don't reveal this betrayal, there will be consequences. If you continue to ignore me, then you're no better than that criminal Leonard Ziehner . . .*

Jan didn't need to read any further.

When he looked up, his gaze met Köllner's. The Inspector's eyes were wide – the young man had cottoned on immediately.

Jan couldn't read the signature at the bottom of the note. 'What's the name of the guy who wrote this?'

Viola Backes narrowed her eyes. 'Francesco Zanetti. He wanted Marek to write a story about some publisher. Apparently, he was scamming authors in a big way.'

She put both palms on the table, her posture tensing. 'The bastard sent one of his books with it. I took a look inside. Total crap.'

Köllner could scarcely contain his excitement. He kept inhaling deeply and kneading his hands. 'Did you ever meet him?'

The young woman shook her head.

That didn't matter. Jan took out his phone and scrolled through his contacts. Rabea had to be told straight away.

A man who'd threatened one of the victims and quarrelled with the other. Could they have hit a bullseye already?

# 14

The basement was definitely not what Rabea had expected. It was neither dim nor dusty, and it didn't smell of damp. Shrink-wrapped books were stacked chest-high on dozens of pallets. Three fluorescent tubes lit the room. One was flickering, throwing diffuse plays of shadow across the walls.

'Give me a moment.' Frau Ziehner opened a file and skimmed through it.

Rabea crossed her arms. The weariness she'd felt in the car was gone. Her heart was pounding. Could they have struck gold already? Was it really this simple – a serial killer well-known to one of the victims?

'Here it is!' Frau Ziehner tapped a page. 'Francesco Zanetti. Print runs in the thousands. They're on one of the pallets over there, on the far left.'

Ichigawa nodded and walked across, picking up one of the books at random. Her eyes narrowed, she read the title aloud: *Letters of Death*?

Rabea's heartbeat quickened. She crossed the basement and picked up a book. The words Ichigawa had read aloud were printed in a silver serif font on a black background.

She tore off the plastic shrink-wrap excitedly and opened the book.

The print was so tiny the lines almost looked like thin lines. There were no paragraphs and no punctuation. Apparently, nothing but muddled fragments.

She skimmed one of the lines: '—blood-red fear death love deep black thought evil sorrow—'

Total confusion. No wonder the author had had to reach into his own pocket to get these scribblings published.

'Did you ever meet Herr Zanetti?' asked Ichigawa, who was still staring uneasily at her copy.

'No, thank God.' She was looking at the desk, but her eyes seemed to be peering through it. 'But my husband went to see him once because he fell behind with his invoices. Zanetti didn't want to pay – he called my husband a fraud and a schemer. Said he was going to contact some journalist to bring the truth about him to light.'

The old woman was supporting herself on the arm of an office chair. Her self-control was crumbling. Her whole body was trembling. 'The man's insane.'

An idea struck Rabea. 'This journalist, the one Zanetti was going to contact – was his name Marek Lünner, by any chance?'

'How did you know that?' Frau Ziehner wheeled around.

Instead of answering, Rabea turned to Anita: 'We've got to call Stüter immediately!'

She was just stuffing the book into her jacket pocket when her smartphone vibrated.

A glance at the display. Jan.

'We've got a suspect,' they said in unison.

'Francesco Zanetti—' said Rabea.

'You've got his address?'

'Yes.'

'Then tell Anita and Stüter. They should get a search warrant, put off that bloody press conference and get a SWAT team on standby. We'll meet in twenty minutes in Hachenburg.'

'Got it, see you soon.'

'See you soon – and Rabea: good work!'

Her heart leapt. When Jan had mentioned the SWAT team, she'd realised how serious this discovery was. Most likely they didn't just have a suspect – they had the killer!

She put her phone back in her pocket. Ichigawa was already dialling, while Frau Ziehner glanced indecisively from one to the other.

'A' and 'B'.

*Letters of Death.*

Evidently Zanetti had made his book's title a reality.

Hopefully they could keep the number of victims at two.

# 15

'A, B, C, D, E, F, G
   H, I, J, K, L, M, N, O, P . . .'

*Somebody was singing quietly. A hoarse voice somewhere in the darkness.*

'Q, R, S, T, U, V,
   W, X, Y and Z.'

*Tugba tried to move, but all her muscles were stiff. The back of her head was throbbing. Her bare shoulders were freezing. Where was she? Why wasn't she still in her apartment?*

*The past hours – or days, she didn't know any more – felt like one long black corridor.*

*Her heart was thudding. Who was out there? Who was singing?*

'He – hello?' *The words were barely audible from her parched mouth.* 'Help, I need help!'

*Somebody had to explain what was going on. Around her everything was dark. The air stank. She couldn't place the stench, but it sent a shiver down her spine.*

'Who are you?'

*No answer.*

'Then ABC, the cat's come round for tea.'

*Footsteps. The voice was coming closer.*

*'DEF, the monkey is the chef.'*

*Now it was directly in front of her.*

*'You've got to wait.'*

*The footsteps faded again.*

*Tugba shut her eyes. Her head. Her memory. Everything was empty. She felt nothing.*

*Fell back into nothing.*

# 16

'Dammit, what are they doing here?' Chief Superintendent Rolf Stüter was seething with rage, his eyes glued to the OB van.

Rabea jumped as he hissed.

Still, she understood. There could only be one reason why one of Germany's biggest broadcasters had sent a camera team to the sleepy town of Langenbach: somebody on the investigation team had blabbed.

The two police vans pulled up on a field in the heart of Langenbach, close to Zanetti's house. Without their flashing lights, of course. Ichigawa and the SWAT team were in one while the second held the remaining members of the team.

'Köllner, keep the TV twats out of our hair,' growled Stüter, flinging open one of the sliding doors. 'I need a serious word with Ichigawa first.'

'Off to a great start,' muttered Jan, who was sitting next to Rabea.

They climbed out. The evening was oddly scented with danger – as though some chemical hung in the air, transmitting a simple message: something isn't right.

The SWAT team, practised and silent, swarmed out of their van. In their combat gear they looked as though they'd leapt straight out of some sci-fi movie.

One of them took off his protective helmet and approached them. His black balaclava still covered most of his face. Vigilant blue eyes glinted through the eye slits, beneath black brows.

'Name's Eller. Head of Operations.'

Despite his curt manner, he deliberately shook hands with all of them. When he reached Rabea, she felt the pressure of his hand even through the thick combat glove.

'We spoke on the phone,' said Stüter. 'Sorry the journalists are here. Somebody must have talked.'

'Nothing to be done now,' said Eller with a wave of his hand. 'As long as they keep their distance, I don't care. Were you able to obtain a plan of the target's house?'

The SWAT team leader was like an oasis of calm in their agitated little group.

Stüter shook his head. 'The council didn't respond quickly enough to our request. This is the sticks, remember.'

'No need to be so contemptuous about your home town,' replied Eller casually, before getting back to the topic at hand. 'We'll have to go in blind, then. There's a back entrance, correct?'

'Erm, yes—' replied Stüter, still on the back foot.

'Good, that's all we need for now. One more thing: your people only enter the target's property once access is obtained and the area secured, understood?' His penetrating blue eyes swept across them.

They nodded mutely.

'Right, then—' murmured Eller, putting his helmet back on. He sounded drained – an exhausted warrior who'd already seen too much.

While Köllner and his colleague stopped the camera teams switching on their floodlights, the six members of the SWAT team made their move.

Zanetti's house was set back slightly, almost on the edge of the river Nister. The jagged, deep-black silhouettes of the fir trees huddled along the far edge like a stage set.

The once white façade was covered with crumbling plaster. Faded rugs and sheets hung in the windows, blocking the view inside. There was nothing but dead remnants in the two flowerpots either side of the front door.

As they reached the house, the SWAT team split up. Four of them continued towards the front door, while the other two darted around the building.

Rabea could no longer distinguish Eller from the others.

One of the four at the front held a battering ram; the others readied their HK MP7s.

Only the rustling of the pines filled the night. Rabea swallowed drily.

'Attack!' Eller's voice rang out.

The battering ram slammed home with a crash, and the door flew open.

The SWAT team stormed inside.

'Police!'

'On the ground!'

The torches mounted on their weapons cast grotesque shadows.

The sudden noise and garish light must have totally confused Zanetti – precisely as the officers wanted.

For a few seemingly endless moments, all they could see were the torch beams through the veiled windows. Rabea was so nervous she wanted to shut her eyes and stick her fingers in her ears.

Shouts of 'Clear!' echoed from various parts of the house, until one of the officers yelled, 'Eller, over here!' Unlike the others, the note of detachment was utterly gone from his voice. 'We found him.'

No shots, no shouts. Nothing but a bald statement. Rabea threw a sidelong glance at Jan, who was rubbing the bridge of his nose thoughtfully with his thumb and index finger.

A shadow emerged from the house.

Everybody started. Köllner's hand twitched instantly to his holster.

At a second glance, however, it turned out to be one of the SWAT team. Tearing the helmet off his head, he collapsed to his knees and vomited into the grass. His coughing and retching were the only sounds to be heard above the excited chatter of the TV reporters behind them.

'What did he see in there?' murmured Jan behind her, although his question was addressed to no one.

A light came on in the room to the right of the front door, and moments later one of the officers ripped away the sheet.

The walkie-talkie on Stüter's belt crackled. Eller's voice: 'Come inside and bring the analysts. Zanetti isn't the killer. He's one of the victims.'

# C

'Since we Germans, like the Greeks and the Slavs, express the tenuis of the guttural with the letter "K", the letter "C", taken from the Latin alphabet, is entirely superfluous; hence also why it is absent from the Gothic and Old Norse script. The Slavs use it for "S", the Poles and Bohemians for "Z".'

The Grimms' Dictionary

## 17

The house stank of loneliness.

Of unemptied litter boxes, cold cigarette smoke and spoiled food.

Rabea pulled the collar of her shirt over her nose. Ichigawa, Jan and Stüter followed her down the dim corridor.

Newspapers and magazines were piled either side – the earliest Rabea saw dated from 2007. Beside them were rows of shopping bags filled to the brim with empty containers from microwave meals.

Evidently, Zanetti had been unable to throw anything away.

She frowned. A fear of loss, perhaps originating from his divorce? Or was she jumping to conclusions again?

They entered the living room; or rather, the space that had once been a living room. It no longer held any trace of comfort.

'If this is any reflection of his mental state, then I'm guessing the guy had more than a few bats in the belfry,' whispered Stüter.

The only item of furniture was a sagging leather sofa covered with cigarette butts and burn marks. Piles of books towered like stalagmites from every surface. Rabea saw titles like *The History of Kabbala*, *The Primeval Alphabet* and *The Lexicon of Numerology*, as well as countless copies of *Letters of Death*.

'What's numerology?' she asked Jan.

'The symbolism of numbers,' he replied. 'It's an attempt to reinterpret the letters of the alphabet as numbers in order to decode a hidden message. In the Torah, for example. Searching for God's secret code. Aleph, i.e. "A", is one, Beta – "B" – is two and so on.'

A jumble of letters and numerals were scrawled on the wallpaper with felt-tip pen. Torn-out pages from books were pinned to the wall among them.

The SWAT team officer who had secured the room gestured curtly towards the door on their right. 'He's in there.'

As they got closer, another, far more threatening, stench overpowered the smell of dilapidation.

Rabea recognised it from an autopsy she'd attended shortly after university. Back then she'd rubbed peppermint oil under her nostrils, which had taken the edge off the smell of the body.

Her stomach knotted. She gave a choked cough.

'All right?' asked Jan, who was ashen-faced.

The room, which had once been Zanetti's study, looked like a slaughterhouse.

On the chaise longue lay something more reminiscent of an abattoir's waste than a human body. It was impossible to tell the original colour of the upholstery; it was too soaked with blood.

Rabea managed only a brief look before she had to avert her eyes.

Her legs shook so much that she felt as if she was on stilts.

It wasn't until she'd freed herself from the spell of the bloodthirsty sight that she noticed the walls. The letter 'C' stared back at her, repeated dozens of times.

In blood.

Jan crouched down in front of the chaise longue. 'Overkill. He's been completely disembowelled. This was frenzied.'

'Look!' Ichigawa, pulling on a latex glove, picked up a note from the side table.

'Another quotation?' Rabea took a step closer.

Ichigawa nodded, handing her the scrap of paper.

It took her a moment to decipher the tiny lettering: *When Gregor Samsa awoke one morning from unquiet dreams, he found himself transformed in his bed into a gigantic insect.*

She knew the line only too well. It was a book she'd had to read at school. 'Kafka. The first line of *The Metamorphosis*.'

'It's a fitting sentiment, if a macabre one,' said Stüter. 'Our killer certainly transformed Zanetti into something inhuman.'

'This murder represents a turning point,' groaned Jan, creaking to his feet. His face was twisted, warped with pain and concentration.

'You can say that again,' agreed Stüter sarcastically. 'The point where the shittiness of the situation turns from crap to absolute bull.'

'That's not what I was driving at, although you do put it very poetically,' replied Jan.

'Then please, enlighten me.'

Jan held up his index finger. 'Okay, first observation: he's playing with us. He knew we'd think Zanetti was the killer and that we'd come storming into his house. Probably his way of expressing superiority. Showing us he's one step ahead. Or it's about much more than that, which leads me to my second observation.'

He lifted another finger. 'The killer's motive comes from Zanetti's perspective on the world: the symbolism of letters. "A", "B", "C" and so on. The question is, did he only do so to throw suspicion on Zanetti, or is he genuinely interested?'

Jan raised a third finger. 'Now we come to my final observation: the killer enjoyed this murder.'

'Tell me something I don't know,' said Stüter derisively.

'I will if you let me talk,' continued Jan. 'With the first two victims, the act of killing was simply a means to an end. He was probably as afraid as his victims. This, however – this he really enjoyed. As I said, it sent him into a frenzy.'

'So, we can assume Zanetti is the third victim, time-wise.'

Jan nodded. 'I think the autopsy will confirm that.'

'Well, it's something to be getting on with, I suppose.'

As Rabea forced herself to look back at the corpse, she noticed something on the wrists.

Stepping closer, she took out her phone and switched on the torch.

Yes, she'd been right.

Both wrists were crossed with red lines – pressure marks.

'Zanetti was bound. The house is fairly remote. The killer could easily have kept him here for several days.'

'Makes sense,' remarked Ichigawa. 'That way he could have killed them in the right order and also made sure Zanetti didn't throw a spanner in the works while he was committing the first two murders.'

The Chief Superintendent nodded, visibly impressed for the first time.

Jan gave her a wink, adding, 'Our killer has a plan. I think he already knows who his victims will be. From A to Z, if you want to put it like that. And under no circumstances will he deviate from that plan.'

'That'll make him predictable – might help us.' For the first time, Stüter was eyeing them with a trace of approval.

His phone rang, rearranging his face into its normal, grim expression. 'Our media liaison officer.' He answered. 'Yes, what is it? We're holding a press conference in an hour?'

'Impossible! We need more time at the scene,' said Jan distractedly. He turned on his heel and began to search the room.

'After the conference you can spend as much time here as you like,' replied Stüter, who'd already hung up. His voice sounded husky. 'We're all in this mess together.'

Instead of a lead, all they had to show at the press conference was a fresh piece of bad news. And they were no closer than before to catching the killer.

# 18

A flurry of flash bulbs. Jan shielded his eyes with his hand as he stepped onto the podium, pausing for a moment in confusion.

'Over here!' Anita was waving him over with one hand and pointing at a folding chair on her right with the other.

Gratefully, Jan threw her a weak smile. He edged behind the long table and took his seat.

'Welcome to Hell,' whispered Stüter, who was sitting on the other side of him.

Jan sipped at the water bottle in front of him. He realised he hadn't eaten or drunk anything for hours – possibly another reason for his pounding headache.

His gaze swept across the mob of news people. The photographers in the front row were busy taking pictures, while the cameramen were still assembling their equipment. Those in the back were writing diligently in their notepads or typing into their iPads.

Jan's heart began to race. He wasn't unaccustomed to speaking in front of crowds. He'd given lectures at university, he'd led seminars – he had that down pat.

This, however, was an altogether different challenge.

Anything he said here could easily end up on the evening news. Not to mention that the unwanted camera team outside Zanetti's house had caught their failure on tape.

They'd been pushed into a corner.

*Another Body in Westerwald – Investigators Still Groping in the Dark* was the headline already up on one major news website.

Who'd called the TV crew?

Other than the investigation team, Frau Ziehner and Marek Lünner's girlfriend, nobody had known a thing about it.

Although – that wasn't quite true.

The killer had known.

Had he tipped off the camera crew?

At that moment a piercing whistle signalled that the microphones had been switched on. The whispers in the wood-panelled meeting room in Bad Marienberg died down.

The red-haired media liaison officer leant forwards onto her elbows and raised her voice. 'Ladies and gentlemen, I'd like to welcome you to this press conference with Investigation Team Alphabet Killer. Frau Ichigawa will update you on the most recent turn of events. Afterwards you'll have the opportunity to ask questions.'

Anita summarised the situation. Today she didn't seem to be enjoying the spotlight at all. The strain was obviously taking its toll.

Then came the hail of questions.

The first, addressed to Anita: 'Is this case too much for you?'

The look she gave the bald journalist made Jan momentarily afraid she was going to leap over the table and throttle him.

'The first body was only found this morning,' intervened Stüter before she could reply. 'Did you seriously think we were going to find the killer by now? We have several good leads and places to start, but you've got to understand that this is solid police work here – it's not *CSI*.'

At that moment Jan was grateful for Stüter's gruff manner.

'Was sending a SWAT team into the third victim's apartment too hasty?' A journalist in the front row jumped in.

Stüter's face was gradually turning as red as his tie, which he'd put on hurriedly before the press conference. 'As I already said,' he growled, 'this is solid, decent police work we're doing here, and we would only take such a step if the evidence was convincing, and—'

He got no further.

A loud female voice that Jan now knew all too well cut him short: 'I've been informed by reliable sources that there are deep divisions within the investigation team, especially between the behavioural analysts and the detectives.'

Nora Schneill – the editor of the *Wäller Zeitung*, who had given her card to Jan only that morning – stood up triumphantly from her chair. 'How can that be, after so short a time? Herr Stüter, Herr Grall – would one of you like to comment?'

An excited murmur ran through the room. More camera flashes.

Jan threw a sidelong glance at the Chief Superintendent; he could almost hear the cogs whirring. His jaw was gritted, his narrowed eyes fixed on the journalist.

'That's — I—' he growled.

Before Stüter's reply could end in an outburst of rage, Jan spoke up. 'There is absolutely no basis for those insinuations.'

He took a gulp of water. At that moment, Stüter sprang to his feet.

'You know what, Nora?' he bellowed, pointing at her. 'You're no better than the nutter running around out there, slaughtering people letter by letter. You and your sensationalism, you're just as blood-thirsty and—'

Anita grabbed him by the shoulders and dragged him back down into his chair. 'Be quiet!' she hissed. 'Do you even listen to yourself?'

The babble of voices in the room was growing louder. The photographers were snapping picture after picture.

For a moment the media liaison officer buried her face in her hands, then said tonelessly into the microphone, 'Ladies and gentlemen, the press conference is over.'

Jan went to help Anita manhandle the still furious Stüter off the podium – no mean feat with such a hulking giant.

Once they'd finally grabbed hold of both his upper arms, they dragged him into the adjoining green room, which was furnished with a corner sofa and a table full of snacks and drinks.

'All right, all right. Let go of me!' The Chief Superintendent tore himself free and slumped onto the sofa.

Anita stared at him, shaking her head. 'If you'd only let me do my job.'

As she and Rabea paced the room, Jan put his legs up on the sofa and rested his head against the window. Occasionally he sipped from his bottle of mineral water.

Sleet was sweeping across Büchtingstrasse, driving the reporters and their camera teams into their vans. Particles of ice struck the windows, melting and running down in faltering channels.

'Whoever blabbed to that Schneill woman was definitely a man,' growled Stüter. 'And I can imagine exactly what she offered in return. She's always known how to wrap men round her little finger.' He crossed his arms. 'If I find out who the guy is, he's going to wish he'd never joined the police.'

Rabea rolled her eyes.

'The problem wasn't the informant, it was that you can't control yourself,' said Anita. 'Now you've managed to put the entire Westerwald police force in a bad light. Congratulations.'

It was enough to silence Stüter for a moment. He sat there brooding darkly.

'What if the informant wasn't on the team at all?' suggested Jan.

'Who else would have known about the cr—' Rabea asked, but immediately answered her own question. 'Of course, the killer.'

'He couldn't know about your differences of opinion, though,' objected Anita.

Jan shrugged. 'Perhaps he's bugging the office.'

'That's unthinkable!'

'Just because something's unthinkable, doesn't mean it's impossible.'

Ichigawa frowned. 'Then interview the journalist. You've been waiting ages for the opportunity to give her the third degree again, eh Stüter?'

The Chief Superintendent merely sank lower in his chair. 'Enough of the insinuations,' he said, barely audibly.

'What insinuations?' asked Rabea.

'She's my ex-wife.' Evidently distracted by some fleeting memory, Stüter's gaze grew distant for a split second. 'But we got divorced two years ago.'

Jan wanted to laugh out loud. It all made sense: Stüter's verbal sparring with the journalist, his outburst at the press conference, even the fragility he was trying to hide.

'Repression is a normal psychological defence mechanism,' said Rabea, 'but such a regressive approach only works short-term.'

Stüter waved a dismissive hand. 'Don't give me Freud!'

# 19

The revolving restaurant on the roof of the wildlife park hotel managed only one revolution per hour, but Jan was still feeling sick.

Maybe it was the bodies he'd seen earlier; he still couldn't forget the sight.

It certainly couldn't be the meal. On his trip to the buffet he'd found more than enough vegan food – but he'd scarcely been able to take a bite.

He'd come to the restaurant by himself: Rabea had wanted to phone her family from her room.

Who could blame her?

He wanted to phone somebody too, somebody to talk through what had happened that day. But right now, he had nobody in his life like that.

Over the years he'd had several brief flings like the one with Anita, but none had lasted. On the one hand he liked not being tied down, but on the other he sometimes wished he had a constant in his life.

He swirled his glass of water, watching the reflections in the liquid. He'd stopped drinking alcohol when he left home, but the only effect it had had was to make his hyper-sensitivity worse.

He let his gaze wander across the restaurant. Other than him, its only occupants were two chattering old married couples, a red-haired woman about his age and a business traveller glued to his smartphone.

Outside, the night pressed in with such impenetrable darkness that it looked like somebody had hung the panoramic windows with black velvet. Even so, Jan needed only the points of the compass to tell him which villages lay beneath his feet.

To the west, the river Nister led past Unnau towards Hachenburg. To the south, after Hahn, Grossseifen and Höhn was Wiesensee Lake. Eastwards rose the Fuchskaute, the highest mountain in Westerwald. The villages of Nieder-rossbach and Fehl-Ritzhausen nestled in the shadows at its base. Finally, to the north, were Kirburg and Neunkhausen.

Every one of those names stirred memories inside him. Afternoons playing football with friends, the first shy kiss at a basement party, walking for hours with his father.

Absorbed in his thoughts, he didn't even notice at first that someone had approached his table.

'Bill, please,' muttered Jan, assuming it was the waiter.

'I don't think I can help you there,' replied a female voice.

Jan looked up in astonishment.

The woman who had been sitting alone at a table was smiling down at him.

He frowned. 'Erm, what's up?'

Her smile grew wider, which suited her fine-featured face very well. 'You and I are the only ones sitting here alone. I don't know about you, but I could do with a bit of company.'

Jan's brain sprang instinctively into action. In a split second he was analysing the woman's behaviour. A pathological need for attention?

Barely perceptibly he shook his head. Sometimes he tended to over-interpret even the most harmless everyday situations. A beautiful woman had simply come up to talk to him in a restaurant. It was the sort of thing that happened once in a blue moon, and he wasn't about to let the behavioural analyst in him spoil that.

'I've got nothing against company,' he said with a smile, offering her a seat.

'Tamara Weiss,' she said, once she'd settled in her chair.

'Jan Grall.' He beckoned the waiter over. 'What are you drinking?'

'Gin and tonic, please,' she ordered, then said to Jan, 'I'm on holiday – I'm allowed the occasional treat. You're sticking with water?'

Her torrent of rich red curls was pulled back into a braid. It disappeared into the collar of her black dress, which she'd paired with dark tights and knee-high leather boots. Her grey eyes twinkled alertly at Jan.

'I don't drink. I've already got enough addictions,' he replied. 'So, um, and what job are you on holiday from?'

'I'm a freelance translator in Frankfurt. Mainly English and French literature.'

'I've always had tremendous respect for creative types.' Jan sipped his water. 'My work is creative sometimes too, but in a completely different way. What genres do you translate?'

'Romance, thrillers . . . mainly crime.'

'Ah, then you're in the right place at the right time.' The corner of his mouth twisted humourlessly. 'Since we're on the subject: what made you choose this as a holiday destination? It's not exactly the Maldives.'

'You'll laugh, but I'm afraid of flying. I've only ever got onto a plane once – and it was hell.'

Her G&T arrived, and she paused briefly. Jan had met very few people who spoke as articulately and clearly as she did. Who were so utterly in control of a situation. As though her life were a TV show and she was the host.

'Anyway, I like the peace and quiet here,' she continued. 'You feel so far away from other people at this hotel. Nothing but nature around you.'

'True,' admitted Jan.

Feeling far away from everything. As a young man, that had been a reason why he wanted to get out of this place.

'But I'm just prattling on about myself. What about you? You on holiday too?'

'Work,' said Jan. 'Which brings us back to crime. I'm on the team investigating the alphabet murders.'

Her eyes widened, whether from curiosity or shock was impossible to tell. 'Oh – you're one of the inspectors?'

'No, no. I'm from the Rheinland-Pfalz State Office of Criminal Investigations in Mainz. I put together psycho-logical profiles.'

The professional inside him said he shouldn't really be discussing the case. Yet the way Tamara's monolith-grey eyes were sparkling at him had loosened his tongue.

'Then you're a profiler?'

He shook his head. It was the second time today he'd had to explain the difference between behavioural investi-gative advisors, or behavioural analysts, and profilers.

'I couldn't do that,' she said. 'All that madness. The vio-lence. The only crimes I'm involved in are bad English manuscripts.'

'Well, I couldn't spend the whole day poring over—' He fell silent. Something Rabea had said earlier had struck him.

The victims' professions. Editor. Publisher. Author.

And now he was sitting opposite a translator.

She tilted her head. 'What's wrong?'

'Tamara – may I use your first name? – you ought to be very careful.'

'Why?'

'All the murder victims so far had jobs related to writing. Just like you. And that could be the killer's pattern.'

'I'm a big girl,' she replied with a roguish smile. 'I can look after myself.'

'I don't doubt that. Nonetheless, thank you. This conver-sation has helped me enormously.'

LARS SCHÜTZ | 101

She laughed. 'I haven't done anything!'

'Oh yes, you have – I've got to go through the files again right now. Sorry.' He beckoned over the waiter.

Her eye caught his. 'Shall we meet here again tomorrow evening? Same time?'

'With pleasure,' he responded promptly.

## 20

Rabea put down her iPad and took a deep breath.

If she really wanted to spoil her mood, all she needed to do was sift through the ViCLAS database.

She threw herself onto her bed.

ViCLAS stood for Violent Crime Linkage Analysis System. A sheet consisting of 168 questions aggregated all the missing persons cases and serious crimes involving murder, attempted murder or sexual violence. Sensibly organised and laid out.

It was indispensable for behavioural analysts, recording not only the details of the offences but also the perpetrator's social behaviour and the characteristics of the victims.

All evening she'd been searching for patterns that resembled the Alphabet Killer's. Literary quotations at the crime scenes. Tattooed letters. She'd found nothing, although she'd expanded the search to the last decade.

ViCLAS was more than a tool.

It was torture.

A database of family tragedies, lunacy and death. Every time she worked with it, she came away feeling dirty. To her they weren't just numbers, text and images, but stories seared into her brain.

She looked at her phone. 2.11 a.m.

Her mother would have been in bed for ages by now. She'd have to call tomorrow instead. Maybe she should call her flatmates in Mainz. It was possible Asim or Ricarda might have just got home from a party and would still be awake.

But what would she talk to them about? The case was so engrossing that at the moment she couldn't imagine talking about anything else.

She shook her head softly. No. Time she got some sleep. Getting up from the desk, she took off her blouse and dropped it carelessly on the floor then flung herself backwards onto the bedspread. She hadn't even opened her suitcase. Apart from the laptop on the table, the room looked unoccupied.

She shut her eyes, but instantly realised that sleep was impossible. ViCLAS wouldn't let her go. Somewhere in its depths was a record of her own tragedy.

The reason Jan had wanted to work with her.

She'd read the entry on the case so many times she knew it by heart. In the life of every person there comes a moment when they stop being a child. When they become aware that the world isn't the sheltered and peaceful place their parents told them it was.

In Rabea's life that moment had come twenty years earlier, when her father had walked into her room with a tear-stained face and hugged her so tightly she couldn't breathe. 'You've got to be strong now, little one—'

She realised her fingers were knotted around the bed-clothes. She sat up, and for lack of alternatives she reached for the remote and switched on the flat-screen TV.

A talk show flickered onto the screen; an actor was try-ing to promote some film with a boring anecdote.

Everything seemed infinitely far away. As if from a par-allel world that hadn't been shattered by hatred and death. The actor with his crinkly scarf and perfectly studied smirk. Her flatmates with their parties and broken dreams. Snowy Lucerne, which she'd left only this morning.

She was freezing, although the heating was turned up to max. Sighing, she got up from the bed. It was no good. She unpacked her suitcase, cleaned her teeth and threw on the old basketball jersey, with *24 WYLER* emblazoned on the back, that she always wore as pyjamas.

By the time she crawled under the bedspread, the actor had finished his segment. Now it was the lead singer of some band, pushing some new album.

Jan, Stüter, Ichigawa and she weren't part of that world any more. She switched off the television. Since their arrival here, they'd belonged to the world of the dead. The world of letters and symbols.

The world of the Alphabet Killer.

And she wasn't sure if he'd ever let her go.

## 21

'Everything all right?' The taxi driver was eyeing Jan in the rear-view mirror.

Jan was resting his head against the glass. The only source of light on the road back to Zanetti's house came from the reflective bollards. Where they were missing, people had compensated by hanging CDs from wooden posts. An indecipherable, monotonous Morse code of light. A flood of signs.

'You'll get your tip – no need to bother with small talk,' said Jan absently.

'Just asking.' The driver adjusted his cap.

Jan was already feeling overwhelmed by the interior of the taxi cab. The smell of cold cigarette smoke, of the dog he could tell the driver owned, of pungent aftershave. Then the rancid lambskin covers on the front seats. The driving licence with the decades-old picture and the name Hans-Werner Parigger. The passport-size photo of a small, chubby-cheeked boy on the dashboard, right next to a club pennant for TuS Koblenz.

One dip into the river of signs was enough to decode the driver's entire life.

He'd been unable to sleep at the hotel, pacing ceaselessly around the room. He'd listened to music, and even tried to read something. It didn't help. When he was on a case, his brain had no stand-by mode.

So, he'd called reception and got them to order him a taxi. He'd been planning to visit Zanetti's house again anyway. Why not put his insomnia to good use?

'What's going on here, then?' asked the driver as they pulled up outside Victim C's house.

Mobile floodlights surrounded the detached house, bathing it in a dazzling, celestial light. Forensics vans and other police vehicles had parked on the field outside, leaving a muddle of tyre tracks in the fresh snow. Technicians in plastic overalls were flitting through the rooms like ghosts.

'You'll read all about it in the paper tomorrow,' said Jan. 'You can let me out here.'

'Should I wait for you?'

'Not necessary. I'll probably be here a while.' He pressed thirty euros into Parigger's hand – a generous tip. 'That's fine.'

The stocky fifty-ish driver tipped his cap. 'Look after yourself.'

'I'll do my best.'

Jan got out of the taxi. Instantly the wind blew particles of snow into his face. Now, at two in the morning, the winter was revealed in all its frosty mercilessness.

Wrapping his coat around his body as tightly as possible, Jan walked towards Zanetti's house with rapid steps.

He couldn't remember the last time his teeth had literally chattered with cold.

The head of the forensics team was standing by the dilapidated front door, in discussion with his colleagues. Recognising Jan, he nodded. There was amazement in his deep-set eyes.

'We weren't expecting one of you to show up,' he said. 'If it's results you're after, you're too early. We're still in the middle of our examination.'

'No worries. I'm not here to see you. I just wanted to spend time at the scene.'

'Make yourself at home!' He made an expansive gesture. 'Just, please don't disturb my people when they're working.'

Jan stepped inside the crime scene. The place where the lives of the victim and killer had become one. A place full of signs and clues. Full of meaning.

It was Jan's task to find that meaning – and if he didn't, he had to invent it out of what he did know.

The crime scene was at the core of behavioural analysis. Jan could spend hours there. On one of the courses on operative case analysis, he had been taught lateral thinking using the techniques of Edward de Bono. It was about overcoming ingrained patterns of thought through associative leaps, switches in perspective and the search for deliberately unconventional solutions. In combination with his hypersensitive faculties, it was a highly effective weapon.

First, he climbed the spiral staircase to the first floor. The bedroom was much the same as the ground floor: mountains of junk. Scratched, worn-out furniture. Yellowing paper on one wall, unfinished brick on another. Although the technicians had opened all the windows, the musty stench of neglect still hung in the air.

Jan walked up to the king-size double bed. It was covered in unidentifiable blotches of various colours. He thought he could even see dried blood at the head. On the bedposts he noticed the remains of cable ties, which had been interlocked like the links of a chain. On the bedside table lay tattooing needles flecked with ink and blood.

Had the Alphabet Killer brought the other victims here too? Killed them immediately then tattooed them here? They'd have to wait for the autopsy, but Jan was increasingly sure the tattoos had been done post mortem. Was this mutilation? Desecration of the bodies after death? In Germany that sort of thing happened only five or six times per year.

The killer had deliberately betrayed this hiding place. He must have somewhere else where he could keep and prepare his victims. What if he didn't kill them straight away – what if he already had the next one in his power?

As he stepped out of the bedroom, he beckoned over one of the crime scene technicians. 'I don't want to disturb you, but please pay particular attention to the bed, okay?'

The man nodded, his brow furrowed.

Jan walked into the child's bedroom opposite, the only room in the whole house that was still intact. Clown wallpaper, a white lacquer bed, building bricks on the floor, a spick and span changing table.

A stab ran through Jan. The sudden death of a child. The final trigger. The push that had finally sent Zanetti's sanity tumbling into the abyss. He must already have had an inclination towards conspiracy theories, but the loss of his child must have abandoned him irretrievably to that world.

He leant against the window frame, closing his eyes for a moment and holding his face into the night wind. Laboriously he fished his phone out of his coat pocket and dialled Anita's number.

She picked up after the first ring. 'Jan?'

'I thought you'd be asleep already.'

'Were you just calling to wake me up? I was still racking my brains about those quotations – the technicians found another one in the bison enclosure. It was attached to one of the fenceposts.'

'What was it this time?'

'It was a bright cold day in April, and the clocks were striking thirteen.'

'Hmmm – George Orwell, *1984*. Apart from the fact that all the quotations are first lines, I can't see any connection between them. But I'm calling because I'm back at Zanetti's house. He might have brought the other two victims and tattooed them here. Probably he set up another hiding place ages ago – and I'd bet he's already got his next victim captive.'

'We went through all the missing persons cases in the area. No hits.'

'Then widen the search. Temporally and geographically. And concentrate primarily on people who work with books or have some other connection to language.'

'Explain.'

'Think about the previous victims' jobs.'

'Oh.'

'Exactly. Oh.'

'Anything else?' she probed. 'Oh, by the way. I'm moving into the wildlife park hotel too. Koblenz is a bit too far from the action.'

'Great, we'll finally be sleeping under one roof again,' remarked Jan sarcastically. 'And no, I don't have anything else. I'll nose around here a bit more, though.'

'Fine. Keep me in the loop.'

He put the phone away and wandered on through the house, trying to put himself in Zanetti's shoes. The final hours before his death. Was it he who had inspired the murderer? Had they known each other? If so, then why had the killer treated him as so insignificant? Zanetti was only 'C', one letter out of twenty-six. Not 'A' or 'Z'.

All three victims had known each other, but that didn't mean they also knew the killer. Maybe he'd been watching one of them and found the others that way.

The killer planned where to keep them and where to carry out his crime very precisely, although the way he'd killed them indicated impulsive behaviour. It wasn't a consistent profile. Were they dealing with two killers? A schizophrenic personality?

Jan sighed. He wasn't getting anywhere. He sat down on the steps by the front door. His hand slipped briefly underneath his coat, to the baggie with his joint. He toyed with the thought of taking a few puffs, but it would be impossible in front of his colleagues. Yet it was the only thing that calmed him down. The only thing that temporarily stopped the flood of symbols.

All at once, he wanted to leave.

Somewhere out there, the Alphabet Killer already had his next victim in his sights.

## 22

First came the cold. Then hunger and thirst.

'A . . . B . . . C . . . D.'

The echo of the man's voice roared in Tugba's head. She didn't know what the letters meant.

She didn't know anything at all. Where she was. Why she was lying in the darkness and cold. How much time had passed. She only knew she was in danger.

There's no shame in not knowing, only in not learning. The old proverb her baba had told her.

She needed information. It might be her only chance. She ignored the hunger gnawing deep inside her. The burning thirst that glued her dry tongue to the roof of her mouth. She'd spent the past hours – or was it days? – drifting in and out of consciousness. The last thing she remembered was a feeling of blind panic, of a kind she'd never known before in her life.

What did she know? The five 'W' questions she taught her pupils for their essays.

She'd been abducted. She didn't know when or by whom. She didn't know why. She didn't know where she was.

*With an effort she began to move. Every muscle in her body was throbbing with pain. The cold had stiffened her joints. Her shoulder knocked against a wall made of rotting wooden boards, which split the basement into two rooms. She was in some sort of tall wooden cage. Tentatively, her fingers explored. Wood on one side, unfinished brick on the other. Above her a thin wire grille. Dank air and the stench of something that reminded her of spoiled potatoes filled the room. There were no windows. She was in a basement.*

*Heavy footfalls. The floor above her head vibrated.*

*She held her breath, drawing her legs into her body until she was in a kind of upright foetal position.*

*A trapdoor opened in the ceiling. Deep blue night air flooded in.*

*Through the palm-width gaps between the wooden boards, Tugba could see into the basement room from her dungeon.*

*Her tormentor was climbing down a narrow staircase. He switched on a bare bulb, which flickered on with a buzz. The light burned Tugba's pupils. She squeezed her eyes almost shut, blinking. She could only see vague outlines.*

*He was standing with his back turned to her, the hood of his windbreaker pulled down around his face.*

*He was here to fetch her. To end it.*

*She tried not to make a sound, lifting her numb hands from the wood so that the trembling wouldn't make them creak. But it was pointless. He knew where she was. He was the one who'd put her there.*

*Yet he paid her no heed. All his attention seemed to be fixed on the opposite wall.*

*Tugba peered through a different gap, trying to get a better view, although even that tiny movement made her dizzy. Everything spun. Her legs were giving way.*

*But she had to watch. Gather information.*

*The wall that was so enthralling to her tormentor was covered in dozens of chalk marks. Letters. They were letters. The alphabet. Like in the classroom of a primary school. Beneath each letter was a rectangle.*

*Her tormentor reached into the pocket of his windbreaker and took out several pieces of paper. His fingers quivering, he stuck the pieces into the rectangles under A, B and C.*

*They were photos. Tugba could barely see them. Blurry close-ups of naked bodies. When she squinted a little, she thought she could make out letters. Blood red and uneven.*

*They were bodies. Dead, all of them.*

*Tugba lost her balance, cracking her head against the hard, stained mattress. Her breathing was jerky.*

*She remembered now. She remembered the pain. The buzzing. Outside, her tormentor began to recite the alphabet.*

*'A . . . B . . . C . . .'*

*Her back. There was something on her back. Her lips trembled as she ran her hand along her spine. The contortion exhausted the last of the strength in her brutalised bones.*

*'D . . . E . . . F . . .'*

*She felt it. A fine line of swollen, itchy skin. Like sunburn, but infinitely worse. She moved her other hand to feel more of the tattoo. To find out its shape.*

*It was a—*

*'G'!*

*Her heart skipped a beat.*

*Her tormentor was standing directly outside the cage, his face pressed against the boards. Trying to feel the tattoo, she hadn't heard him approach.*

*His face was in the shadows. All she could see was the glint in his eyes. As though he were waiting for something.*

*Tugba shrank back into the far corner of the cage, burying her head in her arms. Those eyes. She didn't want to feel them on her any more.*

*She was 'G'.*

*The hunger and cold had vanished. All she felt was the burning letter on her back.*

*She'd wanted information.*

*Now she knew far too much.*

# 23

'Apart from having worked through the night, I've not got much to report. No DNA, no signs of a struggle, nothing.'

In the fluorescent light of the autopsy room, the bags under Dr Harreiter's eyes were all too visible.

Jan sighed. 'In a case like this, I almost expected that.'

'Still, we're not completely empty-handed,' added Harreiter. 'Follow me!'

Stüter, Köllner, Rabea, Anita and Jan followed the medical examiner deeper into the white-tiled room.

Back in Mainz so soon, he thought. The Institute of Forensic Medicine at the University Clinic was the nearest place they could conduct a thorough autopsy. They'd set off in the early morning, and Jan had dozed throughout almost the whole journey. The late night was in his bones; three coffees later, he still wasn't back to normal. He'd ignored the newspapers laid out near the breakfast buffet at the hotel – he shuddered to think of the headlines about their disastrous press conference.

Their steps reverberated as they walked through the long morgue, past the three victims, who lay on autopsy tables covered in white, formalin-soaked sheets. On smaller tables beside them were plastic tubs containing the organs that had been removed for further examination.

Leonard Ziehner. Marek Lünner. Francesco Zanetti.

'A'. 'B'. 'C'.

Hopefully there would be no more names and letters.

Harreiter and her assistant paused in front of a stainless-steel table. 'During the autopsies, we found bark inside the mouths of all three victims.'

On the table were three greyish-brown pieces of bark about the size of Jan's thumb, bagged and numbered.

'Any idea what kind of tree they come from?' asked Köllner, resting his chin on his fist.

Stüter threw him a glance that clearly only said one thing: 'I ask the questions here.'

'Judging by the structure, I'd guess a linden or maple,' answered the medical examiner. 'We've already sent a sample to a botanist for a more precise analysis. It'll take some time, though.'

'Ah, well it's not like we're under any time pressure here.' Stüter was back at the helm. 'But we know it's something from the area, nothing exotic.'

'That's my best guess, at least.'

'Okay.' Stüter rubbed the bridge of his nose. 'What else do you have for us?'

'I'm fairly confident that the murder weapons are hunting implements. The incision on the first victim's throat and some of the cuts on the third victim come from a curved blade approximately a hand's length. Standard part of any hunter's kit.'

'And the other two victims?' asked Jan.

'Well, here I'm starting to speculate,' said Harreiter, enunciating the word 'speculate' as though it were a crime. 'If the knife is a hunting blade, the rope used to hang the second victim could be part of a hoist – the kind used to winch up and bleed an animal.'

'And what was Leonard Ziehner killed with?' Jan emphasised the publisher's name. He didn't like the way Dr Harreiter was only referring to the three dead men as 'victims'.

It robbed them of dignity.

He wanted to give them that, at least.

The medical examiner assumed a neutral expression. Cutting herself off seemed to be her style. Distancing herself. That, and the brightly coloured Star Trek T-shirt she wore underneath her white coat.

'The haematoma indicates some sort of bludgeon. Also, not uncommon among hunters.'

'At least now we know what weapons we're after,' said Stüter. 'And this thing with the bark—can you make head or tail of that, Mr Analyst?'

'It's a symbol,' said Jan. 'Something very intimate, or he wouldn't have put it in their mouths. The question is whether there was any intimacy between him and the victims, or whether it's a message to us. But it's different from his previous use of symbols. No connection to letters or language.'

'The victims are supposed to swallow it, if you want to put it like that,' added Rabea, her brow furrowed. 'A very dominant place to put it, almost sexual.'

'Every new piece of information seems to be more worrying than the one before.' Anita crossed her arms. She was pale. Jan remembered that she'd never liked visits to the morgue.

'There's one more thing,' said Harreiter. 'Two, actually. One, the tattoos were done post mortem, as you suspected. The wounds didn't start to heal, and there was no reddening. The areas are also not as dry as you'd normally see with tattoos.'

'And the other thing?' asked Jan.

'The killer didn't use tattoo ink.'

'What did he use?'

'Ordinary fountain-pen ink. The kind you'd find in any school. Probably the tattoos wouldn't even have been permanent. But sadly, that doesn't matter now, of course —'

'Sounds like prison tattoos,' remarked Ichigawa.

'It's another message, in any case. Fountain pen ink, of all things. He really is into writing.' Jan felt a band of pressure around his skull.

'What do you reckon?' asked Rabea.

'I've got to think it over.'

The medical examiner made a bow. 'That's all from our side, folks. You can read all about it in the autopsy report as well. I've already filed it with the senior administrator.'

They said their goodbyes, removed their white coats and left the Institute, emerging back into the realm of the living. Two laughing students came towards them in the car park, while children were throwing snowballs in the park nearby. A total contrast to the white-tiled hermetic silence of the morgue. Jan felt like a foreign body. An apparition from some other, darker world.

'Was worth the trip, anyway,' said Stüter in the car park. 'We now know he owns hunting gear.'

Jan hated raining on people's parades. 'That doesn't help us at all.'

'It's concrete evidence. What else is going to help us?' snapped Stüter.

Jan rolled his eyes.

'Let him talk,' said Anita.

Until now she'd been quiet, typing something abstractedly into her phone.

He threw her a brief, grateful glance and turned back to the group. 'Here in Westerwald hunters are ten a penny. Even my dad and brother had hunting licences. The weapons are a clue, of course, but only a minor one.'

'Plus, the ranger at the wildlife park told us somebody'd been practising by killing animals,' added Rabea. 'If we assume it was our killer, then he's not a seasoned hunter.'

Stüter leant against his car with a sigh. 'You're both right, of course, about the hunting gear—'

'So, we'll focus on the weird bark and fountain-pen ink first, then,' piped up Köllner, his protégé.

It seemed to Jan the investigation team was in free fall, and every tiny twig they grasped immediately snapped. The only question was how long the drop would be.

'Yes, Ichigawa here. What's the latest?' Anita fell back a few paces, her Samsung pressed to her ear. For a moment she lost the usually meticulous control of her expression, and her eyes flew wide. Ending the call a few seconds later, she stared at Jan. 'You were right.'

Jan's heart began to race. 'What do you mean?'

'A missing person has just been reported in Montabaur. Fits your pattern. Tugba Ekiz, thirty-two. Teaches German literature.'

**24**

On one point, science was unanimous: time travel was an impossibility.

Jan, however, had to disagree. As his Mercedes passed the sign announcing their entry into Hardt, the car transformed into a perfect time machine.

With every foot the vehicle rolled over the asphalt, the past opened up before him.

His home village.

The prodigal son returned.

He still remembered the moment he'd left. Two days before the funeral. Too late to avoid all the gossip. Far too soon to silence it.

That had been December, too. The sky that day hadn't been a leaden grey like today, but a clear blue. A total contrast with Jan's emotional world as he'd driven towards Bochum in the rented VW Polo.

Jan tapped the wheel with his fingertips. It would be so easy to turn back. A U-turn – nobody else was on the road anyway – and he'd be headed back to Hachenburg.

But he couldn't do that. His name had been haunting the radio and television waves since yesterday, and his face had even made the front page of several newspapers.

They already knew he was here. Just a brief family visit. He owed them that.

On the way back from Mainz he'd told Rabea he needed to slip away for an hour. That she'd have to do the interview with the person who'd reported Tugba Ekiz missing.

She'd asked, of course, where he was going.

He, of course, had made a secret of it.

Even though he might as well have told her. It made no difference. Yet he'd always been a loner. He preferred to sort things out by himself. Or maybe he was simply better at self-deception than other people.

He turned down Kirchstrasse – Church Street. As a child he'd always asked why it was called that, even though there was no church on it.

When he left there'd only been five buildings on that road, one of which was his family's barn. Now there were more than he could count at a glance.

There were a lot of new-builds. A row of smart detached homes lined both sides of the asphalt. Houses with signs outside that said things like *This is where Papa Dirk, Mama Katja, Finn-Lukas and Ann-Sophie live, love and argue.* Home-owning families who earned loyalty points with all sorts of different shops, who watched *Germany's Got Talent* on Saturday nights, who separated out their recycling with painstaking care.

A life he'd never been able to contemplate.

He didn't even recognise his brother's house. When he left, their parents' former home had been in the middle of renovations and completely covered in scaffolding. His brother had wanted to turn it into a home for his small family. Now it glowed a pale beige, with wooden window frames and solar panels on the roof.

Only the barn, slightly to the right of the house, was as dilapidated as in Jan's youth. Cobwebs hung like curtains in the windows, and the unfinished brick walls were thick with the grime and memories of generations.

As a small child, his brother had told him ghost stories about the ruin, about a haunted place of corpses and headless virgins.

His older brother had always been a good storyteller. Somebody who understood intuitively how to captivate his audience. As would also become apparent later in their lives.

Everything had always been about Gero. Jan had merely been the tiny satellite that orbited him. In school, where he'd had to follow in his much-too-big footsteps. With girls, who'd only ever used him so his brother would notice them.

He sighed, brushing the memories aside. His thigh was aching again. The old phantom pain. He halted the Mercedes outside the front door. The first chords of *Driving Home for Christmas* were already playing on the radio as he switched off the engine.

He followed the path, neatly shovelled clear of snow, through the front garden. A plastic figurine of Santa's sleigh was parked to the right of the paving stones, harnessed to six reindeer. In the Christmas decoration competition that had apparently broken out in the neighbourhood, however, the solitary vehicle lagged behind. He was about to climb the steps to the front door when the barn door opened with its familiar squeak.

A lanky young man in jeans and a leather jacket emerged. Early twenties, give or take. He was pushing an acid-green moped, and his beanie was drawn down low over his forehead.

'Morning!' He raised a palm from the handlebars and waved. 'Do we know each other from somewhere?'

Jan needed only a brief glance at his face to realise they definitely knew each other. With those high cheek bones and dark eyes, he looked like a younger copy of his brother Gero.

It was Maik. His nephew. The last time he'd seen him, he'd been hip-height and still playing with building blocks.

'I think we know each other better than you imagine.' Jan walked across, his hand outstretched. 'I'm your uncle.'

Maik shook hands. A weak pressure that spoke of uncertainty and didn't suit his strong build.

'I only have vague memories of you.' A reticent smile crept across Maik's face. 'But I've certainly *heard* a lot about you.'

For a moment that felt like an eternity, they merely looked at each other in embarrassment. Jan's eyes fell on the moped.

'I had one like that. In matt black. The small petrol tank always got on my nerves, though. How far can you get on that?'

'A full tank is enough for a ride to Burger King and back.'

Jan grinned. Out here, young people measured distances not in miles but in the distance to the next pillar of civilisation.

'Is that still in Hachenburg?'

Maik nodded, smiling.

Something about the young man irritated him. How much he resembled Gero. Jan felt like he was having a conversation with the past.

'I was just about to drive to Marienberg,' said Maik, trying to hide his local accent. 'Pick up a few spare parts.'

'Oh, is something wrong with it?'

'No, no. I just like tinkering with mopeds. I've set up a little workshop in the barn. Do repairs for friends sometimes.'

'Fair enough, then I won't keep you.'

Maik swung onto the bike and pulled on his racing-striped helmet. Only his blue eyes – exactly like Gero's – were visible. They were fixed again on Jan.

'I saw you. On the TV,' said his nephew. 'You're here because of the murders.'

Jan nodded.

'I hope you collar the bastard. We knew Herr Lünner, the reporter. He interviewed my little sister once about her school.'

With these words he flicked down his visor and the engine growled into life. Stepping on the accelerator, Maik jolted off towards the street.

Jan stared after him, blinking.

He had a little sister?

## 25

Gero's wife Katharina greeted him formally, but it wasn't anything like as bad as he'd imagined it might be.

'When I heard you were helping out with the investigation, I thought you might show up here,' she said, guiding him down the corridor.

The years had left her somewhat broader, but the extra pounds suited her.

Weight and hair colour might change, wrinkles might appear and skin fade, but some features always remained the same. For Kathi Grall it was her full mouth, her large, dark eyes and her black mane of hair, which made her look Spanish. Jan could certainly see why his brother had fallen for her back then.

'You've got thin,' she said. 'You look almost emaciated.'

'I'm vegan. And I've never eaten that much.'

'Vegan—' she repeated. In her mouth it sounded like he was part of some cult. 'Er, would you mind taking off your shoes?'

'Over the years I've seen my fair share of what people are capable of doing to each other. Believe me, at some point you stop wanting anything more to do with blood, death or captivity.'

He removed his trainers and put them beside the other shoes in the hall. Among them he saw a pair of men's shoes that clearly didn't belong to Maik.

'You remarried?'

'I have a boyfriend.' She showed him her hand, on which she still wore the ring Gero had given her on their wedding day. 'I swore I'd never marry again after him. And I've kept that promise.'

'It wasn't an accusation—'

'Fine.' She waved a dismissive hand as she led him into the open-plan kitchen. 'You can meet Stefan – he'll be here any minute. He always drops in on his lunch break. He's rather late now, actually. I thought it was him when you rang the bell. He can be so forgetful sometimes.' She laughed a fraction too hysterically. 'Do you want anything to drink? Coffee? Tea?'

'Coffee, please. Black,' said Jan absently. He was absorbing the atmosphere. Although the kitchen barely resembled his childhood memories, he felt like he'd come home. The family photos on the walls, the obligatory plate of homemade Christmas cookies on the table, the kitschy décor.

Not a single photo of himself or Gero, he noticed. His eyes rested on a family portrait taken in a studio before a white-and-grey background. Kathi and a small, chubby-cheeked girl were beaming broadly, as though the photographer had just cracked a joke. Maik, who wore a black slouchy jumper, reminding Jan of his own fashion rebellion, was only half-smiling.

'Emilia, that's our daughter's name. Four years old. A clever little thing.' Kathi threw a capsule into the coffee machine and pressed a button. The black brew flowed with a gurgle into the cup.

Jan directed his attention to the fourth person in the photograph. Kathi's new life partner. The hulking man was twice as wide as she was. His dark suit made it impossible to tell whether his size was due to fat or muscle mass. His shoulder-length hair was tied back neatly into a ponytail, his beard trimmed. There was not the trace of a smile to be seen on his lips.

Jan squinted. He was overcome with a feeling of déjà-vu. He pictured the man without his beard and ponytail, and at least twenty kilograms lighter.

Stefan. A common name. Could it be him?

'Is your boyfriend *the* Stefan? Schomar's Stefan?'

'That's the one!' said Kathi, pottering around the kitchen. 'I didn't know you remembered him.'

'Of course, he was one of my brother's best friends. They got their hunting licences together,' said Jan, settling down on the corner bench. He added under his breath, 'I remember a lot. Too much.'

She put the cup of coffee in front of him on the table, then sat down herself. 'Life goes on. Stefan was there for me, right from the beginning. Comfort, support, everything. And at some point, we decided to build something together. He's a divisional manager at WW Insurance in Bad Marienberg. Very considerate. Kind.' She sighed. 'But where there's light, there's always shadow.'

Jan leant forwards. 'What do you mean?'

'Maik. He was six when Gero died. Just after he started school. It wasn't good for him. He's always had problems at school. Like you. The first one in the family to go to university, even though you struggled with concentration when you first went to school, and you nearly had to repeat a year.' She lowered her eyes. 'It gave me hope.'

For a moment Jan shut his eyes. He'd never been able to concentrate on anything or anybody at school. Life and all its stimuli had rained down on him mercilessly. Back then he'd not known how to spread a protective shield across his mind.

'I met Maik outside. He seemed quite bright.'

'He is,' she said with a surge of pride. 'There's no one quicker at working with his hands. He's always had these little odd jobs. But nothing permanent's ever come out of it.'

He slumped inwardly. Guilt crept like a worm into Jan's guts, eating at his chest, deep into his heart. 'It didn't have to be like that.'

Kathi shook her head. 'You know what I think? You're the only one of us who hasn't escaped the past. For whom life didn't go on.' She threw out her arms. 'Look at you! Gaunt, harassed, constantly dealing with murder and death. You've tortured yourself with guilt since Gero's death – and it only exists in your head!'

'But you weren't there!' thundered Jan, leaping to his feet. He bumped into the table and the cup tipped over, its contents pouring across the surface. 'You didn't see it. Experience it. You – you——'

She hadn't known what he'd known. And she could never find out.

Kathi stared at him, her eyes wide.

'I should go.' His fingers trembling, he righted the coffee cup before hurrying out of the kitchen.

She called after him, 'You'll never be at peace with yourself this way!'

His trainers jammed under his arm, he flung open the front door. As he did so, his head almost collided with Stefan's chest.

'Jan? I don't believe it!' roared the bear of a man, whose build was even more colossal in reality.

'I was just on my way out.' He made to push past Stefan, but the man blocked his path.

'Hang on, let me look at you! How long has it been? Oh man, you could do with a little meat on your bones.'

Stefan's effusiveness completely overwhelmed him. The giant was watching him intently, and Jan took the opportunity to study him as well. Stefan looked significantly more tired than in the family portrait, with bags under his eyes almost bigger than the swollen eyes themselves and skin that was sickly pale.

'You really won't stay? Kathi has a lentil stew left over from yesterday, with sausage. A dream.'

'No, I'm really sorry. I've got a meeting to go to. I'm vegan, anyway. I don't eat any animal—'

'Oh, come on, Jan! You don't need to explain to me what a vegan is. This isn't a total backwater.' Stefan stretched out his arms, knocking into the doorframe with his briefcase. 'How's the investigation going?'

'I can't talk about that, I'm afraid. I hope you understand.'

'Of course, but I'm allowed to be curious.'

They edged past each other. Now Stefan was standing in the house and Jan, still in his socks, was on the ice-cold path. Now Jan saw Stefan smile for the first time, he realised why he hadn't done so in the family photograph: it looked horribly forced. Unnatural. Like a studied performance.

Exactly like everything else about Stefan. The effusiveness was nothing but a mask for the tension behind it. Jan fixed his gaze on Stefan's watery eyes. What was he hiding? 'So, why don't you come over for a beer or something one day?' Stefan shrugged. 'For old times' sake. I'm just looking through Gero's old things. Maybe you'd like to take a peek too.'

This time the mere mention of Gero's name hit Jan like the crack of a whip. He winced.

'Sure, I'll drop by some other time!' He waved at Stefan and Kathi, who had come into the hallway, then turned to leave.

He walked to his car in his soaking wet socks. His heart was pounding against his ribs.

'You'll never be at peace with yourself this way!' Kathi's words shot through his mind.

How could he ever be at peace with himself? He'd killed his brother.

## 26

'Nihal Ekiz, correct?' Rabea sat down opposite the woman at the plastic table. 'My name is Rabea Wyler, behavioural investigative advisor with the Rheinland-Pfalz State Office of Criminal Investigations. You're Tugba's sister?'

The little woman nodded, her gaze fixed on her lap. Her hands were tucked between her thighs.

'I still don't understand why your colleagues in Montabaur sent me to you.' Frau Ekiz's deep smoker's voice was at odds with her fragile frame. 'You're on the big investigation team, aren't you?'

'Listen—'

Ekiz looked up. Tears shimmered in her eyes. 'Do you think something's happened to my sister?'

Rabea held up her hands reassuringly. 'This is just routine. At the moment we're checking all missing persons reports in the area. Everything else is just speculation.'

That wasn't quite the truth, but Rabea needed Nihal Ekiz focused, not hysterical. The young Turkish woman's hands were no longer in her lap; now she was fiddling with the small gold ring in her nose.

'I can't believe I'm sitting here. I don't want to believe it.'

'That's what everybody thinks when they find themselves in this situation.' Rabea knew what she was talking about. She thought of her entry in ViCLAS. Of a blood-flecked raincoat, the final sign of life. Of waiting, afraid, which turned at last into the numbness of certainty. 'I promise you, we'll do everything in our power to find your sister. But you'll have to tell us absolutely everything you know. Everything.'

Ekiz brushed her dyed-blonde fringe back from her forehead and sipped at her plastic cup of water. 'I understand. Where should I begin?'

Before Rabea could answer, the door of the improvised interview room – which was actually nothing but an old office – opened. Anita Ichigawa bustled in, introduced herself briefly to Ekiz, then lowered her mouth to Rabea's ear: 'Do you have any idea where Jan's got to?'

'He didn't want to tell me. And he should have been here half an hour ago.'

'Strange. Can you text him again?'

Rabea nodded. Anita's gaze wandered to Ekiz. 'I'll leave you two alone.'

It wasn't like Jan to be late. Was it time to start worrying? Why had he been acting so mysteriously?

*where are you? I could use you at Ekiz's sister's interview,* she texted him.

'Sorry about that,' she said to Nihal Ekiz, leaning forwards onto the table. 'It's best to begin with the last time you saw your sister.'

'That was two weeks ago. I'm a hairdresser in Koblenz, and I live nearby. She's in Montabaur. We try to meet up every other Sunday. Grab brunch, bake together or something.' She swallowed drily. 'But in the meantime, we're always texting on WhatsApp and stuff, of course. I got the last message from her on Friday evening. At first, I thought nothing of it. We'd already agreed to meet up on Sunday.'

Rabea nodded. Absolutely understandable.

'But when I went to the bar on Sunday evening, Tugba never showed up.' Ekiz picked at her pastel-coloured acrylic nails. 'I called loads of times. No response. Then I drove to her apartment and rang the bell, but nothing.'

'You arrived at the police station in Montabaur at four in the morning. What were you doing until then?'

'Well, obviously I didn't instantly assume the worst, although I did have a bad feeling. I called everybody on her list of friends, I called my family. It just isn't like Tugba to pull a vanishing act like this.'

'At some point you decided you had no option but to go to the police.'

'Yeah. And now I'm sitting here.'

Rabea was taking notes on her iPad, although the pauses in the conversation were more important to her than what she was writing down. She needed time to organise her thoughts. Worst case scenario, Tugba Ekiz had been in the hands of the Alphabet Killer since Friday. Her chances of survival depended on what letter he'd allocated her, assuming he was keeping her prisoner like Zanetti.

'Did your sister ever mention being afraid of anybody over the past couple of weeks? Anybody stalking her?'

'No, not a word. I mean, she's a teacher through and through. Her colleagues and her parents love her. Absolute sunshine.'

'Did she have a boyfriend? Anybody she was seeing?'

Nihal Ekiz hid her trembling hands under the table once more. 'If so, she never mentioned it to me. I don't know if she would have had time, given how dedicated she was to her job.'

Rabea ran through her list of remaining questions with the hairdresser, but nothing salient cropped up.

They'd have to search Tugba's apartment, maybe even visit her place of work. The killer must have left clues somewhere.

'You'll let me know as soon as you know anything?' asked Nihal Ekiz as Rabea walked her down the corridor.

'Of course, we—' She broke off when she saw Jan. He was crouching on the floor, his knees drawn up to his chest. His face was the colour of the chalk-white wall. His shirt was hanging half out of his trousers. His whole body looked as though gravity were dragging him earthwards with greater force than normal.

'What's the matter with him?' Köllner, who had just come to escort Ekiz outside, stood there open-mouthed.

'Family stuff,' whispered Jan feebly. He pulled himself upright, holding onto a cupboard. His legs wobbled. 'Are you finished already, Rabea? Shall I help you with the interview?'

In half a second Rabea was beside him, taking hold of his arm. 'You're not going anywhere.'

'I'm all right, trust me,' he replied, but meekly allowed her to support him while she sent Köllner away with Ekiz.

Everything about him was screaming for help.

'Okay, first I'm taking you somewhere you can rest,' she said, dragging him into the car park outside the station. 'Then you're going to tell me quietly and calmly why coming home has knocked all the stuffing out of you.'

# 27

Café Wäller was the beating heart of Bismarckstrasse in Marienberg. People flocked to the round, glass-windowed space in order to see and be seen. On top of that, they had delicious cakes and coffee.

Rabea closed her lips around the first forkful of chocolate torte, shutting her eyes for a moment. The more stressful the situation, the more she needed sugary treats. The torte tasted divine. A catastrophe for her figure, but a culinary first-aid kit for her nerves.

As usual, Jan limited himself to an espresso, which he drank in tiny sips. He still looked dishevelled. His eyes were bloodshot, his shirt rumpled.

'I'm supposed to unburden my soul now, I guess,' he whispered to his espresso cup.

'Don't put it so dramatically.'

It was early afternoon, and the first pensioners were drifting in for their ritual coffees. Servers and patrons knew each other by name here, and if somebody didn't show up then their neighbours would be asked whether everything was all right. Rabea had grown up in the Swiss countryside – she knew the social wickerwork of a place like Bad Marienberg all too well.

'My brother was a few years older than me,' began Jan. Speaking about him in the past tense did not bode well, thought Rabea. 'When I turned eighteen, he was already working for our father's logistics company. He had a wife and child and had started renovating our parents' house for his family.'

When he raised the cup to his mouth, the trembling of his hand made it shake too.

'A car accident. On my birthday, of all days. Gero died on the scene. After that I couldn't take it here anymore. Didn't even go to the funeral. I just wanted to get out.' He forced the words out from between his teeth, avoiding her gaze.

Rabea leant back and put down her fork. She'd lost her appetite. 'Do you want to tell me any more?'

She sensed that wasn't everything. Jan might be good at reading other people, but he'd always been an open book. He'd told her only part of the truth – if that.

He was kneading his hands. 'It was the middle of December, and the streets were like they are now. Slippery. Unpredictable.'

The way he spoke, it sounded like he'd been at the wheel himself.

'Anyway, I understand your behaviour better now.' Rabea drew herself up. 'I'm so sorry.'

'It's okay.' He waved his hand. 'It's all so long ago. It's just that the past has a nasty habit of sticking to you like glue.'

'What's your relationship like with your family?'

'Non-existent. When they needed me most, I bolted.'

If it hadn't been for their difference in rank – and dozens of other reasons – Rabea would have simply given him a hug. That tall, fragile, profoundly sorrowful man.

'My brother was always the popular one. With girls, with teachers, everyone. I almost felt some people wished I'd died instead.'

'If it's affecting you like this, then ask them to take you off the case.'

He shook his head vehemently. 'We're already in too deep. And I'd be running away, again. I've got to face up to it all.'

'Okay.' She reached out her hands a few centimetres. Towards his. Then, catching herself, she pulled them back. 'Köllner just texted. They're headed for Tugba Ekiz's apartment. We're supposed to join them. Only if you're up to it, of course.'

'Hey, hey, hey, you don't need to handle me with kid gloves.' Throwing back his head, he gulped down the rest of his espresso. 'I'll be all right. I'm good at sorting these things out for myself.'

That was probably the biggest lie of all, thought Rabea.

## 28

As darkness fell, Rabea and Jan were entering Horressen, where Tugba Ekiz had lived. During the journey Rabea had described her conversation with the sister.

Jan was certain. A literature teacher from Montabaur. It fitted the story the Alphabet Killer was telling. It fitted the way he thought. This had to be the same person.

'Feeling any better?' enquired Rabea once more.

'We've all got to function.'

Since their chat in the café, she'd been looking at him differently. Before, there had been curiosity and some-times even admiration in her gaze – at least, he thought he'd glimpsed the latter during an attack of megalomania. Now all he saw in her eyes was concern. It should be the other way around, he thought, feeling horribly macho at the idea.

He'd revealed only a little of the truth, but already even that seemed too much.

Jan parked the Mercedes in a space outside the building. As he slid the key out of the ignition, he took a moment to get a feel for the environment in the isolation of the car. Quiet suburb, upper middle class. People kept to themselves.

A few neighbours had furnished their windowsills with pillows and were observing proceedings. Some were even standing in groups on the pavement. This would certainly provide the residents of this Montabaur suburb with something to gossip about for years to come.

What sometimes depressed him even more than the crime scene was the quiet, empty rooms of the victim. Imagining all the things they'd planned for their lives which might never happen now.

It was never the past that ran you down.

It was what remained behind.

An infernal thundering noise made him jump. Stüter was standing at the back of the Mercedes, beating wildly on the roof with his fist. With the other hand he beckoned them out.

'Has he finally blown a fuse?' groaned Jan.

Rabea only rolled her eyes.

'Good to see you too,' said Jan, climbing out of the vehicle.

'Spare me the platitudes. We found something.'

Rabea cocked her head. 'What do you have?'

'Just come!' He marched ahead, down the main corridor. Jan and Rabea struggled to keep pace. Along the way they nodded to Köllner, who was questioning a young couple – probably neighbours.

The stairwell smelled of citrus cleaning fluid, cooking fat and cold cigarette smoke – the typical melange common to more or less every German block of flats.

After slipping into plastic overalls, they stepped inside the life of Tugba Ekiz.

Instantly, Jan was besieged. Stimuli danced across his field of view like the ultraviolet spots you get when you rub your eyes.

The smell of bolognaise sauce was still hanging in the air, although the crime scene technicians had long since flung open all the doors and windows. Photos stuck to the wardrobe in the hall, Tugba with her mother and sister. Among them were a few yellowing images of her as a young girl with a bald man, probably her father.

Jan ignored Stüter and Rabea, who had already gone further into the house, and stepped closer to the wardrobe. Among the photographs hung a printout with Turkish words in a florid script, and beneath it the name of a tattoo studio. Had Tugba had the words tattooed on her? Could there be a connection to the studio?

'Grall, where've you got to?' Stüter's voice reached his ears.

The living room wasn't exactly reticent about the story it had to tell. It was a simple, archetypal story. The story of a lost struggle.

A shattered glass on the laminate flooring. Dried red wine on the sheepskin rug. Torn women's clothing scattered around a scratched, flecked area, like elements of a ritual circle.

'Looks almost like the aftermath of a rape,' commented Anita, who'd been waiting for them.

'No, no, no,' disagreed Jan. 'He was after a different kind of satisfaction. Those are flecks of ink on the floor, aren't they?'

Stüter nodded. 'Odds are it'll be fountain-pen ink again.'

Jan crouched down, pointing at a radiator underneath the window overlooking the back garden. Cable ties. 'He trussed her up like he did with Zanetti, so he could tattoo her in peace. Then he took her.'

'But why tattoo the letter onto her here?' asked Rabea. 'He risked being discovered the whole time.'

'Satisfaction,' repeated Jan. 'For him the tattooing is part of the act. It excites him. He let go of his inhibitions, he couldn't help it. He *had* to do it. Right here.'

'Now we get to the interesting part,' said Anita, sitting down on the chaise longue – beige, like the other furniture in the room – with a sigh. As always when she was stressed, she pulled a face and moved her head in jerks. 'Neither the front door, the garden door nor the windows were forced. How did he get in?'

Jan's gaze fell on the open DVD case of *The Notebook*. 'Tugba's sister didn't mention a lover or a boyfriend. That means she wasn't going to watch the film with a man, but most likely alone or with a female friend.'

'You're saying she wasn't expecting anybody?'

'Right.'

'If there are no signs of forced entry, then she probably let him in,' said Rabea. She'd closed her eyes, but the lids fluttered. Her mind was racing.

'He could have made something up. A simple lie,' said Stüter.

Jan sat cross-legged in the centre of the group, tracing his fingers along the grain of the laminate. 'Or – and this would turn everything on its head – Tugba knew the killer.'

## 29

*A plastic cup of tap water and a bowl of soggy oatmeal in sour milk. Tugba's tormentor had given her nothing else.*

*Her first meal in days. She gulped down the oatmeal in a few bites. Instantly her empty, shrunken stomach rebelled. She retched but was able to keep herself under control.*

*She sipped her water, leaning her head against the brick wall. No more pictures had been added to his wall. She still had time. And time, at the moment, was the only currency she valued.*

*Nihal or one of her friends would have gone to the police ages ago. They'd be looking for her. They'd be on her tormentor's trail.*

*Why her, of all people? Because she taught literature? Was that the only reason?*

*He'd seemed familiar. That face – she knew it from somewhere. Otherwise she wouldn't have opened the door. But where did she know him from? Who was he?*

*Try as she might, she couldn't remember.*

*All of a sudden, she heard the clumping of his booted footsteps.*

*Was he taking the plastic crockery away already?*

*Hastily she emptied her cup. Her constricted throat made it hard to swallow.*

*He came towards her cage. Again, those eyes, which burned like the tattoo on her back.*

*There was something in his hands.*

*Her lips trembled. The next letter.*

*But he didn't go up to his wall – instead, he shoved it through the wooden boards, and it landed with a slap on her quilt. It was an exercise book with a red pen tucked inside.*

*'Work!' he whispered.*

*Before she could reply, he was climbing back up the ladder. This time he left the bulb on.*

*Confused, Tugba crawled towards the book. It was a small-format exercise book, the kind normally used in primary school classes. She opened it.*

*Her eyes flitted across the pages. Again and again, the same words, etched in a scrawl between the lines: house, house, house, house . . . cat, cat, cat, cat . . . car, car, car, car . . .*

*It had to belong to a child in Year One.*

*She slid her fingers over the pen. Was she supposed to go through the book and correct it? Give the whole thing a mark? Maybe her tormentor had a child and was trying in this perverse way to teach the alphabet.*

*Tugba put the book aside and began to unscrew the pen. She had a much better idea for what to do with it.*

# 30

'I saw you on the television,' said Miriam, smacking her lips. 'You seem to be pretty stressed out down there. It's turning into something out of *Seven* or *Silence of the Lambs*.'

Jan stretched out on his hotel bed and pressed the phone to his ear. 'Everything okay with you? Those guys been giving you any more trouble?'

'Nah, it's all chill,' she replied. 'They don't know where your house is.'

'True. What are you eating? You been raiding my fridge again?'

'Think I'm an idiot?' she replied, munching indignantly. 'You've got nothing but some random vegetables and bits of tofu in there. I ordered a pizza.'

Jan rolled his eyes. 'You mean artichokes, kohlrabi and top-quality smoked tofu.'

'Ugh, tofu's tofu whether it's smoked or not. All that veggie crap's got nothing on a decent salami pizza with a cheese-stuffed crust.'

'Such a picky eater. How long are you staying, then?'

'I just want to give things another few days to settle. That cool?'

'Fine. I've got no idea how long I'll be stuck here, anyway.'

She took another noisy bite of pizza. 'Okay, then have a great evening – and don't drink everything in the minibar.'

'Haha. Me and the minibar.'

She groaned. 'Yeah, that was the joke.'

'I know. Good night, Anarchist.'

'Don't call me that!'

He hung up with a grin and put the phone on the bedside table. The conversation with Miriam had done him good. She grounded him. He'd been planning to go to the restaurant and see Tamara again, but he was simply too exhausted.

He drank the last sip of the Coke he'd taken from the minibar and shut his eyes, thinking about their hypothesis in Tugba's apartment. Was the killer one of her—?

A soft knock at the door. Jan blinked, wiping away a thread of saliva. Had he been asleep for ten minutes or several hours?

He unwound himself from the bedclothes. Who wanted something from him now? Was it Rabea? Or somebody from the hotel?

'Who's there?'

'It's me.'

Tamara's voice.

His heart skipped a beat. 'What are you doing here?'

'Open the door,' she said. 'I'm not here to kill you.'

He opened it. Although he was wearing only a vest and jeans, he didn't bother putting anything else on. If you go around knocking on hotel doors in the middle of the night, you have to reckon with sights like that.

Tamara wore a hotel dressing gown. Her hair was loose, making her red locks look even more overwhelming.

'You didn't come to the restaurant.' There was no accusation in her voice.

'I think the bags under my eyes are justification enough. Tough day.'

'I can't say the same of mine,' she said. Without waiting for an invitation, she walked into his room. 'I spent most of it in the spa.'

'I could do with that myself right now.'

She took a step towards him and leant forwards.

'What about this instead?' she whispered.

Her fingers slid across his chest, down his belly and onto his hips. She smelled of some kind of aloe vera massage oil, combined with the slight scent of cigarettes.

Her touch paralysed him. Still half-befogged with sleep, he was in shock. It was all happening so quickly.

Without resisting, he let himself be pulled towards the bed.

'You're one of the tidy ones, eh?' she observed, glancing at his neatly folded clothes and at the desk, which was organised to clinical perfection.

'Everything else might be spiralling out of hand, but at least I want control over my room.'

'You're going to lose that too.' Her hands wandered over his chest, warmly caressing his skin.

'Isn't this going a bit too—?'

She silenced him with a kiss, nibbling at his lower lip and slipping her tongue into his mouth.

Then she pressed him gently down onto the mattress.

## 31

The rustling bedclothes dragged Jan out of sleep.

Tamara had sat up and was putting on her slippers.

His ran his index finger down her back, following her spine. 'You're leaving already?'

She turned to him with a grin. 'Don't worry, I'll put your money on the bedside table.'

'Now I really feel used,' he laughed, pinching her side. 'I've never had the honour of being someone's holiday fling before.'

'That's too bad – you acquitted yourself pretty well.' She pulled the dressing gown back on.

'How long are you actually staying here?' he asked, his head resting on his fist.

'Until Thursday. I'm only two doors down. Number 102.' She winked. 'In case you're ever in the mood for a trip to the spa.'

He rubbed his eyes. 'This was all a bit quick. Is it always like that with you?'

'Not always. But I know what I want. And how to get it.'

She stood up and pulled back the curtain a crack, her eyes vigilant as she gazed down at the wildlife park. The pale moonlight made her skin gleam.

'I'm not a relationship person,' she said. 'Tried often enough, failed often enough. But this sort of thing is fun. How about you?'

'Similar.'

'But you're a man.'

He chuckled. 'No, I'm just Jan. Sometimes I'm so absorbed in human psychology, so preoccupied with all the ricochets our brains produce that I can do without all that at home. All I want is to be alone.'

He searched for a reaction in her face. Had it sounded like inner strength, or merely sad?

'You took the words right out of my mouth,' she replied, drawing back the curtain. 'Somehow I never got over my very first boyfriend. Sounds silly, eh? Back then I was still a naïve little girl. Maybe that was why we fell in love so intensely. So intensely that even then I knew we wouldn't last long.' She crouched down in front of the minibar and took out a bottle of Glenfiddich.

'What happened?' Jan sat up.

'That's a fiasco best left to another evening. And this is on the house, right?' She twirled the tiny bottle of whisky. 'Let's treat ourselves to some alone time.'

She left the room, but she wasn't leaving him alone. His head was whirling with too many questions. For the first time since arriving in Westerwald, the case had been pushed into the background. Crossing his arms behind his head, he shut his eyes and enjoyed her warmth, which he could still feel underneath the bedclothes.

# 32

'There was a woman at breakfast kept winking at you,' said Rabea. 'Anything going on there?'

She noticed with amusement that Jan quickened his pace. Her question seemed to have provoked a subconscious instinct to flee.

'That's private, my dear,' he murmured to himself.

She could barely understand him above the deafening noise in the playground at Mons Tabor High School.

Break time. A classic object-lesson for any amateur psychologist. The formation of social groups, outsiders' attempts to break in, couples frantically groping each other. A symphony of glances and gestures, gossip and giggles, snubs and genuine friendships.

You had to dive into the stream of signals. That's how Jan had put it once, in his typical, slightly muddled style. Here, amid the microcosm of the playground, she understood the meaning of his words.

She watched three boys playing basketball around a single net. The last time she'd held a basketball was more than six months ago. She'd had neither the time nor the opportunity since moving from Switzerland.

'Lots of parents have kept their kids at home today, since they found out about Tugba's disappearance,' said Köllner, who was walking just behind them.

The Inspector had escorted them to Montabaur while the rest of the team went through the responses to their public appeal for witnesses.

Jan glared at a couple of teenagers who were imitating his jagged gait. 'It's all scaremongering.'

'I can understand them. I'd do the same thing with my daughter.'

Rabea pricked up her ears. 'You have a child?'

She was looking at the Inspector with fresh eyes.

The way Stüter picked on his subordinate sometimes made Köllner seem younger than he really was.

'My girlfriend's six months pregnant,' he said. 'Technically it wasn't planned, but we're taking it in our stride. We're planning to marry before the birth.'

'Will Stüter be invited to the party?' Jan winked at him.

The Inspector merely smiled to himself.

'Congratulations, anyway.' Rabea patted him somewhat awkwardly on the back. 'Enjoy your paternity leave, once all this is done and dusted.'

Having kids. Köllner was only a year or two older than her. It was an issue on her mind, too. But should you really bring children into this world? She thought of ViCLAS, the database of violent crimes. There would always be a danger that her child's name might appear in there someday.

She surveyed the deserted school building. A weedy boy was sitting cross-legged outside one of the classrooms, scribbling in his notebook as if his life depended on it.

Doing homework just before class. The image brought a smile to Rabea's face. She'd used the same tactic herself, and it had never made a difference to her grades. School had never been a challenge. Some of her classmates had even suspected she was studying in secret.

'Do you still think Tugba knew her assailant?' she asked Jan, as they walked towards the administrative offices.

'Occam's razor,' he replied.

'Could you be a little more cryptic?'

'You know what it means, don't you?'

Of course, she knew! She recited the scholarly principle: 'When several theories explain the same facts, the simplest is always preferable.'

'If we apply Occam's razor to the Alphabet Killer case, the situation is quite clear,' continued Jan.

'He didn't know the victims personally,' said Rabea. 'Too tangled. Makes the situation too complicated.'

Jan snapped his fingers on both hands. 'Exactly.'

'You've dismissed your hypothesis, then.'

'Like I always say: never fall in love with an idea. You've got to be able to kill it as soon as you've created it.'

She'd always admired how dispassionately he could simply knock down even vast mental constructs that had been pieced together over hours. They marched towards the office. Köllner knocked on the door.

'However, if she did know him, it was through work. There's been nothing from her private life as yet. Hardly anything worth mentioning besides the meet-ups with her sister and a few female friends,' said Rabea. 'Maybe a chat with the headmistress will bring something to light.'

Jan's mouth twisted. 'You've got to be able to kill your hypothesis, but you can never bury them.'

His mood had markedly improved overnight – Rabea could imagine why. The woman from breakfast.

Occam's razor.

The simplest explanation was usually correct.

## 33

Life was a masked ball.

The words shot again through Jan's mind, as melo-dramatic as they sounded. Every person you met wore a mask. Gisela von Esch, headmistress of Mons Tabor High School, wore a mask of professionalism. The dark red of her short haircut seemed to have been carefully matched to her rouge and lipstick. She had squeezed her body into a marine-blue trouser suit that she must have bought some time ago, before she was carrying ten kilograms of extra weight.

'Frau Ekiz is one of the pillars of this school. As qualified as she is humane,' she said, giving her high voice the tim-bre of a eulogy. 'She's the kind of person you have to advise to switch off occasionally. I do hope we'll see her back here safe and sound.'

On her desk, a delegation of hideously tasteless porcelain birds kept watch over the office.

While Köllner and Rabea sat opposite the headmistress in the visitors' chairs, Jan paced the room, arms folded. He let his gaze sweep across files and class photos, coming to rest on calendars and framed awards. He wanted to get a feel for the school. To understand how Tugba had functioned in this system.

'And you're absolutely sure Frau Ekiz was kidnapped by this Alphabet Killer?' asked von Esch.

'That's our understanding at this time, yes.' Rabea shifted in her chair. 'She fits his victim profile.'

'Are – are the rest of our staff under threat?'

Jan had noticed initially that von Esch's red-varnished fingernails were chewed to the quick, and her hand now flew to her mouth. Then she seemed to remember she wasn't alone, and merely brushed her lips.

Köllner shook his head. 'We don't currently believe so. He's targeting specific people who work with the German language. But he's not focused on teachers.'

'Understood.' Von Esch leant back, her chair squeaking pitifully. 'You're here because you're looking for clues, is that right?'

All three nodded. Rhetorical questions – was she speaking to them like she'd address a class of schoolkids?

'You may already have discovered this in the course of your investigation, but there's something in particular about Frau Ekiz that might have attracted this monster's attention.'

Jan felt like telling her she didn't have to keep them on tenterhooks. It wasn't a lesson.

'And that would be?' Köllner expressed himself rather more diplomatically, of course.

'Perhaps it's too banal.' Von Esch's little finger slipped between her lips. 'Frau Ekiz taught literacy classes. In cooperation with an organisation here in Montabaur. Mainly for children from Sinti and Roma families. On top of her work here with us.'

Jan stepped up behind Rabea and Köllner, gripping the backs of their chairs. 'Did we know about this?'

Both said no.

'Then you've been a tremendous help, Frau von Esch,' he said. 'We'll need the name of the organisation and their contact details.'

He and Rabea exchanged an eloquent glance.

While the other two continued the discussion with von Esch, Jan inspected the photograph of 7D – her class. Unlike the other pictures, the children had draped their arms around each other's shoulders, like a football team. Tugba wasn't standing to one side like the other teachers, but in the middle of her pupils. People like her were few and far between. Tugba Ekiz's friendliness and dedication were no mask – and that might have been her undoing.

# 34

Back at Hachenburg police station, Jan and Rabea barricaded themselves into an empty office.

Turning the key twice in the lock, Jan leant against the door with a sigh. 'Peace at last!'

Rabea, her fists resting on her hips, glanced around the room, every square metre of which was filled with filing cabinets and desks. 'Let's make ourselves at home!'

They pushed the furniture into one corner of the room. As they did so, Jan found a biscuit tin full of pennies, a pocket calendar from 1992 and a Gameboy with a scratched screen, which still had Tetris loaded. 'Still works,' cried Rabea, when she switched it on and heard the familiar tune. 'I'm taking it, anyway. The odd bit of gaming helps me think.'

Jan chuckled. 'I've rarely seen you so enthusiastic.'

'Wait until I get the new high score.'

She put the Gameboy down and they began papering the walls of their refuge with documents and notes from the case.

Writing on the wall in thick felt-tip pen, Jan drew the letters 'A', 'B' and 'C'. Underneath each they gathered the information about the respective victims.

Jan settled cross-legged on the floor in the middle of the room, his joints responding achily. He groaned. 'At least I can think straight in here. No Stüter, no Anita constantly breathing down our necks.'

Rabea remained standing near the area of the wall she'd dedicated to Tugba Ekiz. 'Do you still think we'll find our man on the literacy course?'

Copies of the list of participants were hanging immediately under the photograph of Tugba. They were exclusively Romanian adolescents and a few Syrian refugees.

'This isn't just about one murder – he's staging something. It's a very special kind of drama. None of the participants would have a reason to act like our killer.'

'You're making him sound almost like a director.' Rabea, turning, sank onto a sagging grey sofa that had appeared during all the furniture-moving.

'From his perspective, he is. Westerwald is his backdrop, the victims are his protagonists and we – well, so far, we're nothing more than extras. That's got to change.'

'But isn't it too soon to start putting together a profile?'

Jan tilted back his head, staring at the ceiling. 'I know, I know. But time is a luxury we can't afford right now.' His eyes flitted to the photo of Tugba. 'There's too much at stake.'

Rabea leant back on the sofa and nestled her head against the armrest, as though she were visiting a shrink. 'How do you want to proceed?'

'Simple.' Reaching into the inside pocket of his black blazer, he drew out a yellow, hole-picked foam ball. It was so worn from use that one eye of the smiley face printed on it was gone. A marketing toy from some conference. 'We'll tell each other stories.'

Jan chucked her the ball. Surprised, she jumped. It landed on her stomach, rolling off the sofa. She could just reach it. 'What's that supposed to accomplish?'

'Do you remember the first assignment I ever gave you?'

'Of course, how could I forget!' She squeezed the ball, tossing it from hand to hand. 'To write a short story. I felt like I was back in German class, not with the police.'

'And do you remember the moral of the story?'

'You're sounding so didactic again.' She rolled her eyes. 'But yeah, it was about creativity.'

'More than that. About telling stories. Coming up with narratives. Filling the gaps in our knowledge with hypotheses. That's precisely what we're going to do now. Toss the ball back and forth, quickly. There's no right or wrong. Nothing's off the table.'

'You and your brainstorming methods!'

'Stop bellyaching and get going! One or two keywords!'

She sighed and pressed the ball flat against her forehead. 'Okay, we're not dealing with one killer, we're dealing with a group. That would explain the high frequency.'

'Very good! There we go!' Jan tore a leaf out of his note-pad and wrote it down.

As he looked up, the ball smacked him on the nose.

'Oh, sorry!' cried Rabea, unable to hold back a giggle.

'No harm done.' He rubbed his face. 'I'll keep going. The killer sees himself as an artist. He wants to create a unique font, a unique typeface with his alphabet. Arial, Calibri, Times New Roman, the font of death.'

He chucked the ball back towards the sofa.

For the next two hours they continued inventing stories, until the floor around Jan was littered with scraps of paper. Stüter and Köllner kept coming to knock. At first, they shouted that they wanted to be left in peace; but at some point, they simply started ignoring their colleagues.

Of course, Jan knew ninety percent of the hypotheses he'd jotted down were groundless. But if only one of them led to a solid profile, then the brainstorming session had been worth it.

'That's enough,' he said at last, as the ball became increasingly sluggish and their theories increasingly abstruse. 'Tomorrow we'll put all this together with the rest of our notes to create the profile.'

'I can start writing it up tonight,' offered Rabea.

He sat down next to her on the sofa, putting the ball away. 'That would be a huge help. Thanks.'

'I couldn't help thinking just now about the first time we met.' She shot him a sidelong glance.

'Oh yeah?' His mouth twisted. 'You wanted to take the first train back to Switzerland, I bet.'

'Can I just go through the facts again? You locked us in a room for four hours without food or drink, and you confronted me with the worst traumas of my life like we were having a cosy chat.'

'You must have thought I was a psychopath.'

'An arsehole, more like.'

'It was a test. A highly unconventional one, I must admit. And you passed with flying colours. I have had candidates who simply broke down. You were upset, you wrestled with yourself, but you kept yourself under control.'

'It was tough. Bloody tough.' She swallowed audibly. 'Especially when we got to my sister. The way she vanished. I understand why you did it, but I wouldn't wish it on anyone else.'

He felt his guts twist. 'I shouldn't have gone that far. But I had to know whether you could deal with it. Always being at the limits of psychological resistance. It was for your own protection.'

She placed a hand gently on his forearm.

They said nothing. It felt good, thought Jan, not to speak for once. He closed his eyes, relaxing his eyelids. When he awoke with a start from his doze, he felt a weight on his shoulder. Rabea had fallen asleep too, her head resting against him.

For a moment he kept still, listening to her regular breathing. He stroked the hair back from her forehead.

She blinked.

Blood rushed to his cheeks. What was he doing?

'Sorry,' she said, wiping away some drool that had trickled onto his blazer. She moved away and stretched her limbs.

'I think we should call a halt for today,' he said. 'And I'm sorry.'

'For what?'

'Our first meeting. Everything I did. And what I might still do.'

## 35

*5<sup>th</sup> December, evening*

Room 102.

It was the right room, no doubt.

Jan knocked a second time, but nobody answered. Tamara wasn't there. He'd already looked in the revolving restaurant, the lobby and the spa, but she was nowhere to be found.

He shrugged and went back to his suite. Possibly she was in town or going for an evening stroll. In his room he tore out a page from his Moleskine notebook, grabbed a hotel biro and scribbled on the ivory-coloured paper: *Just knock if you're ever sick of solitude again. – Jan.*

He folded the piece of paper in half, went back to her suite and slipped it under the door.

Back in his own room, he took his CD player and a stack of discs out of his bag. He needed music. Rabea had digitised her music collection ages ago and always carried it with her, on her iPhone. Probably she'd laugh at him if she saw him still lugging CDs around on his travels. But he liked the haptic element to listening to music. Putting on his headphones, he flung himself onto the freshly made bed and flicked through the CDs. Depeche Mode. Pink Floyd. Bruce Springsteen. There he stopped and put *Born to Run* in the CD player. As the first notes of *Thunder Road* sounded, he closed his eyes. On the journey back from the hotel, Anita had called again and asked what they'd been doing all that time in private.

She and Stüter needed results. The local administration and the public prosecutor were breathing down their necks. But there were no quick results in this case.

They had to stop playing their parts as panic-stricken, passive investigators so perfectly. If they only did what was expected of them, the killer would always stay one step ahead. They had to do something unexpected. Something even he couldn't predict.

He was overlooking something. Something crucial. Right in front of him.

# D

'"D" conveys the thin and sharp sound "T" with the aspirated "TH". It is positioned fourth in the Greek–Latin alphabet between "G" and "E" or "C" and "E": in the old runic alphabet, which consists of only sixteen letters and has a very different arrangement, it doesn't appear, as "Þ" and "T" suffice instead.'

The Grimms' Dictionary

# 36

*5ᵗʰ December, night*

A long-drawn-out scream.

Jan woke with a start, tumbling out of bed with his CD player and duvet. Ignoring the pain in his back, he got up and tore off the headphones. Listened.

Had he been dreaming? An animal calling from the wildlife park?

'Heeeelp!'

Again. A woman's voice. This time further away.

He grabbed his mobile and dialled Rabea's number, striding across the room. He flung open the door.

And froze.

He lowered the phone.

'Jan? Jan, what's wrong?' came his assistant's faraway voice down the line.

On the wall opposite his room was a red letter 'Z'. Three slanting lines, the thickness of an arm. The ink was still wet – he hoped desperately it was ink, and not blood. Whoever had put it there, they had to be nearby.

He was 'Z'. He was the final letter.

He held the phone to his ear. 'Rabea, listen! The killer's here, he's here at the hotel! Call Stüter and Ichigawa and be extremely careful.'

When he hung up, he turned right.

The door to number 102 was wide open. Gingerly, he entered Tamara's suite. Instantly all hope vanished. The mirror in the corridor was shattered, the desk swept clear, the armchair in front of him overturned, the bed rumpled. The white bedclothes were spattered with blood.

Jan's pulse, having been abruptly dragged out of sleep minutes earlier, was racing. His veins were pulsing so fiercely it made him dizzy.

He dashed out of the room, glancing up at the ceiling in the corridor. Fuck, no cameras! No matter – perhaps they could still catch the killer inside the hotel.

The door of the neighbouring suite opened.

Jan jumped. But it was only a plump woman in her mid-sixties, sticking out her head.

'Wha– what's going on here? It's three in the morning!' she asked, blinking at him.

'Didn't you notice anything?' snapped Jan. 'The woman next door has been kidnapped!'

'Oh God!' Her hand flew to her mouth. 'I did hear some banging and thudding, but I didn't think anything of it, could just have been a bit of hanky panky – until she called for help.'

'Fine.' Jan waved a dismissive hand. He'd already wasted enough time.

He hurtled down the corridor towards the lifts and staircase.

If the killer had carried Tamara's lifeless body out of here or forced her to leave, he would most likely have taken the lift. But to which floor?

As he ran down the stairs, taking the steps two at a time, Jan thought feverishly. He certainly couldn't have just waltzed past reception, so that ruled out the ground floor.

He nearly tripped over his own feet but caught himself on the banister.

What other exits were there?

'Give Yourself a Break: Spa on LG' he read out of the corner of his eye. Of course! By the swimming pool there was a door that led onto the terrace. At this time of night, it would be deserted.

He took the final steps to the lower-ground floor in a single bound, swallowing drily. As an analyst, he didn't carry a gun.

It would be wisest to wait for the police at reception. But it was sure to be another fifteen minutes before Stüter and his colleagues arrived, and by then Tamara and the killer would be long gone.

Taking a deep breath, he pulled open the glass door that led to the spa. The pleasant scent of massage oil and saunas hung in the air, macabrely out of place with the current situation.

Jan crept past the massage room and the sauna towards the pool.

All his life he'd sat opposite killers, seen blood-soaked crime scenes – but it had only ever made him shudder. It had disgusted him.

But this. This was something else entirely. Now, for the first time, he was in mortal danger.

The sharp reek of chlorine reached his nose. The light of the sickle moon flooded through the panoramic windows, breaking against the water in the pool and throwing diffuse, bluish shimmers on the ceiling. Other than the gurgling pumps, all was silent.

Cautiously he began to put one foot in front of the other, moving across the slippery tiles. Wobbling briefly, he glanced down at his bare feet and saw several dark flecks right in front of him.

He dropped to his knees and squinted. Blood. Tamara had to be injured. The trail of blood continued unevenly, leading towards one of the glass doors to the terrace.

Perhaps he would have noticed the trail in the hotel corridor, if he'd been more perceptive.

Jan pushed his way through a few deckchairs towards the door. Ajar. Again, his heart skipped a beat.

An icy wind whistled through the chink, slipping underneath his T-shirt; but his blood was already running cold.

He couldn't let him escape. Couldn't let Tamara fall into his hands. Not another person.

But what could he do all by himself?

There was no time to hesitate. Compressing his lips, he pushed the door open.

Beyond the terrace was an empty slope. If you turned right, you ended up in the hotel car park.

The Alphabet Killer was somewhere in the darkness.

'Hey! Stay where you are!' he suddenly heard a male voice.

He knew it from somewhere.

An ear-splitting bang. In the gloom outside the window there was a flash of light. Jan jumped.

His brain needed a few seconds to draw the right conclusion. A shot. That was a shot.

A second bang. The window to his left burst in an explosion of shards.

Jan staggered backwards. Cover – he needed to find cover! His bare feet felt the edge, and then he lost his balance. Helplessly flailing his arms, he toppled into the pool.

Instantly, he started swallowing water. His eyes began to dim. Jan kicked his legs madly, trying in vain to reach the surface.

Suddenly, a tug. Someone had grabbed his T-shirt and was pulling him upwards. His head broke through the water. He gasped for air.

'Jan! Jan, it's me, it's all fine,' Rabea was saying. She looked exactly like he felt: her face ashen, her eyes wide with fear, her short blonde hair dishevelled. Panting, they left the pool.

At least she'd managed in her haste to throw on a pair of jeans and a black pullover. Even in his agitated state, he noticed that. He was only wearing boxers and a T-shirt.

'Hey, put this on!' She handed him a hotel bathrobe that somebody had abandoned on a deckchair.

'Did you hear the shots?' he asked.

'Hard not to.'

'I heard somebody scream. Somebody tried to stop him.'

'Then probably the bullets weren't meant for you.'

'When is Stüter getting here? What about Anita?'

'Ichigawa was still at the station. She and Stüter will be about ten minutes, I think. But he told me somebody was already on the scene.'

Jan paused. 'Who?'

'Not a clue.' Rabea narrowed her eyes and peered into the darkness. 'Should we go outside? Or do you think he's still there?'

'Those shots were meant to buy time. He's gone.' The sight of Rabea – and, oddly, the dunk in the pool – had done him good. He could think clearly again.

His assistant pursed her lips. 'Great.'

Crouching, they moved stealthily out through the door. The night wind whipped through Jan's wet hair and underneath his bathrobe. He was shivering but pulled himself together.

'What were you thinking, chasing that guy all by yourself? Were you trying to scare him into submission with your chicken legs?' whispered Rabea.

He only grunted. How could she make jokes at a time like this?

Jan trod quietly through the snow. He was so cold his teeth were chattering.

Rabea was getting further ahead of him.

'Here!' she cried breathlessly. 'There's someone lying here.'

'Who is it?'

'Oh no,' was Rabea's only answer. 'Oh no, no, no—'

## 37

The young Inspector lay on his back, his eyes fixed on the starry sky – which in Westerwald really lived up to its name. A gorgeous sea of lights.

The pool of blood lay around his head like a red pillow, melting the snow. The entry wound sliced across his neck. The bullet had completely severed his carotid artery – he must have been dead in seconds.

'What was he doing here?' Jan crouched down on his haunches.

The day before yesterday he'd been giving the young man advice about his future. Yesterday he'd been telling Jan about his children.

Köllner still had his Walther P99 in his hand. It hadn't even been fired.

The tall policeman's chest attracted Jan's attention. His leather jacket was open, his shirt torn. On his hairy sternum the killer had scrawled a messy red 'D'. The same ink as in the hotel corridor.

'He doesn't want to deviate from his pattern,' murmured Jan.

In the distance they heard the howl of sirens, which were getting louder. Two patrol cars and Stüter's Mercedes were streaking down the narrow hotel driveway, spectral apparitions in the flickering blue light.

'The cavalry has got here too late, I'm afraid,' said Rabea tonelessly, stroking Köllner's hair.

With a squeal of tyres, the column of vehicles pulled up in the car park. Slamming doors were followed by frantic yells. Six people came storming down the slope, pistols at the ready. Stüter was at the head, closely followed by Anita Ichigawa.

Jan waved at them. 'Relax, relax! Danger's over!'

The officers lowered their weapons. One of them was even carrying a machine gun. When Stüter saw the body, he quickened his pace, skidding in the knee-deep snow.

'Is it – is it him?' he called out breathlessly.

Jan dropped his gaze. 'Köllner tried to stop him.'

An inarticulate cry forced itself from Stüter's throat, something between a howl and a wail. Flinging his weapon aside, he collapsed.

'Rolf!' It was the first time anybody had addressed him by his first name. Anita made to put her hand on his shoulder.

'No! No!' Stüter shoved her away, crawling through the snow towards Köllner's corpse.

Jan was paralysed. All of Stüter's abrasiveness had fallen away. No more higher reasoning to filter his emotions. He consisted only of furious sorrow. Nothing but a twitching muscle.

Reaching Köllner, he hugged the man tightly, pressing him close. It didn't seem to occur to him he might be destroying evidence.

'What have you done, lad?' he sobbed. 'My boy, my boy—'

Threads of saliva flew out of his mouth. His tears were already freezing on his skin, making his cheeks gleam.

He was weeping for Daniel Köllner as though he'd been not merely the son of an old friend but his own blood.

'Did you see which way the killer went?' asked Anita, turning to Jan.

'Towards the car park. He had a woman with him, so he'll have escaped by car.'

'Got it.' Anita pointed at one of the officers. 'Dahlmann, radio HQ. I want checkpoints on all major roads within a thirty-kilometre radius. He's not slipping through our fingers. And while you're at it, tell the crime-scene lot and the medical examiner to get out here.'

Dahlmann, an angular man with a machine gun, paused. 'Shouldn't that be Chief Superintendent Stüter's decision?'

'I don't think he's in any state to make decisions at the moment.' Anita's gaze swept across Stüter, who was crying over his dead protégé as though he'd lost all control of his senses.

Dahlmann nodded agreement.

'Could you give me a description of the woman?' Anita asked Jan.

'Tamara Weiss, red hair, slim, grey eyes, late thirties. Translator from Frankfurt. Has a distinctive heart-shaped birthmark on her right temple.'

'That's – very comprehensive,' she said, after Dahlmann had noted everything down.

'We got to know each other a bit – but that doesn't matter now. Why was Köllner here alone?'

'He was still at HQ in Hachenburg when the call from Frau Wyler came in. He set off immediately, without waiting for the rest of the team. We – we didn't have the chance to stop him.'

Anita lowered her eyes. For a heartbeat they simply stood there in silence. 'You should put on some clothes or you'll catch your death,' she said at last.

'I'm fine,' he answered dismissively.

'He's taking increasingly big risks,' said Anita. 'I mean, Köllner nearly got him, you nearly saw him.'

'He's realised how much better his fantasies are in reality.'

'What do you mean?'

Rabea, who'd been trying to calm Stüter down, walked up to them. 'With a lot of serial killers, they're trying to make their fantasies a reality. They follow the guidelines of their imagination to the letter. Afterwards they relive the act over and over, which satisfies them for a while.' Rabea swallowed and hugged her arms around her body. 'But memories fade, as everybody knows. The ecstasy of the murder ebbs away. He has to repeat the act in order to get back that feeling. That's what leads to serial violence.'

'But there are also killers,' said Jan, picking up the thread with chattering teeth, 'whose fantasies involve more than one murder. Killers whose fantasies aren't satisfied until they've committed a whole series of murders.'

In his mind's eye he caught a flicker of the letter painted on the wall in the hotel corridor.

'Z'.

The letter meant for him. Why? Why was he the one who completed the alphabet?

Anita nodded. 'Understood. From "A" to "Z",' she said. 'Come on, let's go back to the hotel before you get me frozen to death.'

They trudged up the rest of the slope and sat down on the deckchairs by the pool. Jan wrapped towels around his calves and feet, rubbed his hands and used the mug of tea brought to him by hotel staff as a temporary source of warmth.

Rabea continued the conversation, her eyes lowered. 'I'm afraid our killer won't be satisfied until he's got through the whole alphabet. Individual acts mean nothing to him.'

'At first I thought the insane frequency of the murders was a kind of frenzy,' said Jan. 'But then he wouldn't deviate from his pattern. No, he's realising a story he's told himself a thousand times. Now he really wants to complete it. That's why he's moving so quickly.'

Anita made another jerky movement of her head. 'You mean, if we don't stop him, we'll have another twenty-two dead people on our hands. Including Ekiz and Weiss.'

Jan and Rabea nodded mutely.

And he was one of them too.

'Good Lord—'

'The fact that he painted a "D" on Daniel Köllner also indicates he wants to finish this,' said Jan. 'After the Zanetti disaster I was sure he had his victims picked out and a clear order for the killings. That's why he simply abducted Tamara, not killed her. Just like Tugba. I believe he's got something planned for them later. Normally Köllner wouldn't be in the running as a victim – he wouldn't be worthy of a letter. He wouldn't deserve it.'

'Don't talk about him like that!' Anita's eyebrows knitted.

Jan raised his hands soothingly. 'I'm only speaking from the killer's perspective. His victim profile focuses exclusively on people who have something to do with writing or reading. That's why Tamara also fits perfectly. She's a translator.' He sighed and ran his fingers through his wet hair, still dotted with crystals of ice. 'But how I fit in, I'm not sure.'

Rabea's eyes widened. 'Jan, what are you talking about?'

'He painted a giant blood-red "Z" on the wall opposite my hotel room. You could call it various things: a threat, a clue, a warning. The message remains clear. I'm his last victim.'

Stroking his shoulder, Rabea gazed at him in concern. 'But why? What does he want from you?'

'I don't know,' said Jan.

Fragments of that night rushed through the pathways of his brain. Tamara's screams. The 'Z'. The chase through the hotel. The hammering shots. They were still booming in his skull. Booming. Booming.

Slowly, slowly. He couldn't forget it was his job to ask *why*.

Suddenly he realised he'd tipped onto his side, his head resting on his upper arm. His whole body trembled.

Everything was spinning.

## 38

'You can pick a lock with almost anything. Main thing is, it's got to be thin and metal.'

Benny had been Tugba's first boyfriend. Their relationship had lasted precisely the first six months of Year Nine, until he'd dropped her for a girl from another class. At first his bad-boy attitude had made her – a nerdy bookworm – curious. Quickly, it had also made her hate him. She could count her good memories of him on the fingers of one hand.

But now he might be about to save her life.

Benny's parents had been unemployed, so he'd financed his designer clothes by stealing bikes. One time he'd taken Tugba with him and showed her his technique. She'd felt bad for weeks afterwards.

As she wriggled the clip of the pen back into the padlock, she tried to remember the sequence of movements. She bent it even more so that it fitted better. This wasn't a cheap bike lock – but surely it had to function the same way.

She'd been making attempts for hours, constantly in fear of discovery. But her tormentor hadn't come back since the morning, when he'd brought her more thin porridge.

*She kept levering the clip around, sometimes gently, some-times with more force. Nothing happened.*

*'Fucking shit!' Exhausted, she sank back and drew out the piece of metal. All her muscles hurt.*

*She'd never be his letter. Never. But then, she didn't have to be. She rolled the clip between her thumb and forefinger.*

*It was going to hurt. But anything was better than giv-ing up.*

*She twisted her arm, reaching backwards with the metal clip.*

*Towards the tattooed, still inflamed letter 'G'.*

*She took a deep breath. Closed her eyes. Then she scratched it across the tattoo with as much pressure as she could. The pain bit into her flesh. Reflexively she arched her back and gritted her teeth, feeling a mixture of blood and half-dried scabs running down her skin.*

*She had to persevere. It might not make the tattoo disap-pear completely, but at least it would spoil his photograph.*

*Resistance. Resistance by any means.*

*She kept going, raking the clip across her back. Inhaling sharply.*

*There was a violent thud above her.*

*Tugba jumped. The piece of metal slipped out of her hand and landed on the floor with what sounded to her like an unbelievably loud clatter.*

*He was back.*

*She listened, scarcely breathing.*

*From upstairs there came a barely perceptible whimper – a woman in despair.*

*He wasn't alone. Another letter? Another abduction? The clank of heavy metal, and the whimpering grew louder.*

*What was happening up there?*

*Tugba hid the pen clip under her mattress. She cowered.*

*Then came the first screams. First shrill, then increasingly choked.*

*Tugba couldn't explain how, but the tortured sounds of the second woman made the situation even more real. More palpable.*

*They were both in the same prison of screams and pain. Tugba dropped her head onto her knees. Only now, after all this time in the dark, came the tears.*

## 39

*6ᵗʰ December, morning*

They were finished.

The words had been flitting through Rabea's head since last night, and again they popped into her mind as she parked the Renault in the large gravel car park.

A dead policeman. A kidnapped woman. A Chief Superintendent on the verge of a nervous breakdown. And a death threat against Jan. As if they hadn't had enough catastrophes already.

She got out of the car loaned to her by the Hachenburg police, immediately zipping her soft-shell jacket up to her chin. Clouds of condensation drifted from her mouth with every breath. The day had begun with a radiant blue sky and a bitter cold that crept even through her thick thermal underwear.

By the time the crime-scene technicians and, inevitably, the media had arrived last night, she and Jan had already gone back to their rooms. The hotel had given her boss a new suite. His whole corridor was cordoned off – it was part of the crime scene.

She hadn't got much more sleep. Instead, she'd tossed and turned, trying to drive all the images of the dead man out of her brain. A hopeless task.

At some point around eight she'd got a text from Jan: *not going straight to the team HQ. At my old stadium, if you're looking for me. Need to think.*

What old stadium? was the first thought that crossed her mind. She did need to speak to him. There was something he urgently needed to know.

He hadn't responded to her calls, so she'd asked at the hotel reception.

'He must mean the Hardt Löwenzahn Stadium,' said the young woman at the desk after a moment's pause, before giving her extensive directions.

She'd found it after only one wrong turn.

Rabea crossed the parking area, past Jan's Mercedes, and entered the grounds. Looming fir trees encircled the space, casting it into shadow even on this bright morning. On the other side of the pitch, close to the outside line, was a barbeque hut in dire need of a fresh coat of paint. The smell of pine needles was all-pervasive.

Rabea had played club football for several years herself. Striker, a position that seemed made for her. Basketball, too. The sight of the snowy, uneven pitch conjured up memories of ankle injuries and bruised shins.

On a bench by the barbeque hut she spotted Jan, a dark, hunched figure.

As she trudged across the grounds, she saw he was moving his hand to his mouth at regular intervals. Clouds of smoke rose around him.

She frowned. Since when did he smoke?

Then the smell reached her nose, and it wasn't of cigarettes . . .

'Since when do you smoke weed?' she asked as she approached him. It didn't fit with her mental image of Jan. He was controlled in all areas of his life, relying on a clear mind.

'A happy St. Nicholas Day to you too!' Putting the joint to his lips, he inhaled deeply. 'I started at uni. It helped me to tune out the inessentials. I've smoked ever since. Particularly in stressful situations.'

He did look stressed. He seemed – if such a thing were possible – even more beleaguered than yesterday. Heavy bags under his eyes, unkempt hair, pale features.

He blew the smoke into the morning air and watched it dissipate. 'Sometimes it also helps me think further than I otherwise could.' He turned his gaze towards her. 'But what are you doing here?'

'The hotel put me on your trail.' She sat down next to him on the rotted wooden bench, staring for a moment into the soot-blackened firepit. 'There's something you've got to see.'

Unfortunately, it wasn't something likely to lower his stress levels. She reached for her smartphone.

'You want to try?' He offered her the joint.

'I'm driving.'

He shrugged and took another puff.

She opened her email. 'Take a look at this here.'

The subject read 'Date for meeting', and the sender was Nora Schneill.

The message consisted of just two lines:

*I've got to speak to you.*

*It's about Daniel Köllner.*

He flicked the joint away and grabbed the smartphone out of her hand. Skimming the lines again, Jan's eyes and mouth opened wide.

'Schneill,' he groaned. 'And Köllner. You're thinking what I'm thinking, right? Otherwise you wouldn't have come straight out here.'

'Yeah. I didn't want to believe it first either. Köllner was the leak.'

'Hang on, hold your horses!' He gave her back the phone and stood up. Pacing up and down the side-line, he thought out loud. 'What reason would he have had? Stüter kept a beady eye on him twenty-four-seven, for Christ's sake. When would he have had the chance?'

'Maybe he couldn't resist Schneill. But she'll probably tell us herself. Should we invite her down to HQ?'

Jan scratched his chin. 'We'd better speak to her at once. Ask her if she can be in Hachenburg in an hour. But not the station.'

'Men and their womanising,' sighed Rabea, typing the message into her phone.

He looked at her. 'Are you judging me? For the thing with Tamara?'

'Why should I? It's your life, and it's certainly your love life. How could you have known she'd be abducted?'

Jan kicked away some snow. 'Maybe he only took her because she got involved with me. The "Z" was a statement. A threat. As crude as it sounds, maybe the killer didn't want to let me have her.'

'He's got it in for you – why?' She rose too, tucking her hands into her jacket pockets and coming to stand beside him.

'It's not unusual for a killer to fixate on one of the investigators. To want to play, communicate,' said Jan. 'Sometimes they find it interesting that I want to get into their psyches. Maybe it goaded him.'

'Do you think Tamara is still alive?'

He inhaled sharply, as though he'd cut himself. 'Depends what letter he's got planned for her.'

'So many people have died. And we're groping around in the dark. We've still got no suspects, not even a lead. All that's happened is we've lost a colleague – we've got to stop him.'

'And we will. If he keeps going in this frenzied state, sooner or later he'll make a mistake.' Jan stretched his back and cracked his knuckles. 'Let's go back to HQ. How's Stüter doing, by the way?'

'We won't be seeing him again any time soon,' said Rabea as they trudged across the pitch together. 'Nervous breakdown. He's receiving psychological treatment, then he'll probably be sent home for a while.'

Jan wiped his face. As many times as he'd quarrelled with the Chief Superintendent, he had been a capable man. It was a loss for the team.

'If things keep on like this, he won't be the only one to go nuts,' said Jan.

# 40

When Rabea and Jan reached operational command, they found everybody standing in silence, heads bowed and hands folded.

For a perplexed moment Jan thought the gesture had to do with them, until he remembered again the images from last night.

'I'd like to have a minute's silence so that we can commemorate our colleague Daniel Köllner,' began Anita, effortlessly managing to give her voice the necessary gravitas. 'He gave his life in the attempt to save a woman from being kidnapped. This act of bravery revealed him to be a better policeman than I or anybody else in this room will ever be.'

The weed was still affecting Jan's mind, although it was a weak strain mixed with dried raspberry leaves instead of tobacco. He still had to function, after all. Everything lay beneath a matte veil. The other investigators' empty faces seemed even more hollow, the atmosphere in the tube-like room even more oppressive.

Anita continued. 'Daniel was an important part of this investigation team, and he will be sorely missed as a detective. Far more important, however, is that he will be missed as a son, as a partner, as a father, as a family member. And, not least, as a friend.'

The silence in the room sent a shiver down Jan's spine. He closed his eyes.

Could he have prevented this? Saved Köllner's life?

Ever since his brother's death, he knew he shouldn't ask himself questions like that. Yet his brain had never bothered much with what he should or shouldn't do – perhaps that was why he'd become a behavioural investigative advisor.

'Thank you,' whispered Anita eventually. 'Now let's get back to work so we can bring this bastard to justice.'

The operations command sprang into familiar activity. Tapping keyboards, telephone conversations, discussions. Anita threw two aspirins into her glass of water and walked up to them. Last night had affected even her composure.

Hopefully she couldn't smell the cannabis on his clothes.

'It's simply a tragedy.' She gave them a pained smile. 'You've probably been smoking pot, if I know you. Old habits die hard, eh?'

Jan jumped. It wasn't her nose that had found him out, it was her shrewd instincts.

His eyes fell on the tablets fizzing in her water. 'We've all got our narcotics.'

It was impossible to tell from Anita's expression whether the comment had hit home – something that had always disturbed him about her. A person ought to show they're capable of emotion.

'We've got to talk about the information that filtered through to the press,' said Rabea. 'We believe Köllner was the source.'

Anita nearly dropped her glass, but reflexively caught it with her other hand. Water sloshed onto the floor. She opened her mouth to speak.

Yet before she could say a word, she was interrupted by a scream. An investigator hurled away the thick envelope she'd just opened and buried her face in her hands. As it landed on the carpet, something fell out.

It took Jan a few moments to realise what it was.

Then came the surge of nausea.

## 41

'L'.

Two deep black lines.

Connected to form a consonant.

Rabea couldn't take her eyes off the tattoo. It was unmissable on the blanched, blood-encrusted scrap of skin that fell out of the envelope. It was roughly the size of a postcard. The killer had sent them a gruesome greeting.

With a choking cough, Jan collapsed. Many others averted their eyes in horror.

Ichigawa was one of the few to maintain her composure. After taking a deep breath, she beckoned Rabea over. 'Frau Wyler, you have some basic knowledge of forensic medicine, correct?'

She nodded.

'Tell me everything this – body part – says to you.'

Putting on a pair of latex gloves, Rabea knelt down before the envelope, trying to breathe through her mouth.

Ichigawa turned to the appalled detective who had opened it. 'The envelope came through the regular post?'

The woman's lips were still trembling. She'd wrapped her arms around her chest. 'It was in the post box, but it wasn't stamped, and there was nothing written on it.'

'Is the box under any kind of surveillance?'

A shake of the head.

'Rookie mistake.' Anita sighed. 'He must have brought it in the middle of the night. In a case like this we should have assumed he'd try to communicate with us sooner or later.'

She paced up and down, her brow furrowed. 'Frau Wyler, what do you think? I'll be happy with any tiny piece of information you can give me.'

'A piece of skin and flesh roughly one and a half centimetres thick, excised with a very sharp implement. Possibly a scalpel. Possibly another hunting tool.'

'Which area of the body is it from?' asked Jan haltingly, still half-turned away from the envelope.

'From a woman's thigh, judging by the texture of the skin. But I can't say for sure.'

'Could someone survive that?'

'She would have bled profusely.' Rabea inhaled sharply. 'But if the wound was treated properly, her chances of survival aren't bad. We'll have to compare the skin with DNA samples from Frau Weiss's hotel room,' she continued, 'but it's likely this came from her.'

'Thank you. That was very informative. He tattooed an "L" on her, and luckily, we're still quite far away from that letter. He's following strict alphabetical order with these murders. Tamara Weiss isn't up next, but he's taken her already as a precaution, like he did with Zanetti and Ekiz.'

'What do we do now?' asked one of the officers.

'Get some of your people to start researching everybody in the region who works explicitly with language. Journalists, writers, editors, calligraphers, teachers, linguists—'

'There'll be thousands,' said Rabea. 'What are we going to do with all those names?'

'We'll call them. One after another. Warn them, ask them if they've received any threats lately or noticed anything out of the ordinary. We know our killer's preferred victims. Let's use that knowledge.'

The team dispersed. Jan, upturning his chair, dashed retching out of the room, his hand clasped to his mouth. Only Rabea and Ichigawa remained, as well as another officer, who was putting the flap of skin into a sterile box.

'Nora Schneill will be here any moment. We're meeting her at the castle. Do you want to be present when we question her?' asked Rabea. 'I hope Jan isn't too – indisposed.'

'I don't like having my plans messed up by external factors like this. The most important thing is that we speak to a tattoo artist as soon as possible. Find out something about our killer's skill level.'

Rabea thought about what Jan had said about Ichigawa. 'Do you want me and Jan to be there?'

'Definitely. But we'll talk to this journalist first.' Lips pursed, Ichigawa nodded towards the toilets. 'Could you please go and fetch him?'

## 42

Jan rinsed his mouth out with water one more time. The taste of vomit still stuck to his tongue, but it wasn't as intense any more.

Supporting himself on the sink, he lowered his head and closed his eyes. Again, the image of the skin peeking out of the envelope. The same skin he'd been kissing only a few hours earlier. He didn't want to imagine her heart-rending screams of pain when the killer cut it out of her body.

He tore himself away from the basin and stared at his reflection, a pale thing with bloodshot eyes.

'Jan, where are you?' Rabea knocked on the door for the third time. 'Schneill's already there.'

'Just a second!' He wiped his face with a paper towel then went into the corridor.

Rabea eyed him with an expression he'd never seen on her before: searching, wary, almost distraught.

'Why are you looking at me like that?'

She blinked, caught. 'What do you mean?'

'Doesn't matter. Where's Anita?'

'Waiting outside. She wants to find some tattoo artist afterwards. We're supposed to be there.'

'What's that going to achieve? I can already tell you our killer's an amateur when it comes to tattooing.'

'I think she just wants to make sure.' Rabea looked at him. 'She seems very conscientious.'

'You know what else is conscientious? Machines.' He imitated the mechanical gait of a robot.

'You're only messing around to show me you're okay.'

He ground his teeth and started walking normally again.

They stepped outside, and Jan drew deep breaths of clear wintery air into his lungs. The hideous message had sobered him up instantly.

'Feeling better?' asked Anita, who was waiting for them in the car park. Her voice was a monotone.

'Don't ask unless you're actually interested.'

Her face betrayed one of her rare flashes of emotion. This time it was an expression of exasperation. 'I mean it seriously, okay? If you think none of this is affecting me, then maybe you're not the brilliant judge of character you think.'

'I'm sorry,' he murmured, shocked.

The fifteen-minute walk to Hachenburg Castle passed in silence. The building, stocky and powerful, loomed above the small town.

As Nora Schneill trudged across the inner courtyard, she seemed to Jan more vulnerable than before. Small, lost in the depths of her Burberry coat. Her eyes bloodshot, her hair uncombed and greasy. Köllner's death had stripped back her immaculate veneer. She walked hunched and shuffling, as though to her own execution.

'Why didn't you want me to come to the station?' was her only greeting.

'I'm glad you could come,' said Ichigawa, falling into polite clichés. 'It was Jan Grall's idea. We wanted to avoid any unnecessary questions from our colleagues. Also, for the moment we can't rule out the possibility that the killer is keeping us under surveillance.'

Schneill nodded carefully. 'I understand.'

'Okay, so why are we here?' asked Jan, his hands planted on his hips. His voice shook, and he wasn't sure whether it was the shock of Tamara's abduction or simple rage. Schneill had endangered their investigation – and thus the victims.

'I want to help you stop the murders,' explained the journalist. A smile flitted across her oval, fine-lined face. 'What I did with Daniel – with Herr Köllner – hindered your investigation. I'm deeply sorry for that. I realise I might even have helped the killer.'

Ichigawa crossed her arms. 'Did you have a relationship with him?'

'No, absolutely not!' she cried. 'I had something on him.'

'You know we could arrest you for blackmail and obstructing a police investigation?' Ichigawa exhaled a cloud of vapour at the dramatically perfect moment. 'So, it would be best if you had something concrete to offer us.'

Schneill turned away with a sigh, taking a few steps across the courtyard. She was looking towards the valley. On a clear day like this, you could see across to the Sieben Mountains. 'I'll publish anything you want,' she said eventually. 'False information, news about the killer, whatever. The other media outlets trust me. If I write something, everybody else will jump on the bandwagon.' She turned to face them. 'Do you understand the incredible power I'm offering you here?'

'This doesn't mean you're getting any special treatment,' said Ichigawa.

The journalist nodded, not looking them in the eye.

'What you were using to blackmail Köllner—' Rabea began. 'It doesn't matter now whether you keep it quiet or not. Tell us. Then it's out in the world.'

'One of my contacts on the drug scene caught him dealing cocaine. Hard to imagine, right? You should probably check your evidence storage room, anyway.' The journalist swallowed. 'I – I exploited him.'

'Fine.' Ichigawa raised her hand. 'This isn't the time for remorse. Instead let's consider how we can use Frau Schneill's offer to our advantage.'

'Take me out of the equation,' said Jan, initially half to himself. 'A proactive strategy – with an inexperienced killer, it can provoke a hasty reaction. We'll give it a bit of time, then say I've been taken off the case.'

Anita frowned. 'What'll that do?'

'It's obvious: I'm "Z".'

The others were staring, bemused. He sighed. Time to explain.

'The Alphabet Killer seems to be harbouring an obsession with me, for some reason. The "Z" opposite my hotel room was a clear sign. I'm going to be his last victim.' He made an expansive gesture. If we take me away – his "Z" – then it might send his whole world spiralling out of control.'

'But in reality, you'd keep on working for the team secretly?' Anita was struggling to follow his train of thought.

Jan nodded. 'I'd stay here, but not go out in public.'

'How would the killer react?' asked Anita.

'Best case scenario, he'd stop the murders. If I'm beyond his reach, the whole alphabet might lose its meaning. Second-best case scenario, he'll totally lose control, start panicking and make mistakes.'

Schneill piped up. 'And in the worst-case scenario?'

'In the worst-case scenario, he won't let himself be perturbed and he'll continue as before.'

Ichigawa shrugged and turned to Nora Schneill. 'Sounds like we can't lose.' She shook the journalist's hand. 'We have a deal.'

## 43

'Fuchskaute. What's that?'

'The highest mountain in Westerwald,' explained Jan to his assistant. 'An extinct volcano. Although I know a Swiss person is going to laugh at something that high being called a mountain.'

He and Rabea were squeezed into the back seat of Anita's Audi. His forehead resting against the window, he was looking out at the snow-topped peaks of the Westerwald ranges. 'What's the guy called again?'

'Enno Quester. A tattoo artist. Lives in Breitscheid, works in Montabaur,' replied Anita.

She still drove in the same way. Always above the speed limit, but fully in control. She accelerated and braked as perfectly as if she'd been commuting along this route all her life.

'Why are we meeting him at the Fuchskaute? Why not at his studio?' asked Rabea.

'He said on the phone that the Fuchskaute is on the route between Hachenburg and Breitscheid. Probably wants to spare us the journey.'

'Sounds suspicious,' remarked Rabea. 'As though he's got something to hide at home. Didn't you ask more questions?'

Jan saw Anita roll her eyes in the rear-view mirror. 'Think I'm naïve? Right after our call I questioned some of his clients, studied his website and called his house. I'm doing my job. The man's clean. Anyway, this isn't an interrogation, it's just a normal conversation.'

'Sorry,' muttered Rabea under her breath.

Jan sighed. When it came to intimidating people, Anita was in a class of her own.

'Anything new on what happened at the hotel?' he said, changing the subject.

'The gun was most likely a hunting weapon. The cartridges could have come from a .357 MAG hunting revolver. I'm checking whether anybody in the area has registered a gun of that calibre. What's odd is that none of the hotel staff or guests noticed anybody. There was somebody at reception the whole time, so he can't have come in that way. There was no sign of forced entry at the delivery entrance or side entrances. We only have witnesses for the shots and the woman screaming. As though the kidnapper had been in the hotel the whole time.'

'What are you implying?'

Anita rolled her eyes again. 'All I'm saying is that we've got to check the hotel staff and guests thoroughly. You included. That's all.'

'We're making it too easy for him, much too easy,' groaned Jan, more peacefully. 'He's got away not just with several murders but with the next abduction. And our only lead is the hunting equipment.'

'What do we really know about this Tamara Weiss?'

'You'll soon be able to read about my involvement with her in the report.'

'I'm serious. We've not been contacted by any relatives yet. Not even the publisher she worked for. Who was this woman?'

Jan's fondness for deduction meant he occasionally extrapolated the lives of strangers in detail from a few clues. Like he'd done with Tamara.

In his imagination, she lived in a small apartment in one of the trendier areas of Frankfurt. She had her own blog, where she reviewed books. Kept a cat she'd named after a literary character, maybe Samsa or Don Quixote. Met friends from university at the weekend to chat about their latest disappointments with men.

A good, tidy life. And if they didn't act quickly enough, that life would be over.

## 44

Black leather clothing, a long braid, head to toe tattoos. That's how Rabea had pictured Enno Quester.

The slightly built man sitting at the corner table in the restaurant at Fuchskaute didn't fit the tattoo-artist cliché.

With his frame-less glasses, red-and-white checked shirt and crew cut, he could have been a tax consultant – although a few neck tattoos were peeping out from underneath his collar.

He blended seamlessly into the rustic ambience of the restaurant, as though part of the furnishings. Their wait-ress even greeted him by his first name, reinforcing the impression.

'This guy is putting the rest of us tattoo artists under suspicion,' sighed Quester. His voice was barely above a whisper, his local dialect hardly audible. 'I'm glad you didn't take me down to the station.'

'There's no cause for that.' Ichigawa took a folder out of her briefcase and handed it to Quester. 'We just wanted to test your expertise, not whether you're telling the truth. In that file there are images of the victims.'

She paused briefly. 'I should warn you that some of them are very disturbing. Please take your time looking at the tattoos. Tell us everything that strikes you. Every detail, even if it seems insignificant in your eyes.'

Adjusting his glasses, Quester leant forwards and surveyed the photographs. His face was unmoving; only a vein pulsed unevenly beneath his left eye.

'Pneumatic machine,' he said, concentrating. 'Cheap model. Outliner brush. Working very softly. The ink hasn't penetrated far into the skin. Probably the tattoo wouldn't even be permanent.' He sighed. 'But that doesn't matter, of course.'

'Are these pneumatic machines rare?' asked Rabea. 'Are there only particular dealers who sell them?'

'I'm afraid not. They're pretty standard. Some shops only sell to people with business licences, but these days – with auction sites and so on – that's not an issue any more.'

'The killer used ordinary fountain-pen ink. What do you think about that?' asked Jan.

'Makes me think of prison tattoos. Something improvised about it. Something teenagers do if they want to give it a try. But if you're asking why the guy used it, I'm not sure.'

Ichigawa hadn't given up hope. 'Does anything else strike you?'

'Yeah, there is one thing that gives me pause.'

There was silence at the table. Only the country music coming softly from the speakers on the ceiling was audible.

'The lines are halting. Interrupted again and again,' continued Quester. 'He must have taken breaks.'

Jan frowned. 'So, he really is a beginner?'

'Or the reason could simply be that his victims struggled,' said Anita, but she noted down the observation.

Quester shrugged. 'Could be.'

At first Rabea considered this strange detail as unimportant. The quotations proved, at least, that the killer could read.

Ichigawa stood up and shook the tattoo artist's hand. 'Thank you, you've been a big help. If we have further questions, we'll call you.'

It was impossible to tell from her voice whether she was disappointed with the results of the short conversation. Everything was so distanced. Frictionless. Utterly unlike with Stüter.

As they stepped outside, Rabea's phone vibrated. The number on the display had a Montabaur area code. Frowning, she fell back a few paces. Sheltering beside a hut right next to the radio tower, she picked up. 'Yes? Who is this?'

'Frau Wyler, right? It's Chief Superintendent Stüter.'

His voice sounded raw and hoarse. As though he'd been crying for hours. What did he want from her? The sudden call confused her. 'I thought you were in hospital. How are you doing? Shouldn't you be resting?'

'I discharged myself. I'm at home, but they're not letting me work. I'm no good to anybody if I'm lying in hospital – least of all to myself. I want to get him. For Daniel.'

'And what do you want me to do?'

'Listen.' His voice dropped to a whisper. 'Jan can't find out about this conversation. Don't mention me, whatever you do. I'm just asking you to come to my house this evening.' He gave her the address.

Rabea was of a mind to go straight to Jan. 'Why all the secrecy?'

'There are things you should know about Jan Grall,' he replied tonelessly. 'Just come and see me.'

He hung up without another word.

Rabea stared at her phone. Her heart was pounding. What was going on with the Chief Superintendent? What did he want?

Jan came up to her. 'Who were you talking to?'

'Just a flatmate.' The answer was out of her mouth before she could think twice.

'Fine,' he said, without any hint of suspicion. 'I've got something personal to do. I'm going to get a taxi. If Anita asks about me, tell her I'm not feeling well and I've gone back to the hotel.'

Rabea nodded. She didn't want to believe Stüter, yet Jan's personal errands were giving the suspicious part of her brain no peace. 'Okay, but do you really have to come up with a cover story?'

'I know my night with Tamara means they'll be going through my life with a fine-tooth comb, but I want to keep at least a bit of it in the dark.'

*Jan is every bit as dangerous as the people he hunts.* The words popped into Rabea's head – what Ichigawa had said to her on her first day.

What was Jan hiding?

# 45

*Gero Grall*, read the plain gravestone.

*Life is finite but memory inexhaustible.*

Jan was reading the stone epitaph for the first time. Words that were supposed to alleviate the pain of loss, but ultimately were no more effective than a badly-sticking plaster. If that.

Bad Marienberg Cemetery was above the black Nister river, directly adjoining the main road towards Langenbach.

It had been decades since Jan was last there, at the funeral of a great aunt. He'd not been to his brother's. By that point he'd been long gone from Westerwald. The empty words, the empty faces – he couldn't have borne them. Nor the guilt.

The graveyard lay among fields and small copses. A peaceful place with a wide view of the snow-covered valleys.

Twilight was already falling. Jan was totally alone.

He used to hate visiting here. The thought of walking over earth full of skeletons and rotting corpses – many of them people he'd once known – had always sent a shiver down his spine.

Today he was enjoying the quiet and the solitude, far from the never-ending babble of the media.

He'd meant to visit soon after his arrival but hadn't found the time. Or hadn't wanted to find the time.

Weeds crept out of the untended, overgrown patch of earth in front of the gravestone. Katharina didn't seem to care about her husband's resting place. But could he hold it against her, now that she had Stefan? She had left the past in peace.

He was different. The past had never left him any peace.

He'd bought a bouquet of carnations and lilies, which he laid gently against the grave.

He pressed his hands against the cold stone and shut his eyes. His big brother had been his idol. Full of wisdom about girls, the coolest stuff, life itself. He'd taught him rummy and let him win the first few games, shown him how to skip stones and make dams in streams out of sticks. He'd always included Jan in his large circle of friends, his wide knowledge, his great heart.

Everything about him had been big.

Once he'd been hanging out with Gero and his friends. They'd bumped into a guy who'd hit on Gero's girlfriend and threatened her. The others had jumped on him to teach him a lesson, but Gero dragged them off, standing between them and the guy. *That's cowardly. All of us against one, that's just cowardly,* echoed his voice in Jan's head. *We can sort it out another way.*

That kind of big. Gero had been a role model, but unfortunately an unreachable one. He'd never been able to keep up.

The street lamps flickered above the country road, a pearl necklace of lights. Gloom stole across the valleys like a lurking predator. Time to go.

Jan rose, turning up the collar of his coat.

Three days before the fatal accident, Gero had shown him he was far from the role model he'd always thought.

The bad thing, the really bad thing, was that Jan hadn't been able to decide for days whether to bring flowers or simply to piss on Gero's grave.

## 46

The address was correct. No question.

Rabea put her phone away and walked up to the closed restaurant. *Heino's Den* was written in peeling letters above the front door, which was decorated with crown glass. The shutters were drawn down, discoloured like yellow teeth. The terrace was piled with rusty garden furniture.

One of those pubs where old, stooped men had drunk like they were working an assembly line.

Now everything screamed decay.

Was this really where Stüter lived?

Gradually Rabea was regretting coming out there like he'd asked.

Next to the entryway was a dog-eared note that read 'Closed until further notice'. The menu in the display box beside it dated from 2009. Nowhere was there a bell or a letterbox. Cupping her hands against the glass, she peered inside. Was that a faint glimmer of light in the depths of the pub?

Cautiously she knocked on the glass. 'Stüter? Are you there?'

Something moved behind the pane. A blur of shadows and outlines. Eventually a figure came to the heavy door and opened it a crack.

'Frau Wyler. You actually came,' croaked Stüter.

He pulled the door wide. The Chief Superintendent was wearing a red-and-white-striped bathrobe and slippers. He was unshaven, his cheeks covered in black stubble – the first time Rabea had seen any kind of hair on him. His eyes were bloodshot, his lips inflamed and cracked.

'You live here?' she asked as he ushered her inside.

'Only temporarily. But you know how it goes – nothing lasts longer than a short-term solution.'

The musty stench of the pub enveloped her – old wood, ingrained cigarette smoke and beer fumes.

'The pub belongs to an old friend. Been closed for ages. But he can't get out of the lease, so we made a virtue of necessity and I moved in after the divorce. I like it. Made myself comfortable.'

Stüter had pushed most of the tables against the wall, making space for a camp bed and a small group of chairs. Books and clothes were heaped all over the place. On the wall above the bed hung a poster of *Dirty Harry*.

'Want something to drink?' Stüter went behind the bar.

Rabea sat down on one of the stools, resting her forearms on the worn wood. 'What've you got?'

'Everything,' he laughed. 'This is a pub, after all.'

Above him hung rifle club pennants, most of the years dating from the eighties and nineties.

'A Coke'll be fine, thanks,' she said. 'I didn't expect you to be out of hospital so quickly.'

'I want to keep it under wraps for now.' Stüter bent over the fridge and took out a 1.5 litre bottle of Coke, plus a bottle of Hachenburg Pilsner. 'The thing with Daniel – I should never have cracked like that.'

'It's only human.'

'Still.' As he poured the drinks his hands shook so much that most of the Coke missed the glass. He wiped it down distractedly and handed it to her. 'Cheers! I've never been much good at small talk. Let's get down to business.'

'Great – I'm keen to hear what all this cloak-and-dagger stuff is about.'

'It's about Grall. I have information that hasn't reached the rest of the team yet.'

'What information?'

'I still have very good contacts in forensics. I was able to intercept some information. Breach of protocol, I know, but I hope you won't hold it against me.'

'Whatever you think is right,' replied Rabea, unnerved.

'We're talking about the results from Tamara Weiss's hotel room. We found a note there from your boss. They'd agreed to meet the night she was abducted. They also found traces of sperm, foreign hairs and particles of skin on Frau Weiss's underwear. The DNA analysis isn't complete yet, but we're assuming they're from Jan Grall.'

'We already knew they were intimate with each other. I saw her winking at him over breakfast. I don't know what you're getting at, but it really didn't seem like she was scared of him.'

The Chief Superintendent took a piece of paper from his bathrobe and pushed it across the bar. 'A printout of the last text exchange from Frau Weiss's mobile phone.'

She unfolded the paper and read the exchange between Tamara and someone called Nisrin.

'Who's she talking to?'

'Nisrin Dasheni. Just spoke with her on the phone. A friend of Frau Weiss's from Frankfurt. Project manager at a marketing firm. Spent practically the whole conversation in tears. Have you read the whole thing?'

Rabea's eyes flicked to the end of the page. In Weiss's penultimate text she mentioned Jan: '*Just picked up a holiday fling, believe it or not. Interesting guy, but pssst, top secret, what he's doing. Tell you the rest when I'm back in ff.*'

After that there were a few excited questions from Nisrin, all of which went unanswered. Tamara didn't reply until a day later. The last text was dated yesterday at 5.21 p.m.:

'*Coming home early. Back tomorrow. Please pick me up at 4 at the station. So much to tell you. One detail can change everything you think about a person.*'

A whole volley of questions shot through Rabea's head. 'Why didn't Frau Dasheni go to the police?'

'Because she didn't connect the text to the abduction. According to her statement, Tamara Weiss had been having a brief fling, but it must have gone sour. She thinks those words refer to your friend.'

Rabea crumpled up the piece of paper and flung it into the shelf of spirits. 'That's the normal explanation. What else is there to read into it?'

'Reading into things is supposed to be your area of expertise.' Stüter sipped his beer. 'Ask yourself a few questions: what upset Frau Weiss so much that she decided to leave early? Why didn't she want to meet Jan on that last evening?' He leant forwards. She felt his warm, beery breath on her skin. 'She must have discovered something about Jan that shook her to the core.'

'Supposition, nothing more!' Rabea rubbed her temples, a cold prickle of rage running through her body. 'Why would you assume Jan has something to do with all this? I fished him out of the pool myself when – when Köllner was shot. What about the "Z" painted on the wall outside his room?'

'I never said he's responsible for the kidnappings or the murders. But he has a past here in Westerwald. He has roots here. They could go deep. And far.'

He paused a moment, leaning against the bar. 'I've got no idea what Grall's role in this case is. But with all these inconsistencies, I've no doubt it's more than that of a detective.'

Rabea gulped down the rest of her Coke, put down the glass and ran her index finger around the rim. Did she really know her boss?

Was this really still a question of loyalty?

She decided against it. 'Let's eliminate suspicion before it drives me even more crazy. Let me sleep on it.'

Stüter emptied his beer. 'I'll try to keep the text exchange from Ichigawa as long as possible. Better we sort this out before Jan comes under a cloud. Speaking of Jan's roots. Do you know what happened with his brother?' asked Stüter.

She nodded. 'Jan told me. He died in a car accident.'

'That's all he said?'

'Why?'

Stüter placed a yellowed newspaper clipping from the local paper on the bar.

The photograph showed a completely burnt-out wreck. When Rabea read the headline, she had to hold onto the bar.

*Fatal Accident: One Brother Dies, Other Survives, Minor Injuries*

Stüter snorted. 'Jan told you his brother died in an accident. But not that he was sitting in the car with him.'

## 47

*Ludovico Einaudi – Fuori Dal Mondo* appeared on the playlist on Rabea's phone. She turned up the volume, tilted back her head and listened to the piano chords.

Shortly after eleven o'clock, the hotel lobby was deserted. Only the receptionist kept her company, throwing her the occasional glance that said: 'Go back up to your damn suite and let me play solitaire in peace.'

Rabea had ordered a white wine at the bar, made herself comfortable in one of the leather armchairs, put her feet up on the glass coffee table and tucked her earbuds into her ears. Luckily, she hadn't seen Jan again that evening. She doubted she was capable of having a normal conversation with him.

She didn't want to go to her room. Not after last night. After the killer had simply waltzed in so easily. She knew that kind of behaviour was childish. That four police officers were now keeping the building under surveillance round the clock. She'd just seen one of them walking across the restaurant terrace.

Even so, she couldn't imagine anything worse than lying in her bed in the dark room. After what had happened to her sister, years ago, she hadn't been able to stand it either. She'd spent many nights in her parents' bed, or only able to sleep with a night light and a private zoo of stuffed animals.

Her mother had been the director at the Konzerttheater Bern, introducing her early to piano and chamber pieces. Music in which she'd sought solace after the disappearance of her daughter.

As a teenager, Rabea had listened not to Linkin Park or Britney Spears but to Bach, Chopin and Holst. Especially when she was going to sleep.

Simply sitting here, with Einaudi in her ear and a chardonnay in front of her, was absolute relaxation. She was completely self-sufficient. Cut off from all her troubles.

The Alphabet Murders, with their spider's web of fear, unforeseeability and questions receded into the far distance, washed away by wine and music; as though it wasn't an immediate part of her life but only an especially gruesome story on the eight o'clock news.

Her smartphone's ringtone cut through Einaudi's composition, breaking into Rabea's mental refuge. It was Asim, one of her flatmates. He was thirty-three, the bassist in an indie band who also worked as a projectionist at a small cinema.

'Everything okay in Mainz?'

'Can't complain. But Ricarda and I are getting a bit worried about you.'

'There's no need,' she replied confidently, and was surprised how easily the lie escaped her lips. 'The hotel's better guarded than Fort Knox.'

'Still. Isn't there somewhere else you could stay? A holiday cottage or something?'

'And you think I'd be safer there? All alone in some isolated chalet?'

'Well, when you put it like that—'

She smiled briefly, then grew serious. She was still haunted by Ichigawa's warning about Jan, and Tamara Weiss's last, ambiguous text. She urgently needed a second opinion. 'You've only met Jan once, right?' she asked. 'When he invited us and Ricarda over to his place.'

'Yep. The guy with the big stereo system and the even bigger film collection.'

'The only thing more incredible was the organisation of it all,' added Rabea. Her boss was one of the most structured thinkers she knew, and he carried this quality into all areas of his life.

'What's up with him?'

'Did anything strike you about him? Something that maybe made you feel uneasy?'

He was silent a moment. 'Well, he's a bit laconic, and very serious. But I think that's normal. Listening to you talk about him, he sounds like some kind of genius.' She heard him scratch his curly head. 'One thing did strike me. There were a crazy number of pain meds and psychopharmaceuticals in his bathroom cabinet. I'm no expert, but I think they were pretty strong medications.'

Rabea sipped her white wine. Was it conceivable that someone as controlled as Jan was abusing prescription meds? Was weed perhaps not the only thing that dulled his hypersensitivity?'

'What were you looking for in the cabinet?'

'Dental floss,' replied Asim awkwardly. 'I hate it when I've got something stuck between my teeth.' Now there was unease in his voice. 'Why do you ask? Has something happened?'

'No, no. Just something somebody said about him made me wonder.' She preferred not to mention her conversation with Stüter. She didn't want to worry her friend unnecessarily.

'People talk about each other all the time, that's just how it is. I'd rather not know what Ricarda says about me.'

He and the young philosophy student had fun needling each other. Rabea occasionally caught herself thinking the two of them were involved. 'But you don't think Jan's dangerous?'

'Babe, now you're really making me nervous. You don't think he's your killer, do you?' He laughed anxiously.

'Don't be silly. I shouldn't have asked you in the first place,' she said.

He pretended to be huffy, as awkwardly as only he could. 'Sorry!'

'It's fine,' she said. 'I'm just slowly starting to wonder whether I know this person at all. If I know *who* Jan Grall really is.'

# E

'. . . a non-original, therefore fluctuating, ill-defined vowel that has run rampant in our language and disrupted its harmony. [. . .] such monotony is barely possible in other tongues and was once alien to German too.'

The Grimms' Dictionary

# 48

*7ᵗʰ December, early morning*

'Om bhur bhuvah svah, Tat savitur vareniyam,' Jan sang to himself. He was sitting on the bed in his hotel bathrobe, in the lotus position. Briefly opening his eyes, he let his gaze sweep across the treetops in the wildlife park, half obscured in the morning mist.

He repeated his mantra, concentrating fully on enunciating the syllables. Forming words whose meaning he didn't even know – but meditation wasn't about that.

'The effect of such mantras is subversive,' his Indian uni friend Vikram had explained once. 'It arises through the rhythm, the constant repetition. What it means is irrelevant.'

Vikram, a mechanical engineering student, had written the text of the mantra on a napkin during one of their nights in a Bochum bar.

He'd recommended meditation when Jan told him that nothing helped combat his inner unrest – not 'psych meds', not a wide variety of calming teas, not breathing techniques.

Yet meditation, astonishingly, had helped him find peace.

To forget, for a brief moment. To forget that Tamara was out there somewhere. Skinned, weakened, vulnerable.

Yesterday evening after his visit to the cemetery he'd joined the search some volunteers had organised. Alongside the leaders – a forest warden and a soldier on leave – he'd come up with a plan to scour the woods between Bad Marienberg and Rennerod. He still knew his way around the area as well as in his childhood days. That local knowledge, together with his analytical expertise, had proved extremely useful.

Supported by several dozen helpers, they'd combed the woods deep into the night, until cold and darkness finally drove them back. He gave a racking cough. The effort of pursuing the Alphabet Killer the night before last had taken its toll. It was only a question of time until the tumble into the pool followed by all that standing around in the cold made itself felt.

At the moment, getting sick simply wasn't an option.

He rose from the mattress. As he disconnected his phone from the charger, he saw six missed calls. All from Miriam in Mainz. His heart, still in stand-by mode, began to race. What was wrong? His fingers shaking, he misdialled twice before finally getting through.

'Jan, they were here! They were here!' she shrieked into the telephone, in floods of tears. 'Somehow they must have found out I was at your place.'

'Calm down, calm down. Who was there?'

'Diver and his guys,' she whimpered.

'Who?'

'The ones I owe money to.'

Jan sank onto the bed with a sigh, his hand pressed to his forehead. 'Oh, fuck. Are you okay? Did they do anything to you?'

'Luckily I wasn't here when they came,' she replied. 'But they broke down your patio door and – and – smashed up your DVD collection.'

Right then he couldn't have cared about anything less than his furniture. All that mattered was Miriam's safety. 'Call the police, okay? I'll come straight back. Do you know where this Diver lives?'

'Yeah, but I'm not telling the police anything,' she replied. 'They don't call him Diver for nothing.'

'Doesn't sound particularly dangerous,' he said.

She took a deep breath, sniffling. 'There's this abandoned swimming pool a little way out of the city. Empty. He's known for making people jump off the three-metre diving board there. It doesn't kill you, but you end up with at least a few broken bones.'

'And you borrow money from guys like that. Dammit, what did you even use it for? How much was it?'

'Fifteen hundred. It wasn't for me, it was for my sister. For her class trip. Clothes. Some other stuff. Long story.'

'Okay, tell me when I get there. I've got to tell them I'm leaving, then I'll set off straight away.'

'Jan—'

'Hm?'

'I'm sorry.'

## 49

Anita Ichigawa took the few final strokes to the steps. She climbed nimbly out of the pool, her dark eyes fixed on Jan.

A glance at his watch had been enough to know he'd find her here. She ticked along as precisely as an atomic watch.

He was astonished the hotel had already reopened the pool. The broken window was taped up with plastic film, the shards of glass swept away.

'What's up?' Anita undid her plait and wrung out her damp hair.

From seven to seven thirty she was always in the pool. She'd been that way for years. Her self-discipline was part of the reason why her body was still breath-taking, the skin as smooth and tight as her dark blue bikini, her musculature defined.

He realised he'd let his eyes rest on her a fraction too long. The way his memory lingered a split second too long on the moments she'd pressed him down onto the bedsheets, sat astride him and got what she wanted from him.

He felt like giving himself a clip round the ear. That was all ancient history. Better that way for both of them, he reminded himself – now wasn't the time to get distracted.

'I assume you're not just here to relax.' She wound a towel around her body. 'I know that face. Something's not right—'

'I'm sorry, but I've got to go back to Mainz at once. Not long. Give me one day. But there's something I need to sort out urgently.'

'I'm not your boss. At most I can ask you to do something. I can't give you instructions.'

'Sure, but I'm not keen to get on your bad side.'

She wound a second towel around her head like a turban. 'Okay, then I'm asking this: stay, at least for the next few hours. I'm going to need you.'

'What's wrong?'

'There's a new victim. "E".'

Jan froze. 'Where?'

'Marienstatt Abbey. Near Hachenburg.'

'How long have you known?'

'About an hour.'

His eyes darted to the pool. 'And you still went calmly for a swim?'

'I don't like to break my routine,' she explained. 'Anyway, being over-hasty never helps an investigation.'

He shook his head barely perceptibly. There it was again. The enigma Anita had so often posed to him. 'Sometimes I feel like I've never really understood you.'

For a moment she seemed to give way to her sentimental side. She winked. 'You're the one who's come closest, anyway.' Then instantly her features hardened. 'So, are you coming to the abbey?'

He turned her down, telling her about Miriam, his drifter, who was in trouble. 'You probably find the whole thing silly,' he finished. 'Me doing something so irrational.'

'No,' she said slowly, her head cocked. 'It's just who you are. An impulsive analyst. A cynical do-gooder. A paradox, plain and simple.'

'Sounds almost poetic, the way you put it. I'll stick to that – I'm going. Rabea can take charge in the meantime.'

'I'll keep you in the loop, Jan,' she said. 'And since we're on the topic of Rabea, does she know what really happened to your brother?'

His heart convulsed. 'You're still the only person who knows about that.'

'All these years, and you're still dragging that ballast around by yourself.'

'If I hadn't told you, we probably wouldn't have split up,' he replied, trying as best he could to keep all trace of wistfulness out of his voice.

'That wasn't the reason I ended it!' The familiar vein began to pulse in her otherwise flawless brow. 'But I can't be with a man who's capable of keeping such a secret. That's what makes you so dangerous.'

'You think I'm dangerous?'

'There was a period when I thought you were a psychopath. But unfortunately, it takes a psychopath to understand other psychopaths.'

'That's a nice summary of my craft.'

He was feeling so exposed that he couldn't help taking refuge in sarcasm.

'I've got to go. The team's waiting,' she said, instantly as emotionless as usual. As she left, she glanced over her shoulder. 'You know, for a psychopath you're not so bad.'

## 50

The moment had come. Rabea had feared it and longed for it ever since she'd entered the State Office of Criminal Investigations. She had to stand in for Jan. She had to prove herself as a solo analyst.

Wiping her sweaty palms on her jeans, she leant her head against the window of Ichigawa's Audi.

They were following a road that led out of Hachenburg and into the Nister Valley. The snowploughs hadn't reached this far yet. In some places along the windy road it was difficult to tell where the asphalt stopped and the earth began. Anita was concentrating hard, hunched over the wheel.

The woods began to clear either side of the road. For the first time, Rabea had a clear view of the abbey. It was like looking through a window into the past. If it hadn't been for the car park, the complex of buildings could have been straight out of the Middle Ages.

'That might be Brother Timotheus up there,' said Ichigawa. 'He's going to take us to the crime scene.'

Her gaze was resting on a Cistercian brother in a white-and-black habit, who was herding a group of schoolchildren near the bus stop.

They climbed out and approached the monk.

'Markus, I can see that sharpie!' roared the bearded monk. 'If I see a single line on that bench!'

When he saw them, his tense features relaxed. His cobalt-black beard and chin-length mane of hair made Timotheus look older than he probably really was. Rabea estimated him to be in his mid-forties.

'Sorry, I'm under a bit of stress right now,' he said, shaking hands. 'We ended the lesson early and I have to make sure the children get off all right.'

'No problem,' replied Ichigawa, throwing a glance at the children that made it clear she would never be a mother or a housewife.

Timotheus glanced at them both. 'Isn't Jan here? I thought he'd be dealing with the behavioural analysis.'

Rabea raised her eyebrows. 'You know Jan?'

'Only a little. I knew his brother Gero better,' explained the monk. 'We were best friends. We got our hunting licences together.'

For a moment Rabea held her breath, exchanging a look with Ichigawa.

'Jan had to leave at short notice to take care of a personal matter,' she explained, careful to give nothing away. 'But I'll do my best to be an adequate substitute.'

'Hunting, eh?' Ichigawa spoke with deliberate casualness. 'Being a servant of the Lord seems a far cry from target practice.'

'The road to repentance can be a long and stony one, if you'll permit me such a hoary old Catholic platitude.'

Rabea grinned inwardly. She had to hand it to Timotheus: for a man of the cloth, he had an unexpected degree of self-irony.

'Brother Timotheus, who found the body – and when?' she asked.

'Please, call me Timo. The students do too.' The monk winked at them. 'No reason to be formal.'

A school bus pulled up. With clear, strict instructions he shepherded his charges into the vehicle. Once the whole rabble – constantly on their mobile phones – had vanished onto the bus, his attention turned back to them.

'One of our novices, Benedikt, found it this morning while he was out jogging. Right on the Nister.'

'We'll need to speak to him,' said Ichigawa.

'Of course.' Sighing, he gestured for them to follow him. 'Let's get this over and done with.'

They crossed a bridge so old it had probably been trodden by knights and dukes, then followed a path. There was a wonderful view over the radiantly white abbey, which looked like an ice palace in the snow.

Timotheus turned to Rabea. 'Tell me, how's Jan doing?' he asked. 'I imagine it's difficult for him being back. After everything that happened back then.'

'He's managing,' she replied, deliberately concise. 'Visited his family, briefly.'

'I get it,' said Timo. 'What's that line? "All happy families are alike; every unhappy family is unhappy in its own way".'

Rabea nearly tripped over a root.

The monk caught her upper arm. His touch left an ice-cold prickle on her skin. 'Everything all right?'

'Yes, of course. Your – knowledge of literature surprised me, that's all.'

## 51

'I knew you'd be back.' Katharina Grall manoeuvred the coffee cup onto the kitchen table and said with a smile, 'And please don't break this one. Otherwise I'll soon be running out of cups.'

'I promise,' murmured Jan towards the table top.

He shouldn't have allowed himself that slip-up the last time he visited his sister-in-law. And he called himself a psychologist.

Hardt lay on the route to Mainz. He'd wanted to get to Miriam as quickly as possible, but this geographical fact had thwarted his plans. He had to make a stop. Apologise. Clear the slate.

'I don't have much time, as I said,' he explained, running his forefinger along the grain in the table. 'But I did want to apologise. Gero's death is still so incomprehensibly terrible. For us all.'

His sister-in-law leant against the kitchen unit, her arms crossed over her chest. She rubbed her elbows, a clear sign of tension.

'For me it isn't, to be honest, not any more. Not for a long time,' she said. 'I wasted fewer tears on him than you might think.'

He stared at her.

'Sometimes I wonder whether you knew Gero at all.' Her mouth narrowed. 'He had a lover.' Kathi stepped away from the countertop, her fists balled and her voice hard. 'Some young idiot from Weidenhahn. Must have started about a year before the accident. She moved to Frankfurt later.'

Jan sipped his coffee. He could barely swallow. How many secrets had his brother been keeping?

'I only found out after the accident. When I looked through his phone.'

'Did you ever meet her?'

Kathi shook her head. 'After Gero's death she took off.'

'Sounds familiar.'

There was a hesitant knock on the doorframe. 'Mum?'

Kathi turned around. 'Ah, Maik. How long have you been standing there?'

Jan's nephew gestured vaguely. 'Not long. Less than a minute.'

Again, the young man's appearance confused Jan. His resemblance to Gero was overwhelming. It was like staring straight through his face into the past.

Maik handed his mother an envelope, whispering something into her ear.

'Yeah, fine. It's from the insurance company. We'll go through it together in a minute,' she replied.

Her son blushed, his eyes flitting to Jan.

Kathi put a hand on his shoulder. 'Maik has similar problems to the ones you used to have. Concentration. But it's nothing to be ashamed of, is it?'

Maik simply nodded sullenly.

'It's all right. You can trust me. I'm part of the family.' Jan forced a smile. It sounded so strange. Family. 'Grades don't tell you anything about intelligence. Don't let it ruin your life.'

The corner of Maik's mouth twisted, just like with Gero.

The sight made his heart jump. He should have spent more time with his nephew. He turned away and stood up. 'Sorry, but I've got to go.'

'At least you didn't knock over a cup this time.' Kathi gave him a brief hug.

A knock on the veranda door made them both jump. Stefan Schomar, her new partner, waved at them. Snowflakes clung to his outdoor jacket, and his cheeks were burning red.

'One second.' Kathi pulled back from Jan, sprinted across the living room and pushed open the door.

'Sorry, forgot my key,' Stefan greeted her, giving her a peck on the cheek.

He seemed even more tired than the last time, like a soldier coming home after a hard-fought battle. His eyes, which seemed marked with a deep sorrow, fell on Jan.

'Back again!' The hint of a smile. 'I've just been on one of the searches. The weather isn't exactly helping.'

'Don't you have to work?' asked Jan.

'Took the day off. We can't roll over our holiday at work, so I'm using them all up before it's too late.'

'Daaad!'

There was a clatter on the hall stairs. A girl in purple pyjamas, curls flying, raced in and threw herself on Stefan. Jan guessed she must have just started school.

'Princess Emilia! You're still in your jim-jams!' For the first time, Stefan's voice sounded more relaxed.

'She's been playing Nintendo all morning,' explained Kathi, raising her eyebrows.

'Oh? And? Did you beat the final boss?'

Emilia shook her head. 'You've got to help me.'

'And what are you up to, big man?' Stefan gave Maik a nudge, which prompted a halting smile.

'Just driving into town. Mum wanted me to pick up a few things.'

'Helps his mother, what a gentleman!'

Despite Stefan's false jollity, the chemistry between him and Maik was not the same as between him and his beloved daughter.

Emilia was eyeing Jan, her head cocked. 'And who are you?'

'Oh, that's—' Kathi paused. She must have realised mid-sentence it wasn't easy explaining his role to a child.

Jan leapt in. 'I'm Maik's uncle – Jan.'

He gave her his hand, which she hesitantly took. He shook it with comical exaggeration. 'Wow, you have a really firm grip,' he said, rubbing his fingers.

Emilia giggled.

'I think you need a coffee,' said Kathi to Stefan.

Stefan sat down at the table. 'You got that right!'

For a moment Jan absorbed this family idyll, although it was nothing but a performance – improvised am-dram; then he made his second escape attempt. He had to go to Miriam.

'As I said, I've got to go.'

Stefan threw out his arms. 'Disgraceful! We keep missing each other by a hair's breadth. Don't forget – my invitation still stands.'

Emilia was swinging around on her chair. 'Will you show me your gun when the man's gone?'

Instantly Jan's mind shifted up a few gears. 'What gun?'

'Oh, she saw me taking my shotgun out on the search this morning. I promised her she could take a closer look later.'

Kathi was open-mouthed. 'She's four!'

'I was only going to explain how it works.' Stefan shrugged. He hid his hands underneath the table, but Jan could see they were shaking.

'What were you planning? To shoot the killer?' Kathi nearly raised her voice, but then seemed to remember Jan's presence.

'I was worried about my safety!' Stefan kept his eyes lowered.

'Why didn't you bring it back?' enquired Jan.

'Hm?'

'When you came in just now – you didn't have a gun with you.'

'One of the other volunteers didn't think it was a good idea having it with me. We left it in the village hall. I forgot it there.'

You don't forget a gun that easily, thought Jan, but he left the words unspoken.

'Sorry,' he said. 'It's getting to be a habit, constantly asking questions like that.'

'No worries.' Stefan took his first gulp of coffee. 'You could probably do with some holiday too, eh?'

'That'll have to wait.'

As he left, he clapped Maik on the shoulder. 'We'll have to meet up once all this is over.'

Surprise glimmered in the young man's eyes. 'Yeah, sure,' he said in his listless voice.

Jan winked at him. Perhaps he could be a good uncle yet.

## 52

*For a long time, I used to go to bed early. Sometimes I closed my eyes almost before the candle was put out, so quickly I had no time to think: 'I'm going to sleep now.'*

Ichigawa's eyes rested on the note, which was pinned to one of the oak trees. 'The beginning of a novel. Of course. I'm starting to feel like I'm in a book club.'

*In Search of Lost Time,* breathed Rabea. 'Proust. At first, I thought the quotations were connected to the victims, but now I'm beginning to think they're chosen at random.'

'But a serial killer would want to express himself. Communicate with us. It doesn't make sense.'

'Maybe it's not about the content, but the writing. About positioning himself. Our killer tattooed letters on his victims – he's more interested in the act of writing itself.'

One of Rabea's hobby horses during her training at the Bern ViCLAS Centre had been to leave well-trodden paths. To think laterally. A skill she'd praised during her first conversation with Jan: 'I'm also able to think out of the box.'

Jan had simply laughed. 'Outside every box there's just a bigger box.'

At this moment, however, her mentality was paying off. Giving her a self-confidence that rushed ever-stronger through her body.

She and Ichigawa turned again towards the crime scene on the riverbank. The Nister was almost completely frozen over, gurgling faintly like a hibernating animal.

Tape separated one section of the river – an arena of death. The coroner, Diana Harreiter, was kneeling over the dead man like a sorrowing clown. Even at a distance Rabea could see the deep red 'E' on the back of the corpse, the lines as shaky as though drawn by a child.

'Could you tell me the dead man's name?' asked Harreiter as they approached.

Ichigawa crouched down beside her. 'Does it make a difference to you?'

'I always like to know the names of the people whose chests I'm about to saw open.' Today, small Death Star earrings were hanging from her earlobes. 'Dr Michael H. Ehrberg,' said Rabea, putting an end to the squabble. 'Brother Timotheus knew him. He was a literary scholar, an expert in biblical mysticism and Christian superstitions. He was supposed to be taking a break here in Marienstatt.'

'A longer one than planned,' remarked Ichigawa unemotionally.

Rabea stared at her.

Ichigawa merely shrugged. 'Dr Ehrberg is part of my job. And I don't let emotions get tangled up with work.'

Rabea felt like rolling her eyes.

The scholar's face had been in the river, the head and neck bloated. His hair hung in soaked, bloody hanks. An oval laceration yawned on the back of his head.

The skin on the rest of his body was grey and puffy. His limbs were scrawny, almost those of an insect. The irreverent thought of Gollum from *Lord of the Rings* popped into Rabea's head.

'Was he beaten to death or did he drown?' asked Ichigawa.

'When I raised his head, I noticed there was water in his lungs,' replied Harreiter. 'The blow to the back of the head must have put him out of action, but the cause of death was drowning.'

'Time of death?'

'Judging by the discolouration and blanching, I'd say around two in the morning. And there's no indication he was moved. The victim must have got here under his own steam – either because he was forced to or of his own accord.'

Rabea surveyed the body, which lay before her on the icy gravel bank. Had he met the killer here? Had he known him? If so, how?

Ichigawa patted Harreiter on the shoulder. 'Thanks, that's a big help.' She turned to Rabea. 'Let's go and see our monk again, shall we?'

Brother Timotheus didn't notice them until they were standing right in front of him. His hands tucked into the wide sleeves of his habit, his head bowed in humility, he resembled a Renaissance statue of some martyr.

'Apologies for my obvious question but was there anybody at the monastery who had differences with Dr Ehrberg?' murmured Ichigawa, suddenly an entirely different person. As though she'd put on a mask.

'I can't remember any quarrels,' said Timotheus from underneath his beard. 'Although – there was a rumour among the brothers that he was homosexual.'

Ichigawa tilted her head. 'What's your opinion of his work? Christian superstitions. I suppose a topic like that has to be treated with kid gloves?'

Rabea's eyes flicked back and forth between them. It was all-too apparent that the team leader was zeroing in on the Cistercian. She too found the monk's behaviour suspicious, but she could hear Jan's voice echoing through her brain, warning her not to jump to conclusions.

'Ehrberg's area of research was controversial, true.' Timotheus cleared his throat. 'These days the Church is criticised on all sides, attacked, undermined from within its own ranks. We don't need somebody else coming along to take apart our holiest of holies – the word of God – piece by piece.'

Ichigawa's expression had darkened with every word. She gave a chilly smile. 'Timo, would you have any objection to continuing this conversation in your cell?'

## 53

The Virgin Mary, holding a sceptre and the Baby Jesus, gazed balefully down at Rabea as she followed the others through the monastery gate. She wasn't particularly religious, but magnificent sacred architecture like the baroque staircase always prompted in her a certain degree of awe.

Timotheus greeted two of his brothers, who observed the group in wide-eyed silence, and led them up the branching staircase to the monks' retreat. A world normally barred to outsiders.

'I don't know exactly what you want to know from me,' said Timotheus as they walked down the corridor, their footsteps echoing. 'Or what you think you'll find in my cell. But I have nothing to hide, so please—'

He paused outside a plain oak door and pushed it open. It wasn't locked. Nor was there much to steal inside the cell: a simple bed, a desk, a wardrobe, a few books, a glasses case, and the obligatory wooden cross on the wall. It smelled like freshly laundered bedding and a vague purity.

Ichigawa stepped inside without waiting to be asked and sat down on the only chair. Her gaze swept across the books arrayed on the desk. 'You really are well-versed in world literature.'

Timotheus sat down on the bed. 'For me there are more books than just the Holy Scripture.'

Anita tapped the wardrobe. 'May I?'

'If you must.'

Rabea's interest was elsewhere. 'When was the last time you saw Jan?'

'What's that got to do with anything?' asked Ichigawa, peering through the contents of the wardrobe.

'If you literally mean seeing, then the last time was the day before yesterday, in the newspaper. I scarcely recognised him. The years have left quite a mark.'

There was genuine concern in the Cistercian's voice, making Rabea even more doubtful he was capable of violence.

'Frau Wyler! Look at this!' Ichigawa stepped away from the wardrobe.

Rabea came to stand beside her. Ichigawa had put on latex gloves and was now crouching down.

'The wardrobe has a false floor.'

There was a tiny hole in the far-right corner of the wooden panel. Ichigawa poked her finger inside and pulled it back to reveal a cavity the width of a hand. Inside was a Stone Age Nokia.

'Nothing to hide, eh?' said Ichigawa triumphantly.

Even behind the thick beard, it was obvious the monk had blanched.

Picking up the phone, Ichigawa switched it on. 'Can you tell us what we'll find on here?'

'The phone?' stuttered Timotheus, real confusion glinting in his dark eyes. 'I lost it a few days ago.'

'How convenient – it seems to have turned up again. Aren't you pleased? Who else knew about this secret compartment besides you?'

Timotheus merely stared open-mouthed at them.

'Go through the texts,' said Rabea breathlessly.

Ichigawa's fingers rippled across the keys, then she passed Rabea the phone.

*I am at the nister. waiting for you. your timo.*

'Who was this to?' asked Rabea.

'Michael. As in Dr Michael Ehrberg.' Ichigawa turned to the monk. 'Brother Timotheus, I'm arresting you on suspicion of murder.'

She took the handcuffs from her belt and stepped towards him. No trace of his composure remained. He rose from the bed, arms flung wide.

'I – that – that's impossible—'

Rabea followed what was happening as though watching television. A passive witness.

It was too simple. This wasn't right.

They were making a huge mistake.

## 54

'Finished?'

Tugba's tormentor's eyes flashed in the darkness. His leather gloves cracked as he gripped the boards of her wooden prison.

He'd torn her out of an uneasy doze. The kind of sleep that brings no rest, that takes it. Luckily, she'd been lying with her back to the wall, so he didn't see she'd already scratched away half the G. She had no idea what he would do. She didn't want to find out.

He kicked the boards.

'Are you finished?' he repeated, this time more sharply.

She nodded vehemently. 'Yes—' She could scarcely get a word out through her parched lips. Her tongue felt like a dry sponge stuffed into her mouth.

She moved her cold-stiffened hands, balling and opening them again, then reached underneath the mattress and took out the book. She had marked the exercises, which somebody had completed in a smudged childish hand, as normal. Putting ticks, correcting mistakes, giving marks. What was he planning? Who had filled it out? His child?

When she passed it to him, trembling, he ripped it instantly out of her hand, then jerked it open and leafed impatiently through it. In a flash he seemed to have forgotten all about her.

She was about to withdraw to her mattress when suddenly he raised his hand. 'The pen!'

Tugba's throat clamped shut. He hadn't forgotten after all. Again, she slipped her fingers under the rough material of the mattress.

All her exhaustion fell away. Adrenaline pumped through her veins. The cheap plastic pen was cool and light in her sweaty palm. She ran her thumb over the place where she'd broken off the metal clip.

'Here.' She reached out her arm.

Impatiently he grabbed the pen. Looked at it. Paused.

Tugba scrabbled back onto the mattress in panic. No, no, no! She couldn't breathe. He had noticed. Sensed immediately that something was wrong. How could she have been so stupid?

He put the pen back into his pocket and turned away, his eyes fixed on the book.

Tugba didn't dare exhale until he'd climbed back through the trapdoor. He must have been so absorbed in the corrections that he didn't notice the missing clip.

She fiddled around inside the small hole she'd torn in the mattress, stroking the metal clip and the half of the refill that she'd broken off.

*She was going to see daylight again. She was going to eat ice cream with her sister. Laugh with her students. Live on. She let the images pass like a mantra through her mind. She still had time. Her letter hadn't come, not yet.*

## 55

'Do you know about the Lincoln–Kennedy mystery, Frau Wyler?'

'I'm not here for a history lesson.' Rabea got up from her bar stool. 'I need a second opinion on the arrest.'

Stüter was crouching on his bed, clad only in an undershirt and baggy jogging bottoms. A checked woollen blanket was draped around his shoulders. The word 'neglected' had shot through Rabea's head when she saw him at the front door of Heino's Den. But that wasn't quite accurate. He was freshly showered, smelled of aftershave, and wore clean clothes. She just had to get used to seeing a controlled person like Stüter look so casual.

'I'm not giving you a history lesson, I'm giving you a maths lesson. One of my little foibles.' He pointed at a pile of books next to his camp bed. Rabea, peering at it, read titles like *Mathematical Phenomena*, *Fundamentals of Statistics* and *The Mystery of Pi*.

'Sounds a bit better. Why are you so interested?'

He flung out his arms. 'Look around you! I live in a pub. My daughter is on a gap year in Australia. I only hear from her once in a blue moon. My best friend's son was murdered on my watch, and his killer's still out there. The whole world is in chaos, and it's getting worse. Numbers have always given me something to hold on to. Order. Control. They're so different from what we deal with at work. Don't worry – I'm not going to give you some boring lecture. My question is connected to what I think about the arrest of this Cistercian brother.'

Rabea stepped behind the bar. 'How do you know about that?'

'The same way I knew about what was found in Tamara Weiss's hotel room,' he replied with a humourless chuckle. 'I have my sources. Why did you come to me and not to Grall, anyway?'

She avoided his gaze. 'You know why. In any case, he's unavailable at the moment.'

'Unavailable? Interesting choice of words.'

'Lincoln and Kennedy, what about them?'

Obviously Stüter noticed her clumsy change of subject. He raised the corner of his mouth, making it look like a wolf's maw.

'The Lincoln–Kennedy mystery is about a series of weird coincidences involving the two presidents. Here's a couple: Lincoln was shot at the Ford Theatre. Kennedy was assassinated in a Ford Lincoln. Lincoln was elected to Congress in 1846, Kennedy in 1946. Abraham Lincoln became president in 1860, Kennedy in 1960.'

'Sheer chance,' remarked Rabea. She didn't understand what Stüter was getting at.

'Correct, correct. You can find just as many coincidences between Kennedy and any other random president, if you search for long enough. In mathematics we call this a phenomenon – that you can find people with the same characteristics even in a small group – the birthday paradox.'

'I heard about that during training.' She ran her finger ruminatively along the stainless-steel tap. 'If you're in a room with more than a certain number of people, the chance that two of them will have the same birthday is greater than fifty percent.'

'Absolutely right. The number is twenty-three, to be precise. At fifty people, the probability rises to seventy-nine percent. Incredible, isn't it?'

'Sure. But please tell me what this has to do with the Alphabet Killer.'

Stüter got up and stood on the other side of the bar. 'You and Jan have been straining to find similarities between the victims. There's nothing so very wrong with that, initially. But as we both know; such similarities can be deceptive.'

'But that's where the killer's motivation is hidden.'

'I don't think it will lead anywhere. We'll just get lost in a web of apparent connections. The Cistercian isn't the killer.'

Rabea glanced at her phone. She hadn't owned a watch for years. 'I'm due to be at his interrogation. So, what's your opinion then?'

'I think we should concentrate on one victim and fully explore every facet of their life. And that victim should be

Tugba Ekiz. The literacy course. The fact that there were no signs of a break-in at her apartment. She must have known the killer. We've not had the chance to investigate all that thoroughly. Events have moved too quickly.'

Rabea put it on her mental to-do list. The Chief Superintendent might be right.

He closed his cold, rough hand around her forearm. 'One more thing: be careful. You saw what happened to Daniel.'

'Thanks. I'll watch out.' She put on the most confident smile she could muster.

Not her most convincing one, she had to admit.

## 56

Jan's apartment looked like the aftermath of a massacre.

Shards everywhere, shattered DVDs. They'd not spared his TV, either – the screen was covered in a rose-shaped web of cracks.

His life. One big heap of rubble.

Again, he swept his gaze over the shards of his film collection, worth several thousand euros. But what could be less important now?

'Thank God, there you are!' came a voice from underneath a mountain of pillows and blankets on the sofa. It took Jan a second to see Miriam.

Her head poked out. Her jet-black hair was shorn on one side and chin-length on the other, her lip pierced, her neck tattooed with stars, her eyeliner smudged from crying.

In three paces he was beside her, hugging her much-too skinny shoulders. 'Everything is going to be fine.'

'People are always lying when they say stuff like that,' she said, her lips quivering.

He didn't reply, just drew her a little tighter. When he let go, he looked into her light green eyes. 'Were the police here?'

She nodded. 'Yeah. They took a load of notes. I told them I was your niece, so I didn't get into any trouble.'

'That's what you are to me.'

He glanced around, sighing. This place had been his refuge. The centre of his life. It was where he'd gathered strength. Lost himself in old Tarantino films, eating Turkish falafel. He'd not needed anything else. Now even this sanctuary of silence had been desecrated.

'You look so sad,' said Miriam. On the street she'd learned a good instinct for body language. 'I'm really sorry I got you dragged into this.'

'There's nothing you can do about it. Just one thing: I want the truth. Why did you borrow money from him?'

'My sister— '

'She's still living with your father, isn't she?' he asked, the word 'father' laden with contempt. He didn't want to know what that man had done to Miriam.

She nodded. 'She needed money. For the class trip. For food, even. My father doesn't give a shit. Wastes it all on betting and boozing.'

Jan rested his chin in his hands. 'Why didn't you come to me?'

She lowered her eyes. 'I'd never want to be in your debt. I'm too proud for that.'

'Pride isn't much help when every bone in your body is broken.'

He was relieved, however, that she'd borrowed the money for her sister and not for drugs again. Not that he had much moral superiority there. His eyes fell on the drawer of his large walnut desk. There was at least a month's supply of weed in there.

'Look.' Miriam took a picture from the coffee table and handed it to him. 'They smashed up the chest of drawers and some pictures fell out.'

He examined the photograph. It depicted him and his brother when Jan was still a child and Gero a teenager. Gero, looking fit and muscular with his flashing eyes and dimple, was proudly holding up a fishing rod, while Jan held their catch – a giant trout – with a faint smile on his lips.

'Who's that next to you in the picture?'

'My brother.' He dropped it back on the table.

She stared at him in astonishment. 'You never told me you had one.'

'He died when I was eighteen. Car accident.'

'Oh, I'm sorry. I didn't mean to reopen old wounds.'

'They're not the kind of wounds you're imagining.'

She looked at him for a moment in confusion, then said, with a hint of pleading in her voice, 'I don't want to stay here alone.'

'You don't have to.'

'What do you have in mind?' Miriam leapt up from the sofa, cheerful once again. 'Just one thing: if you call in the welfare people, I'm running away. They don't care anyway. I guess you have to go back to Westerwald, right?'

'Right.' He took a deep breath. 'But I'm taking you with me.'

He already knew it was a bad idea.

## 57

*7th December, midday*

'Two hours until the press conference! We're getting everything ready!' The media liaison officer clapped her hands.
'Once again, good work, Ichigawa.'

She gave the team leader a thumbs-up. Anita simply gave
an exasperated flap of her hand.

The operations centre was in a fever of activity – Rabea
had never seen anything like it. It felt like they were all
grimly battling their own downfall.

Timotheus wasn't the killer. All the odds were against it.
She could see that even without Jan.

'Come on!' Ichigawa marched past her. 'Where were
you? I had to do the first interrogation without you.'

Together they walked towards the interview room.

'Sorry, I just had to get some facts straight.' She didn't
mention her brief trip to see Stüter.

'I'll have to tell Jan. That sort of thing is unacceptable.'

Rabea rolled her eyes. As if Jan would care!

They stopped outside Interview Room 002.

'Let me do the talking in there, okay? I've just been given some background information on our man of God in there, and I want to play those cards at the right time,' said Ichigawa. 'And don't bother with any psychological magic tricks, okay?'

Rabea merely glared.

They went inside. To call it an interview room was a serious exaggeration. The police station in Hachenburg was so small they'd used a converted office. No observation room behind a two-way mirror, no cold light, no oppressive atmosphere.

Merely a single desk, and the Cistercian slumped at it. So far, he'd refused a lawyer. In the habit of his order, he looked like a man from another age. He wore handcuffs, which Rabea thought was totally unnecessary. He seemed about as aggressive as Gandhi.

He shot them a pained smile. 'Glad to see you again. I hope you're here so we can end this farce.'

Ichigawa sat opposite him and switched on the recording device. 'Oh, I'm afraid this *farce* has only just begun.'

Her voice was so cutting it even sent a shiver down Rabea's spine.

'You know your rights?' Rabea made sure. 'You really don't want a lawyer?'

'People who've done nothing wrong don't need to defend themselves. My lawyer is up there.' He gestured towards the sky. Rabea sighed. Why did people always cling to principles that ended up hurting them?

Ichigawa laughed sardonically. 'We'll see how well your lawyer up there did on his exams.'

Rabea, glancing back and forth between them, interlaced her fingers.

'Yesterday after compline, none of your brothers saw you. Where were you?'

'In my cell. Alone. I was reading. It's not a weak alibi, it's just the life of a monk: solitude.'

Ichigawa raised an eyebrow. 'So why did one of the students see you leaving the abbey at ten o'clock? With a heavy bag?'

Right into the trap, thought Rabea.

Timo rubbed the back of his neck, avoiding their eyes. He bit his bottom lip.

Rabea cocked her head. His body language was that of a liar. Had she been mistaken, perhaps?

'You don't want to answer?' persisted Ichigawa.

Silence.

'As you wish,' she sighed. 'We've got all the time in the world. Let's try something else. You spoke earlier about the life of a monk. Are explicit text messages part of that life too?'

Timotheus's eyebrows shot up. 'I don't know what you're talking about.'

'I doubt that.' Ichigawa leafed through the pile of paper in front of her. 'Here, for example. The fourth of December. Eight minutes past ten. Text to Dr Michael Ehrberg: "I watched you all day again today. Touching myself and thinking of you. Your Timo".'

Even through the thick beard, it was clear the Cistercian was bright red. 'I – I would never write something like that.'

'Then how come that text was sent from your phone under your name? You've been messaging back and forth like that for six days. Sending each other filthy rubbish.'

Timotheus flung up his hands. 'Six days ago, I lost my phone. Going for a walk with a visitor, Tamara Weiss. The woman who was abducted.'

'I'm supposed to buy that? Really?' Ichigawa whistled through the gap in her front teeth. 'And thanks for mentioning the connection with Tamara Weiss – another potential victim – off your own bat. That only makes our job easier.'

Rabea put a hand on her forearm and whispered into her ear, 'Let's take it a bit easier.'

'Take it easier?' replied Ichigawa at a normal volume, her eyes still fixed on Timotheus. 'I've barely started. Why did Frau Weiss visit you?'

'She is – was – Dr Ehrberg's editor. She earned most of her money from translations, but when a subject interested her, she would also do editorial work. They ate together at the brewery then he invited me for a walk. I must have lost my phone then.'

'And how do you explain text messages being sent from the phone after that point?'

'Somebody must have found it and used it! Take fingerprints – that will clear everything up.'

'I certainly will. But I have a feeling the results won't look good for you.'

Once again Rabea tried to rein her in. 'Before you give the press conference, at least wait for the results of the fingerprint analysis,' she whispered. 'So that we're one hundred percent sure.'

'Sometimes you have to press ahead. Didn't Jan teach you that?'

'More the opposite, actually.'

'Typical.' Ichigawa leant forwards and glared at her interviewee. 'Now, Brother Timotheus—'

'May I interrupt a moment? I just want to ask one question.' Rabea made her voice as steely as possible. Time to assert herself.

Ichigawa gave an exasperated groan, but said, 'Do what you have to.'

'Okay.' Rabea made an expansive gesture. 'Please answer my question as spontaneously as possible, no matter how peculiar it seems.'

Timotheus nodded eagerly. He seemed to realise he had an ally in her.

'A man is at his father's funeral. He meets a beautiful woman and gets on with her incredibly well. But they forget to exchange numbers. One week later, he kills his mother. Why?'

The Cistercian's face was utterly baffled. 'Eh? Why would he do that? There's no point.'

Rabea smiled. 'Fine. Thank you very much, that's great.'

'It's obvious. He wants to see the woman again at the mother's funeral,' said Ichigawa with a shrug. 'What's that test supposed to do?'

Rabea's smile broadened. 'Your answer shows that you think more like a psychopath than Brother Timotheus. You showed no emotion whatsoever. You simply followed an unscrupulous if logical line of reasoning.'

Ichigawa waved a dismissive hand. 'Spare me your party tricks. You're supposed to be analysing this man's psychology, not siding with him.'

Of course, the test question was a scientifically dubious little game. Yet it was enough to rattle the Senior Chief Superintendent for a few seconds.

Still, Ichigawa didn't need long to pick up the thread. 'Did you and Frau Weiss see each other again after the walk?'

Timotheus shook his head.

'Did you know where she was staying?'

'Yes, at the wildlife park hotel.'

She was taking notes, writing with deliberate slowness and glancing up at him meaningfully as she did so. 'You have a hunting licence, correct?'

'That's true, although I haven't owned a gun for years.'

'Mhm. And what did you do with your guns? Sold them?'

'Gave them away. To Gero Grall, your behavioural analyst's brother.'

This time it was Ichigawa's turn to whisper to Rabea. 'Gero Grall died in an accident. We'll have to check what happened to the guns.'

'I know about the accident.'

'Jan must really trust you if he told you that.' Ichigawa turned back to the monk. She skimmed through the pile of paper, stopping at a dated list. 'You're not exactly unknown to the police here.' She slid the page of numbered images, organised into a table, across the desk. 'These photographs all date from the time before you entered the order. Back then you were what – nineteen, twenty? Grievous bodily harm. Numerous instances. Rather unpleasant, I'd say. You were a textbook thug.'

Rabea caught a glimpse of the photographs and instantly regretted it. They showed brutally beaten teenagers, their eyes swollen, cheeks covered in bruises and abrasions, and their lips split.

Brother Timotheus coughed.

Ichigawa leant forwards, her eyes ablaze, eager for a confession.

'I – back then I was still – I—' The Cistercian laid his sweaty palms flat on the desk. 'I think I'd like a lawyer now.'

## 58

The most gruesome art gallery in the world.

The thought occurred to Rabea as she paced around her and Jan's brainstorming room. By now the walls and even the window were papered with countless photographs, notes and documents.

She threw herself onto the sagging sofa with Tugba Ekiz's file. Again, she checked her phone. No message from Jan.

For the umpteenth time she read the report. Her eye was caught by the description of a tattoo on Ekiz's left upper arm: *Bilmemek deðil, öðrenmemek ayýptýr.*

The documents included a receipt from a tattoo studio in Montabaur called Purple Heart. Rabea looked up the website. When she saw the name of the owner, a shiver ran down her spine. Enno Quester. The tattoo artist they'd met at the Fuchskaute. By then it was public knowledge that Tugba was missing. Why hadn't he mentioned knowing her? Or had he not remembered her? Instantly it struck her as much odder that he'd not invited them to his studio. Rabea took a deep breath. First, she wanted to check what the tattoo meant. Typing it into a translation app, she read: *There's no shame in not knowing, only in not learning.*

A Turkish proverb. It fitted the image Rabea had of Tugba. She had been a committed, almost obsessive teacher who'd passed her exams with top marks. A picture-perfect humanist animated with the belief that knowledge could be imparted even through the thickest of skulls.

Was it this conviction that would give Rabea the decisive clue and lead her to the killer? Almost any decision a person made could be used to deduce a character trait. Some small psychological basis that inflected every action.

Including the fatal ones.

She went through the young woman's CV, checking once more the list of participants on the literacy course. Concentrating hard, she re-read the background information on the students, most of whom were children. As Jan had already said – nothing suspicious.

And yet – her theory that the murderer might be illiterate was looking more and more plausible. But if so, then how did the quotations fit?

What if the killer's motivation was rage? Rage at everybody who could write? Who had mastered literacy?

In that case, the tattooed letters made sense. So would the choice of victims. Even the literary quotations, which were mere demonstrations – look, I can do it too! It fitted with his increasing brutality. But that profile fitted no one on the list of course participants.

Her head was ringing, her thoughts going in circles. Placing the documents on the floor beside the sofa, she closed her eyes for a moment. Still her mind wouldn't stop whirring.

Her foot jogged against the Gameboy she'd left here last time. Perfect! Snatching it up, she felt herself growing calmer the moment she heard the Tetris theme tune.

For the next few minutes, she distracted her overworked brain by piling up blocks. Only once she reached level 12, with seventy-thousand points, did she finally fail.

'Darnit!' she blurted, before restarting the game and letting her thoughts flow. Midway through level 5, it all became clear.

She switched off the Gameboy.

The killer was acting out of rage at everybody who loved and had mastered the craft of writing – and rage's little brother, its preliminary stage, was shame. Shame at his own failure. His own inability. What if the killer had applied but never taken part? She leapt up from the sofa. Her palms were damp with sweat, her heart racing.

After a few seconds on Google, she'd found the number of Tugba's school and dialled. Thank God, a cheery administrator picked up at once. When she heard that Rabea was part of the investigation team, she could barely get out a coherent sentence because of her agitation and sheer sadness about Tugba. 'Yes, we have a list of all the people who called up but never actually came.'

She promised to fax the list at once – a reminder that Rabea was in Westerwald. It bordered on a miracle that the secretary hadn't dispatched a stagecoach.

Her fingers trembling, Rabea put her phone away and crept out of the room to the fax machine, an ancient monstrosity from the pre-internet era.

For two minutes she leant against the wall, waiting, then the machine gave a piercing beep. Clattering and jerking, it spat out a sheet of A4 paper.

Rabea rubbed her sweaty palms on her trousers before picking it up. Fifteen handwritten names, most of which – like the other participants – weren't German.

But one immediately caught her eye.

## 59

'Remind me again how many people live in Bad Marienberg?'

There was still dismay in Miriam's voice.

'Enough,' sighed Jan.

He was packing fresh clothes into a holdall. He had no idea how much longer he'd be in Westerwald.

'I don't think I've ever been to a place with so few people.'

'Actually, it's relatively busy for the area.'

Miriam slipped theatrically down the wall in the corridor. 'I can't take it. It's Hicksville!'

He flung out his arms. 'You're welcome to stay here.'

'Are you kidding? Diver will kill me!'

'Then it's settled. Not another word about my home town!'

'Oh well. Maybe this Alphabet Killer will get me too.'

'Don't worry, you don't fit his pattern. You're not interested in literature.'

She balled her fists and planted them on her hips, visibly outraged. 'What's that supposed to mean?'

Jan simply grinned and walked back into the living room, the holdall slung over his shoulder. He checked the answering machine.

Four new messages. The same Frankfurt number had tried three times yesterday but hadn't left a message. The fourth call, from another number, had been made early this morning. This time, there was a recording.

'Hello Herr Grall,' came a serious male voice. 'This is Chief Superintendent Altunbas, Frankfurt Homicide. It's about the murder of Arne Sapkowski. He was found dead at his practice this morning. Yesterday he tried to call you several times. Please get in touch with me. We'll need to ask you a few questions as a witness.'

Jan's mouth gaped. The people around him were dying like flies.

What had Sapkowski wanted? He'd never heard the name before. He'd call Altunbas back as soon as his mind was halfway clear again.

'Let's set off,' he said, and he could hear for himself how flat and weary he sounded.

'Hey, you're knackered,' protested Miriam. 'Set a good example and all that – no driving while exhausted.'

He pushed open the front door. 'I've never been a good example.'

'Then don't give me a lecture if I ever do the same thing.'

'Wouldn't dream of it. You're too smart to do shit like that. And anyway, I'm not your father.'

She looked up at him. 'Feels that way sometimes, though.'

He gazed at her, at this confused girl who was being dragged by youth culture in so many different directions at once. Her words were the petrol that the fire inside him sorely needed. Maybe in Westerwald she'd take more care of him than he of her.

Before they got into the car, he checked his mobile phone. A text from Rabea:

*why didn't you tell me?*

Immediately he called. Dial tone. His throat felt tight. He leant against the roof of the car.

'Jan?' Miriam rubbed his shoulder. 'Everything all right?'

'I think I've made a huge mistake.'

# 60

*7<sup>th</sup> December, evening*

Thick clouds of fog hung in the valleys of Westerwald, pooling in them like water in a gutter. A standing army of grey. Jan felt as though the area hadn't seen the sun in days.

After making sure Miriam could check in at the wildlife park hotel, he'd set off straight for Hachenburg.

Still no word from Rabea. His pulse raced. He shouldn't have left her alone.

He thought of the crucial information he'd omitted. How had she found out? Anything, but not that.

The car rushed past clearings and dells, through which hundreds of police and volunteers in lurid yellow vests were combing, searching for Tamara. For other victims. Or simply for another lead. A police helicopter, engine screaming, was patrolling above the hills. Like a hawk on the hunt for prey.

Jan focused again on the freshly salted road. 'In the murder case that has kept Germany on tenterhooks for days, suspicion has fallen on a Cistercian brother from Marienstatt Abbey,' said a voice on the radio. 'At a recent press conference, investigators announced that they have significant evidence. The investigation, overshadowed thus far by mishaps and mistakes, may finally be coming to an end.'

Jan had known Timotheus – or Ben, as he was actually called – since childhood. In his younger years the man had had to endure more than his fair share of tragedies. First the death of his father, then his mother's Alzheimer's. He'd started getting violent. Threatening others. Hanging around with a shady crowd. Not until he met Gero had he got back on track, and his death had prompted Timo to join the monastery. It didn't take a behavioural investigative advisor to exclude him as a suspect.

His phone vibrated. The hope that it might be a text from Rabea made his heart leap. He picked it up from the passenger seat.

It was. Her name was glowing on the bright green display of his Stone Age phone. He opened the text, keeping the road in his peripheral vision.

He nearly jerked the steering wheel.

The text consisted of a single letter.

'F'.

## 61

A *feather mattress. Soft and white.*

*Rabea nuzzled it, pressing her cheek against it. She closed her eyes. This was where she wanted to stay. To fall peacefully asleep.*

*Around her was the rustling of the forest. The hoarse cawing of a crow. She was naked. Free. Liberated. From everything. The only mark on her pale body a tattoo.*

*What had given her the idea to get something like that done?*

*She couldn't remember any more. Yet she was too tired to look. Why the hurry? She'd have it for the rest of her life.*

*There was something else. She felt something rough and hard on her tongue. A piece of wood, maybe. She coughed it out, along with a torrent of saliva.*

*Sleep. If she went to sleep, deeply and soundly, she'd be warm again. She was utterly sure of that. Sleep tempted her, stroking her shoulders with its velvety fingers. An eternally murmuring lover.*

*Yet there was a throbbing pain at the back of her head. Where was she? A brief flash of panic. Her heart rate picked up.*

*Then, exhaustion again. Sleep gave a charming laugh.*

*Now there were feathers falling from above, too. Fluttering gently. Almost like snow. A soft mattress of snow. What a lovely image.*

*Just before the twilight fell, her mind's last convulsion: you must not sleep.*

*Then her father's voice: 'You've got to be strong now, little one.'*

*She'd been strong far too long already.*

## 62

'Locate her mobile phone right now!' Jan thumped his fist onto the technician's desk.

'It's not as simple as you're making out.' The almost anorexic man in his mid-twenties raised his arms defensively.

'Are you even listening to me? Rabea is in mortal danger!' Jan kicked the desk so hard the tech grabbed his wobbling monitor.

Panic gripped the young man's acne-scarred face. His lips quivered. 'I – I'm sorry – I'm doing my best.'

'Clearly your best isn't—'

'Jan!' Anita's voice whipped through the operations room. 'Is that any way to address my people?'

Pumps clacking as she crossed the room, she walked up to him like some goddess of vengeance.

Something inside Jan broke. She had smashed the last dam holding back his emotions. He planted himself in front of her. 'Rabea is out there somewhere!' he yelled, pointing out of the window into the snowy darkness of the night. 'We've got to find her, for fuck's sake, before it's too late!'

'It probably already is,' said Anita, her voice low.

'No!' he spat. 'No, she's still alive. Just like Tugba. Like Tugba. He's threatening us. It's only a threat!'

His knees were giving way, and he sank into a chair with a groan. Rabea was under his protection. He never should have left her.

'I'm sorry, Jan, but I'm simply thinking logically here.' Anita made a clumsy attempt to rub his shoulders.

Her fingers felt like spider's legs through his shirt. Half acting like a human – it had never been her strong suit.

'And she really didn't say where she was going? Who she was meeting?' he asked.

'Not a word.'

He shook off her hand, stood up and crossed to Rabea's desk. Her workspace was unchanged. The same coffee cup, deep black dregs solidifying at the bottom. Resting his fists on the surface, he dropped his head.

'At least we can rule out the Cistercian,' he said tonelessly. 'That was a blunder from square one.'

Anita came and stood next to him, arms crossed. 'Remember the suggestion that there were two killers? That we might be dealing with partners?'

He rubbed his stubbly chin – shaving wasn't exactly a priority at the moment – and considered the question. 'That would explain the extraordinary frequency, true. The planning. But I still don't think Timotheus is one of them.'

'No matter who it is or how many there are, we'll find Rabea.'

'You've changed your tune.'

She put on a smile. 'I didn't mean it like that. We've got to stay functional. For Rabea.' She sighed, thinking for a moment. 'Do you know what's just occurred to me?'

'I'm not in the mood for guessing games.'

'Somebody said Stüter was here, asking for her. Just after Rabea left.'

Jan hesitated. Wasn't the Chief Superintendent still in hospital? Maybe her disappearance was connected not to his secret but to Stüter? Maybe it wasn't his fault at all? Why else would Stüter have asked for her?

'We've got to find out where he is. Right now.'

# 63

Grosse Wolfstein Rock.

In the middle of the night, it was a shadowy monster of weather-beaten stones.

The local Tower of Babel thought Rolf Stüter.

People said the devil had once tried to build a tower to heaven out of basalt rock. As usual in such legends, things hadn't turned out well for the devil. The tower came crashing down, leaving nothing but a rubble of giant stones that children climbed in summer.

Turning up the collar of his leather jacket, he fought his way towards the rocks. Snowflakes as sharp as metal splinters blew into his face. The wind was so strong he could scarcely breathe.

Hopefully she'd be there. If the girl was really out in this, she wouldn't last long by herself.

From the first, Rabea had reminded him of his daughter. Of Ida, who was doing a gap year in Australia. From day one he'd kept a protective eye on her, making sure she was as safe as possible at the hotel and the crime scenes. This concern had been one of the main reasons why he'd immediately taken her into his confidence about Jan.

When she'd left him a few hours earlier, he'd quickly realised she might act too hastily – and alone. An old cop like him could sense impending danger in his bones.

He'd gone straight to the station at Hachenburg, just in time to see her driving away, but he'd chosen the nonchalant path and followed her in secret.

He had failed.

She'd left Hachenburg on the road towards Bad Marienberg. For two or three kilometres he'd been tailing her, but then she zoomed to overtake a tractor – a risky move – and stepped on the accelerator.

It was the moment he'd lost her.

He'd searched every place he could think of and called her several times on her phone. No luck. When the message came through that Grall had received that strange text, he feared the worst.

Yet one chance remained.

Nora Schneill, of all people, editor of the *Wäller Zeitung* and his ex-wife, had given him fresh hope.

She'd called as he was on his way back to Hachenburg. 'Stüter? I just heard something disconcerting.'

'Hmm?' he'd simply grunted, his phone clamped between his shoulder and ear. At that moment she was the last person he wanted to talk to.

'Rabea Wyler, the analyst's assistant. Her car – the plates end in nine-six-one, right?'

'Right.'

'Then one of my contacts has just seen it being driven down a trail deep in the forest north of the wildlife park.'

With a screech of tyres, he'd immediately done a U-turn.

'Did this contact see who was at the wheel? Was she alone?'

Schneill didn't know.

'How do you even know the plates of all the police cars round here?'

'I have my sources,' she replied. 'You of all people should know that.'

He'd gritted his teeth, seeing Daniel Köllner's face before him. It had been hard to stop himself screaming at her. Then he'd hung up. At that moment, what mattered was Rabea.

Managing to find tyre tracks on one of the trails, already almost covered by the relentlessly falling snow, he'd followed them. On and on.

To Grosse Wolfstein Rock.

He'd wondered whether he should call for back-up, but officially he was no longer on the investigation. He'd only end up incurring Ichigawa's wrath. Yet every step took him further into danger. Into the heart of darkness.

As teenagers they'd gone camping by Wolfstein. Toasted marshmallows and cooked sausages over the fire, snuggled up in their sleeping bags, told ghost stories and thought about girls.

None of that seemed to have anything to do with the place he was headed to now. For the first time, Wolfstein struck him as a mausoleum. A colossal, archaic memorial.

The tyre tracks grew markedly deeper – this had to be where the car had parked. Drawing his Walther P99 and his torch, he trudged towards the rocks. The basalt stones were stacked to form little plateaus, caves and cracks.

The beam of his torch flickered across the frozen stones. Icicles hung from the outcroppings.

'Police!' he bellowed into the howling wind. 'Show yourself – immediately! Or I'll use my gun.'

No answer. Nothing. Cautiously he edged around Wolfstein, his narrowed eyes fixed on the tiny sliver carved out by his torch.

Then he found her.

Rabea's naked, pale body lay half hidden under a jutting rock, covered only by a whisper-thin veil of snow. The torch slipped from his fingers. He lurched towards her, tripping over a root before staggering back to his feet.

A mixture of tears, sweat and snow was freezing on his face.

He sank to his knees beside her. Saw the 'F' tattooed on her shoulder blade. Deep black and yawning. The laceration on the back of her head, nearly hidden beneath hair sticky with blood.

He summoned what remained of his hope.

Reached for her wrist.

Felt it. Waited fearfully. Held his breath.

No pulse.

Please, no. Please, please, no . . .

# F

'The shape of "F" is modelled on digamma [...] the Romans were hesitant, however, to designate "φ" with "f" in words taken from Greek, preferring to use "ph", while the Greeks replaced the Latin "f" with their "φ", and in ancient words common to both languages "f" and "φ" each appear. [...] All this indicates that "f" and "φ" often stand in for each other.'

The Grimms' Dictionary

# 64

*8 December, early morning*

*Soon he'd reach 'G'.*

*The alphabet was coming together.*

*Letter by letter.*

*On the basement wall hung photographs of 'D' and 'E'. Blurry images of bare skin, blood and the deep blue of the ink.*

*Only one letter stood between Tugba and death. She'd spent hours scratching the 'G' off her skin, until her arms shook with cramp and her back was sticky with blood.*

*For her the letters were no longer writing. They were symbols of death. Dark marks. Something to be cut from the body like a tumour.*

*She'd tried several times to make contact with the other woman, hissing and whispering, but she'd never got a response. Maybe she was long dead and part of the alphabet.*

*Tugba's eyes darted to the wall of photographs. Was she already up there? Was she 'D' or 'E'?*

*She thought about how she'd taught her students their ABCs. Giving them colourful cut-out letters they could arrange into words.*

'Very good, that's A-P-P-L-E!'

'A-N-I-M-A-L! Absolutely right!'

She swallowed, hugging her arms around her legs. If she tried to make words from the pictures on the wall, all that came to mind were D-E-A-T-H and B-L-O-O-D.

On the floor beside her was a bowl, still with the remains of dried, cardboard-like porridge. She dragged it over, scraped her bloody fingers inside and forced down the greyish brown clumps.

Boots. The trapdoor opened. Bright light flooded inside, burning her pupils. She choked on the porridge, coughing up several chunks.

Her tormentor was enveloped in a thick black jacket, the fur-trimmed hood pulled down low over his face – she couldn't make out his features beneath the heavy fabric. Each step left a trail of snow which rapidly melted into puddles on the bare stone floor.

He stood in front of his wall of letters, legs planted wide. Unzipped his jacket.

Tugba crawled forward, her heart hammering against her sternum. She was breathing in jerks. No, not now! Not yet!

He hung the 'F' on the wall and stepped aside, either deliberately or unknowingly giving her a clear view of his most recent crime. The red letter on a canvas of blanched skin.

Her whole body stiffened. The food on her tongue tasted like ashes.

*Her tormentor turned around. She thought she saw his eyes flash for a split second in the shadows of his hood. Fixed on Tugba.*

*He climbed back up the ladder. The trapdoor fell shut with a crash.*

*Next time he'd be back for her.*

*As soon as his footsteps had died away, she leapt up and rushed to the mattress, reaching into the finger-sized hole she'd torn and pulling out the bits of the pen.*

*She clutched the clip in her trembling hand.*

*Time to act.*

## 65

'Excuse me a moment.' Stüter took his vibrating phone from his pocket and vanished from the waiting room.

'We were bloody lucky.' Anita's eyes followed him. 'A few more minutes and it would have been too late for Rabea.'

Leaning against the coffee machine, Jan sipped at his plastic cup full of the much-too-bitter brew. It was his fourth. Whenever he was waiting for important news, he needed something to calm his nerves.

They'd been waiting for the doctor's diagnosis for two hours. Suffering severe hypothermia and with potential brain trauma, Rabea had been rushed to the University Hospital at Siegen, which had more specialist equipment than the hospital at Hachenburg.

'Did the techs find anything at Wolfstein?' he asked.

'Nope,' replied Anita. 'No literary quotation, as yet. Although in this weather it wouldn't have lasted long anyway. Don't get me wrong – I'm very pleased she's alive, but I'm surprised Stüter found her there. I mean – did he follow her?'

Jan had already formed his own theory. 'He must have given Rabea a clue. Kept investigating in secret. Then he must have realised he'd put her in danger by doing so.'

Before Anita could pursue the issue, the door flew open. The Indian doctor, followed by a nurse, hurried in, white coat fluttering. His sparse, sweaty hair clung to his brow.

Jan went up to him. 'How is she doing?'

'Frau Wyler is out of immediate danger, but her condition remains critical. She has suffered severe hypothermia – her body temperature dropped to below twenty-eight degrees. So low there was no perceptible pulse. It's deceptive. They're only lost for good if they're warm and dead. Now we've got to warm her up using a heart-lung machine.'

Jan exhaled and passed a hand across his face. The answer was only slightly reassuring. 'What about the blow to the head?'

'She suffered a cranio-cerebral trauma, which in combination with hypothermia is extremely dangerous. We'll be keeping her in an artificial coma, checking her brain daily with a CT.'

Jan's knees gave way. He sank down onto a chair. An artificial coma. He never should have gone to Mainz. Never should have left Rabea here alone.

The tears came without warning, streaming as abruptly from his eyes as blood from a fresh wound. His whole body shook with sobs. He covered his eyes with his hands – a last, desperate barrier between himself and the outside world.

'Can – can I see her?' he asked the doctor, without looking up.

'I'm sorry. Not while she's in Intensive Care.'

The answer Jan had been expecting. Even so, he broke into fresh tears. He couldn't remember the last time he'd wept so unrestrainedly. If he'd ever cried in front of other people as a grown man.

He'd always kept others away from his break-downs. Away from all his emotions.

The gentle pressure of Anita's fingers on his shoulder. She stroked him cautiously, as though he were a wild animal that might bite.

'She'll be all right,' she said softly. 'I'm here, Jan, I'm here.'

'Thanks,' he whispered, meaning it with all his heart. 'I – I'd better phone her flatmates. Her family. They shouldn't hear it on the news.'

'There's still a few minutes. Take some time to compose yourself first. Or I can do it, if you like.'

He shook his head. 'No, it's my job.'

'Okay, but then it's going to be your job to get some sleep, okay?'

This time he nodded.

'Then we're going to find him.'

# 66

*8th December, morning*

'Did you really have to bring the kid?'

Jan had entered the operations room about five seconds earlier, and Anita had noticed his companion immediately, of course. 'I'm certainly not leaving Miriam alone in the hotel.'

'Hey, guys, I'm right here!' exclaimed Miriam.

'Just make sure she doesn't get annoying.' Anita seemed barely to notice her. 'A retired couple found Rabea's vehicle this morning in a clearing near Langenhahn. The crime scene technicians are on it, but I'm not holding out much hope for usable evidence. Locating Rabea's phone won't help us much either. We recovered it burnt to a crisp in the glove compartment. The model is the same.'

Jan dropped his head. Two leads gone. What else did they have?

'Stüter told me Rabea went to see him,' she continued. 'They talked about the first kidnapping victim, Tugba Ekiz. She most likely knew the murderer. Rabea must have been following that trail – and it brought her to the killer. So, we'll go through everything we know about Frau Ekiz once more. Associates, distant friends, people from the past. Everything.' Anita's gaze fell once more on Miriam. 'I'm really not pleased you brought the girl.'

With that she bustled off to brief a couple of SWAT officers. Jan put his hand on his protégé's shoulder. 'She can be nice too, trust me.'

Miriam seemed scarcely to have heard him – instead, she was staring straight across the room. 'Are we in *The Da Vinci Code* right now?'

Jan followed her gaze. Brother Timotheus was standing in the doorway, looking lost, flanked by two officers. In his black-and-white habit he seemed as out of place as an altar boy at a Black Sabbath concert.

He'd spent the night in custody. The accusations against him had been dropped, but the possibility remained that he'd been an accomplice. Now he was probably going to be taken for arraignment.

'Timo,' Jan greeted him warmly. 'I'm really sorry about the way they've treated you. You should never have been a suspect.'

The Cistercian waved his hand. 'Forgiveness is part of my remit.'

The monk's calm baritone, and his eyes, which sparkled with genuine interest, made Jan feel he could trust him.

There were still a few minutes until they had to leave for the arraignment. Time enough, perhaps, for Jan to help him explain. In any case, he urgently needed someone to talk to.

'Would it be possible for me to borrow Timotheus for a second?' he asked the officers, putting a hand on the monk's shoulder.

At first, they hesitated, exchanging dubious glances.

Jan sighed. 'I'm hardly going to make a run for it with him.'

'Okay, fine,' said the older officer. 'You've got ten minutes.'

'Let's find somewhere quieter to make use of the time.' Jan gave Timo a reassuring smile.

Somewhere quieter turned out to be in Jan and Rabea's brainstorming room. Her Gameboy was still lying on the sofa. Jan felt a stab at the sight of it.

The Cistercian turned around on his heel, giving a muted sigh. 'I can hardly stand to look at the walls.'

'Even that's enough to make me believe you're not involved in this.' Jan dropped down onto the sofa. 'Be glad it's not your job to examine every detail.'

'You're already beaten down.' Timotheus sat down beside him. His hulking body sank deep into the scratched material.

Jan took his smiley foam ball out of his coat pocket, threw it against the wall and caught it as it bounced back.

'Want something to drink?' he asked.

'No thank you.'

'You're in a bit of a pickle, you know. You've got no alibi. I'm not sure where you were that night, but maybe I can help you. And that's not the only reason I've kidnapped you. I need to talk to someone about Gero. Somebody who knew him as well.'

Throwing the ball. Catching it. Throwing. Catching.

His lips quivering, Timotheus puffed the air out of his cheeks. 'Oh God, I'm afraid those things are more closely connected than you think.'

Jan threw the ball, but this time he didn't catch it. It rolled underneath the sofa. 'What do you mean?'

The Cistercian put one of his hairy paws on Jan's hands. 'First, tell me what you have to say. Maybe it will come out of its own accord.'

'I went to his grave.' Jan traced a burn mark on the armrest with his forefinger. 'Even left some flowers.'

'Last time I went was three years ago. I don't have much time for cemeteries. I prefer to commemorate the dead in church. I feel closer to them there, and to God.'

'You can take confession, right? Meaning you'll keep everything we say here secret?'

Timotheus nodded. 'Right. As long as it doesn't involve a crime, which I'd have to report to the police.' He glanced around. 'Which wouldn't take me too long right now.'

Jan bit his lip. 'I'm an atheist, so I'm not interested in absolution. Only in your ability to listen.'

'Fair enough.' A conspiratorial smile flickered beneath Timo's beard.

The knot that had been forming in Jan's throat loosened. He could breathe freely. 'Thank you – really, thank you.'

There was a brief silence. He admired the monk's composure. Timo had a God he could turn to for solace. Jan had only his comfortless rationality.

'Apart from Anita, nobody knows about this,' he sighed. 'Okay, first I have to ask you something: you used to be one of Gero's closest friends. What did you know about him that he'd told nobody else?'

'I always sensed he was keeping something from me. When I came to visit you, he never let me out of his sight. Got nervous if ever I was poking through his stuff.' He twirled a few stray beard hairs. 'At some point I started to investigate.'

Jan's heart stopped a moment. Now everything was falling into place.

'And I suppose you stumbled across the same thing I did.' Jan kneaded his fingers. 'I was in his study the day of the accident – my birthday. Looking for some stuff on his computer. What I found was something else entirely.'

Timo's eyes widened. 'You knew too?'

In response Jan merely buried his face in his hands. His pulse was racing as though he'd run a half-marathon. They'd taken the first step.

'It was unbearable, wasn't it?' he continued haltingly. 'Torture. Strangulation. Serious stuff. The poor children. And he seemed to have taken a few of the pictures himself. A couple – a couple had even been taken in his bathroom.'

Jan's voice broke. He laid his head on the table. Breathe. Just keep breathing, somehow. He felt Timotheus's hand close over his again. Jan took a deep breath. 'I only found out after his death. When I was going through his things with Stefan. Saw the same stuff you did. Everything I thought I knew about him got flipped topsy-turvy.' Timotheus smiled sadly. 'I never would have thought it of Gero. He was a role model for me. A person with ideals. Values.' He rubbed his eyes. 'I'm constantly shaken by this world.'

Jan stared up at him. 'How can you still believe in God after seeing something like that?'

'This world would be unbearable if I didn't believe in Him. Everything this Alphabet Killer has done. The suffering of those children. I wouldn't be able to stand it if there were no salvation for them. If life with all its cruelty and brutality was meaningless.'

For a moment Jan dwelled on the thought. He clicked his tongue. 'All I can think is that we're intelligent apes whose minds are so degenerate that we can do terrible things to other members of our species.'

'Faith, no matter what it's in, can help.' Timo slapped his palm against the table. 'We both thought we were alone in this, and we probably desperately needed to talk to another person about it.'

'Why didn't you go to the police?'

'I could ask you the same question.'

'I wanted to do something. Call him to account. I had to do something – and in the end, I did.'

'What do you mean?' The monk's eyes narrowed to slits. 'I only knew that your brother gave you that used Golf II for your birthday. You were drunk when you made the first trip—'

'I haven't touched a drop of alcohol since.' Jan inhaled sharply, as though about to dive into a pool. 'I'm sure Cain and Abel mean something to you. My guilt is even deeper.' He was fighting the urge to gag.

'The car accident?'

Jan stared at the floor, eyes expressionless. He shook his head.

The Cistercian swallowed drily. 'Why, Jan?'

Yes, why? The question Jan had been asking himself for years. He'd never found an answer that gave him any relief.

'Why didn't you go to the police?' asked Jan again, trying to give himself a short break.

'Because first I wanted to check something that soon turned out to be true: your brother had an accomplice.'

It was as if he'd opened a trapdoor underneath Jan. At first his brain couldn't process the information. 'Wha – what?' he stammered.

Timotheus continued: 'I talked Kathi into letting me use Gero's computer – told her I had a few files on there. The poor thing had other things to worry about at the time. I copied stuff onto dozens of discs. Plus, I found his emails. I noticed that in some of the photos he was in the picture and somebody else must have been holding the camera.'

'Do you have a name? A picture?'

Timo shook his head. 'The emails were brief and cryptic. And the children and your brother were the only people visible in the images.'

'But that would have been more of a reason to go to the police.'

'You know I had my own problems with the police back then. I was a different person and my faith in your esteemed colleagues wasn't the greatest. But that wasn't the only reason. This accomplice had no idea anybody knew about him. He thought he was completely undetected. I wanted to use that and do my own investigations. I got involved with the scene, asked people about where the photos and videos came from.'

'With no result—' concluded Jan dully.

'True. At some point my efforts petered out. I still have the discs, though. As a reminder. On the night Dr Ehrberg was murdered, I wanted to meet with somebody on that scene in Westerburg, but he never showed up. The fact that I couldn't get anywhere – that's the guilt on my conscience. I deserve to be in trouble because of that now.'

'You've got to explain all this to the police. You can use me as a witness.'

'Maybe they'll finally find the accomplice. I should have done it long ago.' A fresh layer of anxiety crossed Timo's face like a veil. 'Do you know whether he ever did anything like that to his son?'

Jan shook his head. 'I assume – I hope – that the images were everything. That he left Maik alone.'

'These days I'm not so sure. I knew him for years. And I never suspected a thing.'

'That's what horrified me the most,' said Jan. 'The monsters aren't lurking in remote forest cabins. They're among us.'

'I admire your courage, coming back here.'

'And? Would you forgive me if this was a confession?'

'There's no right or wrong here. I can't forgive you, even if I wanted to.' Timotheus rose to his feet. 'You're the only one who can do that. Leave the past behind you, at last. Leave it here, where it belongs – here in Westerwald.'

## 67

'Grall, hang on a minute! Where are you off to?'

Stüter grabbed his shoulder just as he was leaving the operations centre.

He'd pressed the Gameboy into Miriam's hand and sentenced her to stay inside the police station. She'd given an exasperated sigh, but quickly settled into her first round of Tetris.

'What's up?' he snapped at Stüter.

'I only wanted to apologise.'

'After this mess with Rabea that's only appropriate, but now's not the right moment,' replied Jan. 'I'm going back to where she was found. Maybe the technicians overlooked something.'

'I was worried about Frau Wyler. Apparently too worried. I confided my doubts about you, Herr Grall. My suspicion that you might be involved in the case.'

Fine pinpricks dug into Jan's chest. 'And she believed you?'

'Not at first. She took some convincing. Eventually it seems I was able to persuade her not to trust you.' Stüter rubbed his face. 'When she found out something yesterday evening, I guess that was why she didn't tell you – and confronted the killer by herself.'

'Ugh.' He dropped his head and kneaded the back of his neck. He should never have been so secretive with Rabea about his past.

'I can exclude your involvement now,' said Stüter. 'You weren't here when Frau Wyler was attacked. I'm sorry I believed that of you. This case has brought all of us to our wits' end.'

Jan sighed. He didn't hold it against Rabea for mistrusting him. It was his fault, and his alone. Now he might never be able to explain it to her.

He held out his hand to Stüter, who shook it tentatively. 'Time to put our disagreements aside. For Rabea.'

'For Rabea.'

## 68

He'd started climbing on impulse.

Before Jan could think twice about how dangerous it was in this weather, he was already clambering up the first rocky ledge. Several times he slipped on the icy basalt but he managed to reach the top of Wolfstein unscathed.

He crouched down, turning up the collar of his coat against the whistling wind. The first time he'd climbed the rocks as a child, he'd felt as though he'd conquered Everest. Invincible.

Today his feelings couldn't have been more different. He'd come here alone, to where Rabea had been found. Trying to maintain the fiction that he was off the case, he could no longer work publicly with the investigation team.

He was more isolated than ever before. Most distressing of all was that he'd lost Rabea's trust. That she'd actually shared Stüter's suspicions.

What had she discovered? Had she actually found a connection between Tugba Ekiz and the killer? He shook his head, his eyes wandering over the white-powdered pines.

Why had Rabea wanted to confront the Alphabet Killer herself? He didn't know what he'd hoped to achieve by driving out here. The technicians had examined the scene millimetre by millimetre. Although they were only looking for individual pieces of evidence.

Not for connections. Not for stories.

There was an inconsistency in the killer's actions, thought Jan. A mix of panic and planning. Being uncovered by Rabea must have shocked him to the core, but at the same time he didn't want to break his pattern.

In his haste the killer had managed to tattoo the 'F' on her body, but he'd forgotten another part of his signature: the literary quotation at the scene. Nor had he placed a piece of bark in her mouth, as with the other victims.

And serial killers hated nothing more than changing their rituals.

Lost in thought, Jan stared down at Wolfstein, which was permeated with small craters.

He'd wondered many times about the bark, but still it made no sense. The botanist brought in by forensics had identified it simply as wood from a sycamore. That was all the information they had.

It didn't fit with the letters, with the victims, with the quotations. The killer placed it on the corpses' tongues. It might have some sexual symbolism, but Jan suspected it was more about the mouth as a means of communication. He'd literally put something into his victims' mouths. He wanted to share something with the world, just like with the 'Z' outside Jan's hotel room.

It's about me, he realised. But what?

He thought about it. Held his breath.

A piercing whine began to echo through his head. His heart boomed. It couldn't be.

He jumped up and began leaping down from stone to stone. A jabbing pain in his lower back and an increasing shortness of breath soon signalled that he ought to slow down.

Hopping down to the next ledge, he lost his balance. His arms flailed, and he stretched out one leg to stabilise himself.

Something slipped out of his trouser pocket.

And his heart dropped.

His phone landed on the stone beneath him, skittering down to the next until it finally shattered on one of the lowermost basalt rocks, a mosaic of plastic and glass.

He scrambled clumsily down, falling to his knees, panting, before the remains of his phone. A single glance was enough, even for a Luddite like him, to see that it was a write-off. Even though these older ones were supposed to be robust. He took his SIM card out of the device and jumped the final metres into the snow.

He had no time to worry about his phone or anything else. He had to find out. Had to be sure.

Gero's words flitted through his skull: *'Best wishes on your birthday, little brother! How about we take this little sweetheart for a test drive?'*

He knew now what connected him to the sycamore tree.

## 69

The road towards Rennerod.

The last time Jan had driven down it, many years earlier, it had been the middle of the night – and Gero had been in the passenger seat.

The dark silhouette of the sycamore loomed beside the turn-off for another town. A gnarled giant of a tree, it towered above the surrounding roofs and foliage. The closer he got, the more its branches seemed to Jan like skeletal hands, reaching out to grasp him.

He parked on the narrow, steeply sloping verge and climbed out. In his mind's eye he could still see the burned-out Golf II crumpled against the trunk.

The accident had done the giant no more damage than anything else over the past decades; probably it hadn't even budged so much as an inch. He was a mere footnote in its existence. All Jan could make out was a faint shadow on the bark where it had been licked by the flames from the car – and that was most likely his imagination.

He pictured how deep the roots must reach into the earth. They were like the past, he thought. Nobody could simply tear them up and think they could live on without them.

From the side of the road, Jan couldn't see any missing bark. He trudged around the tree, his soaked trainers sinking into the snow. With every step the ache in his thigh grew more intense. The old, long-faded wound. Nothing but a psychosomatic twinge, though he dulled it sometimes with painkillers.

He'd never read the papers from back then, but he could well imagine the headlines: *Family Tragedy – Car Accident: One Brother Dead, One Injured.*

Then he stopped short.

The 'Z', uneven and light brown, was on the other side of the tree. A wound of peeled bark. Another letter.

Jan lurched across to the sycamore and stroked the dry wood with the tips of his fingers, exactly where the Alphabet Killer had flayed the broad trunk.

His throat tightened, and he exhaled jerky clouds of breath into the winter air.

He understood.

In the killer's alphabet, the 'Z' wasn't simply the final letter.

It stood for revenge.

## 70

Being stuck in the middle of the most shocking serial murder case in recent German history was one thing above all else: incredibly fucking boring. Miriam's eyes wandered around the operations room. The same as any other office. A moustachioed police officer whose name she'd already forgotten was on the phone. A PR woman was heaping three sugar cubes onto her spoon and stirring them into her coffee. All of it overlaid with the monotonous sound of tapping keyboards.

Miriam yawned. She felt like she'd gone back in time to when she'd been an intern in her dad's office. Dull days spent inputting numbers into Excel spreadsheets, but mainly just surfing the internet. Six months later her dad had lost his job at the logistics firm because his alcohol problem was getting worse.

She swapped the Gameboy in her hands for her smartphone. Opening her browser, she typed *news serial killer westerwald* into the search engine. If she wasn't going to find out anything new about the case here, then maybe the internet could tell her something.

The very first hit was a bullseye: *Breaking: Profiler Taken Off Alphabet Killer Case!*

Miriam scratched her head. That made no sense. Why hadn't he told her anything?

She tapped the link, which took her to the *Wäller Zeitung* website, and skimmed the article written by someone called Nora Schneill. The journalist cited confidential sources within the investigation team. According to her information, Jan had been dismissed from the team and sent back to Mainz because of deep-seated disagreements between the analysts and the local force.

The atmosphere was tense, that was true. But why should that mean Jan was taken off the case? What was going on?

The bald superintendent – Schlüter or something – stood up from his chair. He turned to a woman with curly hair, who had introduced herself to Miriam as the media liaison officer.

'Ries!?' he barked at her. 'Did you see that bloody Schneill woman's article? How could something like that get through? It's a blatant lie!'

Miriam rolled her eyes. So grumpy! Although it surprised her that the officer didn't seem to know about Jan's apparent dismissal.

The media liaison officer remained entirely calm, and Miriam couldn't help admiring her.

'The Commander didn't tell you?' she asked, raising her eyebrows. 'We're cooperating with Frau Schneill. It's all a ruse to lure the killer out into the open.'

Stüter's face went scarlet. With his spherical head, he reminded Miriam of the rage emoticon on her smartphone. 'How are we supposed to communicate here if I, one of the senior investigators' – he tapped his chest the-atrically – 'am excluded from fundamental decisions like that?'

'Don't make such a fuss! It wasn't my idea. And anyway, you'd been sent home at the time.' Ries raised her hands defensively. 'Maybe it's because of outbursts like this one that people don't include you in stuff.'

Miriam felt like she was in the middle of *Criminal Minds*. But she urgently needed the loo. She got to her feet as quietly as possible, and at that moment the phone on the desk began to ring.

Miriam jumped.

She stood transfixed, staring at the phone. In the general hubbub, the ringing went completely unnoticed. Twice. Three times. Four times. Who was being so persistent?

Fine. She took a deep breath. Picked up the receiver.

'Yes, hello?'

'Am I speaking with Frau Wyler?' came a sonorous female voice.

'Erm, I'm standing in for her.'

'Oh, okay. I'm Frau Bischof, administrator at Mons Tabor High School. I only wanted to check whether the fax with the list of names came through all right.'

Miriam's heart began to beat faster. Suddenly she forgot how badly she needed to pee.

Jan had already told the team they needed to find the clue that had led Rabea to the killer. Miriam was a total outsider, but she could put two and two together.

'Could you please read the names aloud? That would be brilliant. What kind of list was it again?'

'Oh, of course!' Helpfulness seemed to be the administrator's dominant characteristic. 'All the people who applied to the literacy course but never showed up.'

She rattled off the names. None of them was familiar. What else had she expected? Miriam was about to hand the phone to one of the officers when she heard it.

'I'm sorry, would you mind repeating that name again?' she said, hesitantly.

## 71

*8th December, late afternoon*

Back in Kirchstrasse. Back home.

How many times had Jan been down this road? A thousand? Two thousand? On the back seat of his parents' car, at first. With his brother. Playing with his Gameboy, dozing, messing around with plastic figurines. Then on his bike. Sometimes with a girl, either riding beside him or sitting on his bike, her arms wound around him.

Eventually in cars with friends, taking him back from some party completely shitfaced. He could still remember exactly how he'd snuck in through the basement door and slept on the sofa in the den so that he wouldn't wake his parents.

He knew every tiny bump in the asphalt. Every trivial detail.

On none of those journeys had he been so afraid as at this moment. He didn't know what was going to happen in the next few minutes. Only one thing was clear: afterwards this place would never be his home again.

The Mercedes jolted down the hill towards their house. Jan focused on breathing in and out. He couldn't shake the feeling that his coat was strangling him.

This was really happening.

Kathi and Maik were in imminent danger.

If his phone had still been working, he would have called for back-up. But there was no time for a detour to Hachenburg. He had to act.

The 'Z' in the sycamore's bark had made one thing clear: the reason the Alphabet Killer had chosen him as the final victim went much deeper than he'd first supposed.

The murders weren't about letters, rituals or hazy conspiracies. They'd been about him all along. Well, no. Not about him, but about Gero. After all these years, the killer wanted to call him to account for his brother's death.

Those closest to Gero had immediately come to mind. Stefan Schomar, Kathi's new partner, had been a good friend of his brother's. He had a motive. And he still had Gero's old hunting equipment.

Timo had suggested that Gero had an accomplice. What if Stefan hadn't merely been Gero's friend – what if they'd been in it together? And if Stefan was capable of abusing children, what else was he capable of?

He thought of Katharina and shy little Maik. They'd already been through so much, and now they were in terrible danger. His stomach twisted. He had to warn them before it was too late.

And Tamara. Tamara and Tugba. Everything was connected. A web of madness and guilt. Tyres screeching, the Mercedes pulled up outside the old barn opposite his family home. The building, which had been a ruin even when Jan was a child, had always held a grim fasciation for him.

Among the boys it had been a test of courage to creep inside. The locals had told countless horror stories about the place.

Today one of them seemed to be coming true.

Jan remembered meeting Stefan out here.

How could he have been so blind?

## 72

The padlock opened with a click. Tugba took the metal clip out of the keyhole. She had to restrain herself from simply letting it fall. For countless hours she'd worked on the lock with the clip, which was now completely bent. She'd lost faith ages ago. Now she resisted the impulse to simply tear the wooden door open and leave her prison. She hadn't seen her tormentor for a while, but he could appear at any moment.

By now pain had overwhelmed all other sensation. Her whole back was on fire. The scraped tattoo must have become infected again. Whenever she touched the wound, her fingers came away sticky with pus and blood. A rattling, convulsive cough had settled in her lungs. Must be the bitter cold. When it gripped her, she spent minutes hunched and wheezing. A constant throbbing in her skull drowned out nearly all clear thoughts. Her knees were bloody from being perpetually huddled on the floor.

As gingerly as her trembling fingers allowed, she slid the bolt of the lock out of the rusty body. She pushed the door open. The hinges creaked almost inaudibly.

She listened, holding her breath. All she heard was the blood thudding swiftly through her veins.

She put one bare foot outside the cage, leaving the six square metres of blood and despair.

The basement was murkily dark. Only a few streaks of light fell through the chinks in the trapdoor. She edged forwards, moving agonisingly slowly. Her outstretched hands knocked against a table. Fumbling across the surface, her hands found a leather-bound book. A bottle of ink. A handle. She grabbed it. A knife!

She'd never injured another person. Never been in a fight. But if she bumped into her tormentor, she would strike. Without hesitation. Use the last of her strength for one final, desperate attempt.

Holding the jagged knife tightly by its leather handle, she climbed the ladder. She had to get out. Find help, it didn't matter where. Hopefully the place he'd kept her wasn't too remote.

She pushed the trapdoor open a crack. The floor above the basement seemed to be a kind of workshop. Stacks of crates and pallets against the walls, full of spare parts and tools. Directly in front of her were rusty barrels. Hooks hung on long chains from the ceiling. Behind one workbench she thought she could see a motorbike or a scooter. The smell of oil and metal, faint in the basement, hung thickly in the air.

She could see no one. Apart from the howling wind that streamed around the building, all was silent. The windows were too dirty to see outside.

She blinked several times, until her eyes were completely accustomed to the brightness, then she pushed the trapdoor open and took the last few steps into the workshop.

There was no hint here as to what was going on in the basement. On the wall hung a plain calendar beside posters of topless women posing next to cars and motorbikes. In one corner stood an old pinball machine. No signs of a struggle. No sign of the other woman.

Finally, her gaze fell on the wooden door of the workshop, the white paint peeling off in long strips. It was ajar.

The icy pressure around her chest relaxed. For an instant the pain faded.

A way out.

She walked towards the door.

But her footsteps weren't the only ones. Behind her. He was behind her. He must have been there the whole time.

She wheeled around, jabbing with the knife. Missing. Effortlessly he dodged the blade.

Tugba felt something cold around her neck. She kept lunging with the knife, but at that moment the thing tightened.

A chain!

He wrenched at it mercilessly. The links began to squeeze her throat. The knife slipped from her fingers and landed with a clatter on the concrete floor. Her legs thrashed. She tried frantically to get her fingers between the chain and her neck, her screams choked. Everything went blurry.

Her arms dropped. Her lungs constricted. At last her legs gave way. As the blackness descended, all she could feel was the burning 'G' on her back.

## 73

'Try again!'

Ichigawa rolled her eyes. 'This is the fourth time. Jan's not picking up.'

Stüter kicked over one of the office chairs. The one time he actually needed that profiler weirdo, and he'd switched off his phone.

'I spoke to him earlier. He was going to Wolfstein. Maybe he doesn't have any reception up there.'

'Or he's going to his family home and walking straight into the killer's arms.' He leant against Ichigawa's desk and lowered his gaze. 'Like Rabea. Like Daniel.'

It had been Miriam, of all people, that goth girl Grall had found God-knows-where, who had discovered the crucial information by sheer chance.

'Right, I want everybody's attention!' Stüter took a deep breath and peered around the room. It was up to him to brief the team for its upcoming mission. They had no time to lose.

'Frau Wyler was interested in Ekiz's commitment to social causes,' he began, holding up the teacher's CV. 'She came across a list of people who applied to the literacy course Frau Ekiz was running. On it is Maik Grall – Jan Grall's nephew.'

A tapestry of whispers rippled through the team. Stüter rolled his eyes and rubbed his upper arms. Finally, Ichigawa called them to order with a rap on the desk.

Nodding gratefully, Stüter continued. 'All this time we've been assuming the killer is deeply embedded in the world of books and letters. Somebody who maybe worked in the literary or media industry.' Stüter lowered his gaze, his hands stuffed into his trouser pockets. 'We neglected one possibility entirely: what if it was someone who had nothing whatsoever to do with that? Somebody excluded from that world – who had developed an intense hatred for it.'

Ichigawa cleared her throat. 'May I take over for a moment?'

She tapped the files underneath her arm. 'We've assembled as much information as we could about Maik Grall. After his father's accident, he became increasingly withdrawn. He started having such serious problems in school that he's functionally illiterate.'

'And he still managed to get a licence for that scooter? How did he pass the theory test?' asked one of the officers, who was flipping through the documents.

'You can apply to do it orally,' replied Ichigawa. 'Maik Grall has trouble forming and reading words, but that doesn't mean he's stupid.'

Even now, the murmuring hadn't died down. The words 'Jan' and 'Grall' kept reaching Stüter's ears. He raised his hand.

'Before this goes any further, we've got to address the elephant in the room,' he sighed. 'Strictly speaking Grall should no longer be a member of this team, partly because of the conflict of interest but also for his own safety. As it happens, however, he's currently the person most familiar with the circumstances and people in question. So, he stays.' His eyes swept across their ranks.

Ichigawa picked up the thread. 'Maik Grall had more than one connection to Tugba Ekiz. He also helped out at the wildlife park. Opportunity enough to get the animals used to him and practise killing them. It also explains how he was able to dump the body of our first victim in the bison enclosure. On top of that, his father had an extensive collection of hunting weapons. This was enough to get a search warrant.' Ichigawa folded her hands behind her back. 'There's also imminent danger, so SWAT are already on their way. It's time we prepared ourselves to go in.'

When she was finished, she went over to Stüter. 'We've tried Jan several times now. Either his mobile's switched off, or—'

Stüter grunted.

The protective layer of professionalism that surrounded Ichigawa crumbled for the first time. 'Do you think something's happened to him?'

'No, I don't want to believe that,' he replied. 'The place he was last known to be is Grosse Wolfstein. Let's hope he didn't drive straight to see his family and that he didn't bump into his nephew. If only we could warn him somehow.'

## 74

The clouds stretched above the house like the roof of a leaden sarcophagus. Only the muted thunderclaps from the storm some kilometres away broke the silence.

Jan climbed the steps to the front door. If he was right, then Stefan had intended to be caught. The killer hadn't left the pieces of sycamore bark by accident.

He knew he'd never finish his alphabet.

He wanted a confrontation. A clash. A grand finale.

Jan had no gun. He could only hope he'd be able to catch Stefan off guard before it was too late. Just so long as Maik and Kathi were safe. On Jan's last visit, the patio door had not been locked. It was his only chance.

Keeping close to the wall, he crept around the house and peered through the window in the door into the living room.

Kathi was sitting alone at the dining table with a cup of tea, staring in concentration at her tablet. Relief imploded in Jan's chest. He knocked cautiously against the glass.

She jumped and looked up.

A noiseless, 'Jan?' She walked over and pushed open the door. 'What are you doing here? Why didn't you ring the bell?'

He grabbed her arms and whispered, 'Where's Stefan?'

'Upstairs, I think. What's wrong?'

'I'll explain everything, okay? My colleagues will be here soon too.' He looked deep into her eyes. 'You've got to trust me. Stay down here and stay calm. Is that okay?'

Her lips trembled and her eyes had a glassy sheen. 'Wha – what's wrong?'

'Like I said, I'll explain everything. Where's Maik?'

'In the barn. Tinkering around with a scooter.'

'Okay, he can stay there for now. That's fine.'

Slowly he let her go, then took two steps back and held out his hands reassuringly. He still had the element of surprise. Just so long as she didn't call out to Stefan.

'Everything's fine. I just need to talk to Stefan.'

He kept walking backwards through the living room, only turning when he reached the corridor. Taking three steps at once, he climbed the staircase. There was no going back.

He stormed down the hall towards the study, the place his brother had already filled with his darkness.

The door was ajar.

Jan's last fight was so long ago that he could only hazily remember it. Some kind of set-to in a Bochum bar. He was no fighter. Stefan was a broad, powerfully built guy. If he wanted any chance at all, he'd have to be quick.

Jan barged open the door shoulder blade first. The impact of his own movement nearly swept him off his feet.

Stefan Schomar leapt out of his leather chair. Before he could make any more coordinated movement, Jan lunged. With a force he'd never have believed he was capable of, he slammed the Alphabet Killer against the wall.

Stefan's head left a blood-red mark on the white wood-chip paper.

'Jesus, Jan!' he groaned. 'What the hell was that for?'

'Don't give me that!' He planted himself in front of Schomar. 'Just tell me why you did it.'

'Wha – what am I supposed to have done?'

Jan pressed him against the wall. 'You killed all those people. You left sycamore bark at the crime scenes. It was always about me, wasn't it? Always about Gero. Then why the alphabet, Stefan? Why?'

'Are you completely nuts?' yelled Stefan, his eyes wide and his rosy face contorted. 'What would I want with you? And what bark?'

Jan was beginning to doubt himself – but that was probably exactly what Stefan wanted.

'And what about the shotgun? With all the equipment? Why didn't you bring back the gun from the search?'

Something in Stefan's eyes crumpled. His breathing slowed. 'I can't tell you that.'

'Of course not,' said Jan acidly.

Stefan sighed and gestured to the right. 'It's to do with him.'

Above a bookcase hung a picture of Ernest Hemingway. On the shelves were several of the author's novels. Evidently Stefan was a big fan. The first connection that came to Jan's mind between Hemingway and guns was his death.

'Dying standing up,' he murmured.

'Yeah, that's how he did it. Put the barrel under his chin and pulled the trigger.' Stefan bit his lip, suppressing tears. 'You can never tell Kathi.'

'Don't worry—'

'You're right. I wasn't at the search. I was in the forest. Alone. Just me and the gun. I wanted to do it the same way as him.'

'Why?'

'Because there aren't many days now when I feel anything at all. I'm not living; I haven't lived for a long time. And I know what it would do to Kathi and Emilia. But I can't any more, I can't live – but then, as I was standing there in the snow, I couldn't do it.'

Depression guessed Jan. Probably untreated. It explained Stefan's inconsistent behaviour – and ruled him out as the killer.

'I'm sorry, I really am so sorry.' Jan reached out his hand and helped him up. 'I know a colleague I can recommend – wait, you didn't have anything to do with the films my brother made, did you?'

'What films?'

Jan believed him. Stefan had been simply a friend of his brother's, not his accomplice. And certainly not the Alphabet Killer.

But if it wasn't him, then who was it?

His eyes wandered around the study, past the Hemingway portrait and a map of Westerwald to an educational poster of the alphabet.

'Is that for Emilia?'

Stefan shook his head.

It was at that moment that Jan heard the sirens.

## 75

'Test me!'

The chain slackened a fraction. Tugba drew a rasping breath into her lungs. Everything was spinning. She blinked. What did he want from her?

He tugged her back. She choked, her bare feet scrabbling over glass shards and metal splinters.

'The alphabet! The letters! Test me.'

Test him? How was she supposed to do that?

On one of the workbenches she could see a rusty spanner about the length of her arm. If only she could take a step towards it . . .

A pointed blow. A single pointed blow.

'The—' she coughed, 'the first letter?'

'A!'

'A like—?' she rasped.

'Ape.'

'Go on, go on!'

'B, C, D, E, F, G!'

He recited the letters fervently. A prayer. A creed. His rattling, sometimes too high voice echoed through the workshop.

*The alphabet had distracted him. She only needed a few centimetres. No more. Tugba braced herself against his grip, balancing on her tiptoes.*

*'H, I, J, K, L, M!'*

*She managed a few tiny steps forwards; he was so engrossed in the alphabet that he let himself be led. Now. It was her only chance. He wouldn't give her another one.*

*She stretched out her arm as far as she could. Her shoulder ached, the muscles stretched to the edge of what was bearable. The tips of her fingers brushed the end of the spanner.*

*It wasn't enough. Fuck, it wasn't enough.*

*'N, O, P—'*

*He paused. Had he noticed?*

*She threw her whole weight towards the workbench, but instantly he jerked her back and swore incomprehensibly.*

*But it wasn't she who had drawn his attention. He froze. It was like he'd heard something. He breathed shallowly.*

*Tugba tried to ignore her pounding heart and listen. Engines – there had to be several vehicles. Tyres crunching through snow. Followed by the slamming of car doors.*

*Somebody was coming. For her?*

*'Heeel—' Before the word was fully out of her mouth, he clamped his hand over her lips, gripping her jaw with his sweaty, oil-smeared hand and jerking her towards the back of the workshop with the chain.*

*'"G". Now it's time for "G".'*

## 76

The SWAT team came storming out of three vans, every movement perfectly orchestrated. HK-MP5 machine guns at the ready and reinforced Plexiglas shields braced, they swarmed outside. Masked intruders in the place Jan had once called home.

'Jan! Explain to me what the hell's going on here!' Kathi's voice sounded like the howl of a mother wolf desperately defending her young.

She followed him out of the house and grabbed his shoulder. Stefan remained in the corridor, his arms around Emilia.

Jan wheeled around. 'Kathi, please stay indoors. It's not safe for you here!'

'Not safe?' She slapped him. Pain prickled on his skin as though she'd seared him with a branding iron. 'Did you see what you did to Stefan? And now – now you want Maik!'

He reached for her wrists. The situation was overwhelming him. It was too much. Just too much.

'Let! Me! Go!' spat Kathi, her usually friendly, round face twisted into a grimace. 'I want to see my son!'

Before their tussle could escalate, two more vehicles appeared in the yard – a police car and Anita's Audi.

Both officers from the police car dashed up the steps and held Kathi back.

'Frau Grall, please calm down, we'll explain everything. But please come back into the house,' said the female officer, a freckled woman in her mid-forties with a blonde ponytail.

Her colleague turned to Jan: 'Herr Grall, please get into Frau Ichigawa's car with Chief Superintendent Stüter. The SWAT team has instructed nobody be outside the vehicles during the operation.'

'Understood,' said Jan, grinding his teeth.

The two officers got Kathi back into her house, where they were supposed to support the family. Jan jogged over to Ichigawa's car and climbed inside. Rarely had he been so happy to see Stüter.

'Dammit, Grall, what's wrong with your phone!' snapped the Chief Superintendent, flinging an arm around his shoulders.

'It broke on Wolfstein. All I could salvage was this.' He slid next to Stüter on the back seat and showed him the SIM card. At the wheel sat Anita, the SWAT team leader in the passenger seat. 'What's going on? I was sure Stefan Schomar was the killer. But now I'm wondering something much more disturbing—'

'You're right,' said Anita tonelessly. 'Maik applied to the literacy course led by Frau Ekiz. He slipped through the

net first time round because we only looked at the participants. Not all the people who were interested. He also had
a part-time job at the wildlife park. He's connected to you.
Everything points to him.'

Jan pounded his head against the driver's seat.

So, it was true. Maik was the Alphabet Killer. Would
things have turned out differently if Gero had been
alive?

The urge to kill wasn't inborn. It was formed through
outside influence. Maybe it wasn't just his brother who'd
died in that car, but all of Maik's victims as well.

'I'm sorry. I can't imagine what this must be like for you,'
said Stüter.

'You have no idea—'

'It's not your fault,' said the Chief Superintendent with
genuine sympathy. 'Don't think that. Nobody can know
what's going on in the head of a kid like him.'

'I just want to know why he did it. Normally it would be
down to me and Rabea to figure it out for you, but right
now I'm as clueless as anybody else.'

The operations leader interrupted them. It was Eller
again, the man with the blue eyes. From the Zanetti
operation. 'We're going in now. And like I said before:
no matter what happens, stay in the vehicle.'

Without waiting for an answer, Eller swung himself out
of the Audi and flicked down the visor of his helmet.

Jan hadn't been listening. 'How does this all fit together?
The letter symbolism and the end-game, me as the final

victim. If he's functionally illiterate, then the reason can be reduced to one word: hatred.' He paused to let his reasoning sink in. 'This series of murders is an attack on everything Maik hates about his life: on the people who have always excluded him and claimed words as their own. Against letters themselves. And against me, of course. Some kind of event – a trigger – must have released all this pent-up hatred, this frustration.'

'Whatever set this in motion, let's hope we find Tugba and your floozy in one piece inside that barn.' Stüter pressed his face against the glass. Despite his choice of words, there was real concern in his voice.

The safety of the kidnapping victims had top priority. Jan watched as Eller signalled to his men with a few curt gestures to surround the barn. So far it looked utterly deserted: no light behind the smeared windows, no noise, nothing. It seemed as empty as ever.

'Main and side doors secured,' crackled Eller's voice across the radio. 'Ready to enter.'

A SWAT officer kicked open the barn door, while the colleague behind him hurled in a smoke grenade. Bellowing. An ear-splitting bang. Tinnitus. The flash of light was so bright it seared their retinas.

The silence that followed was as abrupt as the assault. The whistling in Jan's ears drowned out everything, even the heavy thudding of his heart. Smoke rose from inside the barn, but otherwise there was nothing to be seen.

'What's happening in there?' murmured Stüter.

Jan grabbed the radio. 'Eller, please report. Do you have visual contact with the target?'

As though in response, there was a sudden cacophony of shouts from inside the barn.

'Police! Drop your weapon!'

'Give up! Let the woman go!'

Jan balled his fists. Tamara. He couldn't let anything happen to her. He flung the radio into Stüter's lap, then stood up and opened the door of the car.

'Grall, what are you doing?' Stüter tried to grab his arm, but Jan tore himself free.

His legs guided him across the gravel as though remote-controlled, heading straight for the barn. Out of the corner of his eye he saw movement. Kathi was watching him from the kitchen window of her house, her expression frozen. The female officer placed a hand on her shoulder and pulled her away from the window.

'Where are you going?' yelled Anita after him. 'The object isn't secured!'

He ignored her, increasing his pace and disappearing into the smoky half-darkness of the barn.

A bulky SWAT officer was posted at the entrance; he blocked Jan's path.

The shouting in the workshop continued.

'Hey, didn't we tell you to stay out of the way?'

'I want to know what's happening.' Jan threw his whole bodyweight against the officer, barging him aside. 'Where is she? Tamara! Tamara, where are you?'

The smoke from the grenade was burning his eyes. He blinked. He could see nothing but outlines. He staggered on.

The SWAT officer grabbed him by the scruff of the neck, his grip as pitiless as a vice. Jan gave a rattling gasp. He swung his fists behind him, but merely brushed the man's hips.

'Tannheim, who've you got there?' came Eller's voice from the depths of the barn. As it had during the Zanetti operation, his voice sounded calm. As though all of this were simply an exercise.

'That analyst!' bellowed the officer.

'Fine, let him go!' Eller gave a long sigh. 'Herr Grall, please come over here. You can help us.'

Reluctantly the officer loosened his grip. Jan entered the barn. Gradually the smoke was dissipating. He could see the silhouettes of four SWAT officers. Machine guns at the ready, they were surrounding someone in the middle of the barn.

Maik was holding a woman in front of him. It was Tugba, not Tamara. Her jet-black hair hung over her face in greasy hanks. She was barefoot, wearing nothing but a stained sweatshirt and tattered jeans. Her body was covered in wounds, and her chest rose and fell shallowly. Her eyelids fluttered as though she were in a fever dream. Maik looked like a different person. This wasn't the boy he'd met a few days earlier. His dark blonde hair, previously carefully gelled, was now sticking out in all directions. His whole body trembled, even more than Tugba's. He had a motorbike chain around her throat. It was his eyes, however, that were most changed. If they had reminded Jan of his brother during his first visit, they now seemed completely alien. Something glinted in them that was beyond all reason. Yet that wasn't what worried Jan most. It was that Maik had hidden it from him so well.

Maik fixed his eyes on Jan. 'I'm taking the letters back, *Uncle!*' he said, jerking the chain taut. Tugba was so weak she barely reacted. Only a pitiful choking sound escaped her cracked lips.

'Maik, listen to me!' Jan stepped forwards. He was now at the same height as the barrels of the machine guns.

'Don't take another step, Grall,' whispered Eller.

In his days as a police psychologist he'd been in similar situations. Yet this was different. In other cases, it had been about creating a relationship with the killer. Now his relationship with Maik was his biggest problem.

'Tugba's sister is waiting for her. It's time she went home,' he began. 'And your mum's in the house. Kathi's beside herself with worry. She's asking whether you're okay.'

For a brief moment concern for his mother flickered across Maik's face, which still had a trace of boyishness. But his madness soon got the upper hand – a predator that could scent any tiny hint of reason.

'You've got no right to talk about family!' Saliva was spraying from Maik's mouth. 'You killed him. You took my father. And the alphabet with him.'

'That's why you want me, isn't it?' Jan took another step forward. He had to change tactics. 'That's why I was going to be "Z".'

'Nobody thought I could do it. They all laughed. All of them. Living in their world of letters.' Maik pushed Tugba ahead of him as he came closer to Jan.

'Stay where you are, or we'll shoot!' roared Eller.

Jan threw out his arms protectively. 'No! Stop! Don't shoot, whatever you do!'

His voice trembling, he turned back to his nephew. 'You were never a part of their world. Their alphabet. So, you made your own. Out of them. Out of everything you hated. But there's nothing Tugba can do about that. Nor Tamara.'

Maik broke into laughter. Hoarse, joyless laughter.

'You don't understand anything, Jan. nothing. You're blind.'

'What are you talking about? Maik, you've got to surrender.'

'The alphabet will be completed.' Maik's face grew firm. He relaxed the chain. 'It will be completed. Whether I'm alive or dead.'

He shoved Tugba away, and she collapsed as her limp body collided with the workbench.

Maik raised the chain above his head, swinging it like a whip, and ran blindly at Jan.

Jan was paralysed with shock. His legs felt like lead. He lifted his arms. 'Don't shoot!'

Too late.

His words were drowned in a hail of bullets.

# G

'"G", the soft guttural (gutturale media), occupying a mid-point between the harsher guttural "K" (gutt. tenuis) and the aspirated "ch" (gutt. apirata).'

The Grimms' Dictionary

## 77

*8<sup>th</sup> December, late afternoon*

A final silence fell across the workshop.

Jan looked up, hands shaking. A high whine had settled in his ears, drowning out all clear thought.

He was still crouching. Everything around him happened in flashes. Impressions rained down mercilessly. Two SWAT officers bending over Tugba's limp body, one feeling for her pulse and putting her in the recovery position.

'Paramedics! We need a paramedic over here!' bellowed the other.

More officers rushed past him, mere black shadows. The clicking of safety catches. Finally, a paw being laid on his shoulder.

'Are you all right?' Eller was standing beside him.

Did that even matter?

'What happened to Maik?'

Eller said nothing, simply stepped aside.

Jan staggered to his feet, staring fearfully at the body in front of him.

Maik was lying on his back in front of him, his arms outstretched like Jesus on the cross. An oval of blood was spreading across the concrete floor around him.

Jan's legs gave way. He averted his eyes, suppressing the urge to gag. His own nephew. He'd been unable to save him.

He couldn't help thinking about Maik's last words. '*It will be completed. Whether I'm alive or dead.*' Was there an accomplice after all? That would explain the high frequency of the murders, at least. They could be at different places at the same time.

Eller was standing over Tugba, who was being wrapped up in a thermal blanket by the officers. The young teacher was unable to speak – her eyes were closed, her breathing shallow.

The SWAT officers turned Tugba onto her side, revealing a mess of dried blood, pus and tattooed lines on her back. It took Jan a moment to realise they were in the shape of a G. Tugba must have tried to scratch it off with some sharp object. She'd fought against the letter to the last.

At least one of the two kidnapping victims was safe. But what about Tamara?

He couldn't think of Maik. Couldn't think of Kathi, who must have heard the shots from the house.

A thought struck him. 'There's a basement room that used to be used for storing food. Over there on the right is a trapdoor – you'll only see it if you look very carefully.'

'We should take a look with your colleagues,' replied Eller. The operations leader flipped up his visor and held the radio to his mouth. 'Object secured. Suspect eliminated. Hostage out of danger. Chief Superintendent Stüter and Senior Chief Superintendent Ichigawa, please join us.'

Jan's colleagues entered the shed, followed by a paramedic coming to treat Tugba Ekiz.

'Oh my God!' gasped Anita. 'Is – is that Maik?'

'Yes.' Jan stuffed his hands into his pockets and took a deep breath that made his whole body tremble. 'He said the alphabet would continue without him. It seems he had an accomplice.'

Anita nudged Stüter. 'Look at his wrists!'

Jan and Stüter stepped closer. A tangle of scars crisscrossed the boy's wrists. The letters of the alphabet. Pulling on latex gloves, Stüter rolled up Maik's sleeves. 'A' to 'G' were carved into his skin up to the elbow. The A was already nearly healed and quite pale, the G fresh and red.

'He tried to teach himself to spell,' said Jan. 'Looks like the victims were nothing but prompts to help him memorise the alphabet.'

'What a crazy reason,' groaned Anita.

'It made sense according to his logic. Maik believed he could solve all his problems at once: the loss of his father, his hatred of me, his illiteracy. The only question is what motivated his accomplice.'

'And let's not forget the second question: where is Tamara Weiss?' added Stüter.

'Maybe they killed her before we arrived,' remarked Anita.

'Or she's in this basement room you mentioned, Herr Grall,' interjected Eller. 'We're going in now.'

They waited breathlessly as the SWAT team tore open the trapdoor and one of them climbed through the hatch.

After a few seconds the officer radioed, 'Clear! Nobody down here!'

Jan let the air out of his lungs. He was grateful they hadn't found Tamara's body, but it still wasn't clear where she was. Had Maik's accomplice taken her to a new hiding place? Was her body already rotting – he didn't want to imagine it – somewhere in the woods?

They crossed the workshop, the smell of benzene and rusty metal reminding Jan of a petrol station. The officer was already climbing back out through the trapdoor. 'There's space for three people, max, so you go down. Some weird shit down there.'

The warning made Jan more than queasy. He nodded to Anita. 'Please, you go first!'

She raised an eyebrow. 'I don't think this is quite the moment for gallantry.'

'Then I'll go bloody first, before we all die of politeness,' growled Stüter, climbing down the steps.

Jan was the next to venture into the basement. It was more than twenty years since he'd been down there. Back then the walls had been covered in shelves, full to bursting with pickles, apples and preserves, which his mother had kept like the family silver.

Now the unfinished brick walls were plastered with dozens – no, hundreds – of pieces of paper, scrawled top to bottom with the same letters. Like the exercises of some manic primary-schooler. Among them were photos of the victims, as well as newspaper clippings about the case. Several times Jan caught a glimpse of his own face on one of the cuttings.

From a wooden cage that had once been used to store potatoes came the stench of faeces. Jan could make out a stained mattress in the gloom. This must be where Tugba – and perhaps Tamara – had been imprisoned.

In the centre of the former storeroom was a wooden table, also covered with countless carved letters. On it were a kitchen cloth, a skinning knife and disinfectant. So, this was where Maik had inflicted his letters. One last set of shelves was still standing in the basement, dusty and over-hung with cobwebs.

'Keep your eyes peeled for clues about the accomplice,' said Stüter.

Jan inspected the shelves more closely. On the lower-most one was a set of hunting equipment. A knife, a hog knife, a pocket sharpening steel. Binoculars, folding stool, box of ammo. There was also a faux-fur rifle scabbard, inside of which were two rifles with scopes. The pistol case, however, was empty.

'Revolver's missing,' said Jan. 'The accomplice is probably armed.'

On the top shelf was a row of leather-bound classics. He could see *Quo Vadis, For Whom the Bell Tolls* and *Murder on the Orient Express*. Standing on tiptoes, he took out the last one and leafed through the yellowed pages. On the first page was a stamp with the name and address of his mother. Most likely Maik had found the books in the attic. Throughout the book, letters had been neatly cut out to make the quotations.

On the shelf beneath he found the tattoo gun. Pneumatic, as Quester had supposed. Beside it were several bottles of ink and a battered, blotchy shoebox.

Jan took it off the shelf and removed the lid. The box was half-full of bits of bark. More than enough to finish the alphabet.

'Seems Tamara's still alive.' Stüter was standing by the wall beside the shelving.

Jan went over to him. 'How do you know—?'

A glance at the wall of photographs and he fell silent. It reminded him of the educational posters you found in primary schools, with colourful letters and cute illustrations. 'A' for ape. 'B' for bear. 'C' for chameleon.

The incomplete alphabet on the wall only reached 'F'. Over-exposed Polaroids of the tattooed letters. Each image the bloody conclusion of a human life. Until 'F'. Until Rabea. Jan could follow Stüter's train of thought. Maik seemed to have hung up each letter immediately after the murder. But Tamara was missing. A glimmer of hope.

'I've got something!' called Anita. Her voice echoed against the walls. 'Come over here!'

She was kneeling beside a metal bucket, the inside of which was grimy with soot.

'What's in there?' asked Stüter.

'Somebody tried to destroy some documents. Nearly everything has been burned beyond recognition – except this.'

She took a scrap of paper out of the bucket, a fragment of which was still legible.

'A train ticket,' muttered Stüter.

Jan caught a glimpse of the fragment. . . . *furt a. M. to Montabaur St.* Immediately below that were the date and time when the ticket had been used: *6.12., 9.28 a.m.*

'A ticket from Frankfurt,' observed Anita. 'Tamara came from there, didn't she?'

Stüter shrugged. 'The killer probably tried to burn everything Tamara had on her when she was kidnapped.'

'Didn't you see the date?' asked Jan.

They paused, staring at the scrap of paper.

'Oh—' breathed Anita.

'Exactly,' said Jan. 'The date is after her abduction. So, it can't be the ticket she used to come to Westerwald.'

'Then one of the killers travelled from Frankfurt that day. But why try to burn it?' asked Stüter.

An itch at the back of Jan's mind. Something deep inside was pressing its way forwards, fighting its way towards the daylight. The sixth of December. St Nicholas's Day. The date had prompted some memory – something connected to Frankfurt.

Exactly. The pieces of the puzzle slotted together. He remembered the message on his answering machine back home. The detective from Frankfurt had said Dr Sapkowski was killed on the seventh of December.

Could it be connected to the Alphabet Murders?

'Anita, I need to use your phone for a second.'

She handed it to him. 'Who are you calling?'

'Thanks!' He put it in his pocket and reached for the first rung of the ladder. 'I've got to call the Frankfurt Police. We might have something.'

On the gravel outside the barn he dialled the number of a colleague at the State Office of Criminal Investigations. As he did so, his eyes fell on his brother's house – and his brain spat out another connection to Frankfurt: hadn't Kathi said Gero's girlfriend had moved to Frankfurt?

'Rheinland-Pfalz State Office of Criminal Investigations, how can I help you?' crackled a voice in his ear, but he didn't reply.

What if they were looking not for another man, but for a woman?

## 78

Miriam walked past the fountain in Hachenburg market square, which was dominated by a golden, two-tailed lion. There were bound to be dozens of stories and legends around it, but Miriam was in no mood for sightseeing. Her stomach had been growling for ages.

She turned down Zeitzengasse, her footsteps echoing off the walls of the houses. The narrow alleyway, still full of tourists and shoppers, wasn't much good if you were claustrophobic. She turned down Judengasse, which finally led into Wilhelmstrasse.

This had to be what passed for their main shopping street. Besides the usual chains there were also plenty of small independent retailers and cute little shops squeezed into the ground floors of the ancient buildings. The window displays, warmly lit and adorned with Christmas decorations, radiated an atmosphere Miriam had only seen in kitschy postcards.

She was bound to find something to fill the hole in her stomach. Dodging a guy dressed as Santa and collecting donations, she discovered a café that adjoined some sort of gallery. They had to have sandwiches or something.

As Miriam stepped inside, she was enveloped in the aroma of coffee and freshly baked stollen. The furniture in the café seemed to date from the fifties. Floral patterns and faux-fur as far as the eye could see.

Ordering a piece of spiced cake and a cappuccino at the counter, she grabbed the last free table in the tiny coffee shop.

Miriam wolfed down the first bite of cake and sipped her cappuccino. It was so hot she burnt her tongue, but right now she didn't care. She leant back and savoured the coffee slowly warming her belly.

An elderly woman with hair as white and bushy as cotton wool was eyeing her from the neighbouring table with an indignant expression.

Sorry my clothes don't fit your boring beige-coloured dress code, thought Miriam, winking at the old bag and raising her cup as though to toast. 'Is there something on my face?'

Cotton-wool lady averted her eyes guiltily. A small victory.

Suddenly somebody was blocking her view of the elderly woman. Miriam looked up. A woman was carrying a cup of coffee towards her table, enormous sunglasses resting on the bridge of her nose.

'May I sit here?' asked the woman with a sugary smile that instinctively made Miriam loathe her. 'The café's absolutely crammed – nowhere else is free.'

Rolling her eyes in irritation, Miriam gestured reluctantly towards the seat opposite.

'I knew you were a nice girl,' said the woman ingratiatingly, sitting down and putting her handbag on the table. Even now she made no move to take off her sunglasses. There were only two kinds of people who wore sunglasses indoors: blind people and arseholes.

She inspected the woman. The half of her face not covered in oversized Gucci sunglasses was almost unnaturally pale and shot through with finely graven lines. Her dark trench coat was typical of what women the other side of forty considered fashionable. Elegant, but understated. Only the sleeves were oddly worn.

'Come here often?' asked the woman.

'Don't bother with small talk.'

Miriam gulped down the cake in record time. She didn't fancy spending any more time than necessary with this weirdo.

As the woman put her cup back in its saucer, her arm jerked awkwardly and she knocked her leather handbag off the table. It thudded to the floor next to Miriam's feet.

'Oh, sorry, I'm so clumsy!' she cried. 'Would you mind?'

Miriam sighed, but bent down and picked up the surprisingly heavy bag. Was the woman taking bricks for a walk?

'Oh, thank you! You're so sweet.' The woman patted dirt and crumbs off the bag before putting it in her lap.

Miriam knocked back the rest of her cappuccino. Time to scram.

'Soooo lovely to meet you,' she purred sarcastically. 'I'm afraid I must be going.'

'You know, I met Jan the same way,' said the lady, just as Miriam was pulling on her jacket. 'I simply came and sat down at his table too.'

Miriam paused. The uneasy feeling that had been nagging her this whole time now surged over her with a vengeance. 'How do you know Jan? Who – who are you?'

'Tamara,' answered the stranger with a grin. 'And I'm glad to finally meet you, Miriam!'

## 79

'Are you currently working on the murder of Dr Arne Sapkowski?' asked Jan when he got through to the head of the Frankfurt Homicide Division. 'I'm sorry to be blunt, but we're under enormous time pressure.'

The woman at the State Office had swiftly put him through to the police station in Frankfurt. He was still hoping his theory was incorrect.

'I'm glad you called, Herr Grall,' said Chief Superintendent Altunbas, whose voice sounded astonishingly young for his senior position. 'We were planning on seeing you anyway, because you were one of the last people to have any contact with Sapkowski.'

'I'm afraid I still don't know what he wanted with me.' Jan sighed. 'But that's not why I'm calling. There's a possible connection between this case and the Alphabet Murders.'

For a few moments there was silence on the other end of the line. 'How can that be?' asked Altunbas finally. 'Sapkowski was found strangled at his practice. Signs of a struggle, including DNA, but no matches in the database. Nor any trace of letters in the apartment or on the body of the victim.'

'It would take too long to explain everything now. I just need to know one thing: is there a woman called Tamara Weiss on Sapkowski's list of patients?'

'Understood. Hang on a moment, I'll hunt out the list.'

Jan lowered the phone. His lips quivered, but he couldn't tell whether it was with cold or agitation. In the distance the mountains of Westerwald loomed dark against the red sunset. He never should have come back here. If his suspicions were correct, it was exactly what the Alphabet Killer had wanted.

'Herr Grall, are you still there?'

He clamped the phone back to his ear. 'Yes, I'm here. Did you find anything?'

'The name was Tamara Weiss, wasn't it? I remember now why it sounded familiar. She's the kidnapping victim in your case, correct?'

Jan's free hand convulsed around the material of his coat. The tension was almost tearing him apart. 'Correct – but is she on the list or not?'

'She is. Her last visit to Sapkowski was on November the thirtieth.'

He'd made an enormous mistake. Like a housefly buzzing straight into a spider's invisible web. Every attempt to wriggle free had only entangled him further.

'Do you need anything else?' asked Altunbas.

'No, no,' murmured Jan. 'That's fine. Thank you.'

Without stopping to hear another word, he hung up. Instantly the truth was as plain to see as the Westerwald landscape.

The whole time they'd been looking for the trigger – the reason why Maik had started killing. Now it seemed as though the trigger and the accomplice were one and the same: Tamara Weiss.

Probably she hadn't merely been Maik's accomplice but Gero's as well, helping out with his video projects. The person for whom Timotheus had searched so long. But why?

'Jan, what's wrong?' Anita and Stüter had appeared beside him. The snow crunched beneath their shoes.

'I had to check something.'

'And? Good or bad news?' asked Stüter.

'Depends.' Jan leant back against the barn. 'I know who she is, the accomplice. But you won't like it.'

Anita cocked her head. 'Hang on, *she*?'

'Correct. We're dealing with a woman. With Tamara Weiss, to be exact.'

Rolf Stüter's jaw dropped. 'How do you figure that?'

'She manipulated us. Primarily me and Maik.' Jan was freezing. The cold was creeping up his legs. Until now his body had felt numb.

Never had he seen Anita's face so anxious.

'Jan, please explain to us what's going on. This is taking on a life of its own, and it's worrying me.'

*Unshakable Ichigawa*, he'd always called her when they were together. If something worried her, the situation had to be serious.

Taking a deep breath, he let the frosty air circulate through his lungs. If only Rabea were here. She knew exactly how to put his unfocused musings on the right track.

'I'm not quite sure how it all hangs together either,' he began. 'But Katharina, Maik's mother, told me Gero had a girlfriend. After the accident she moved to Frankfurt. I'm assuming this girlfriend was Tamara Weiss.' He paused. The shouts of the SWAT officers as they loaded their equipment into the vans had broken his train of thought. And he was thinking feverishly whether to tell them about her possible involvement with Gero's films but decided against it. After a few seconds he continued. 'Clearly Tamara never forgot about Gero, even after all these years. She never processed the shock of his death, and it turned into an obsession that fundamentally altered her.'

Jan looked into the confused faces of Stüter and Anita. What he'd given them so far was an interpretation of Tamara's behaviour, not an analysis. Sometimes human psychology was like an abstract painting: you could read meaning into it, but never decode it entirely.

'Shall I go on?'

They nodded.

'At some point Tamara returned to Westerwald and started looking for traces of Gero and this brought her in contact with his son. Now I can only speculate here, but I believe the two of them entered into a relationship. She saw in him a reflection of Gero. An ally. But also, someone in need of protection.' He gave a sigh. 'With Maik at her side, she could take revenge on the world. For all the injustices apparently committed against them both.'

'Okay, okay,' interrupted Stüter. 'That's the backstory to the whole thing. But answer me one question: why the alphabet? And how come this Tamara was kidnapped by her own boyfriend?'

Anita crossed her arms over her chest. 'And while we're on the subject, why did she sleep with you?'

'There's an obvious reason for the alphabet.' Jan raised his forefinger. 'Maik's anger at people who could write. People who had mastered language. Tamara would have manipulated him in that direction. Who knows what she whispered into his ear. But there's a second, more pragmatic reason.' He raised another finger. 'It was the ritualistic and grotesque aspects of the murders that made you, Anita, think of calling in a behavioural investigative advisor. Otherwise I wouldn't have come. And ultimately it was all about me, for both of them. I'm the epicentre of their hatred. I'm "Z".'

He lowered his eyes, remembering the elegant woman in the revolving restaurant who had surprised him with her urbane sophistication. He was filled with shame and horror in equal measure. How could he have let her pull the wool over his eyes?

'The rest I can figure out for myself,' said Anita. She was the consummate professional once more. 'The kidnapping was staged – a distraction tactic. Cutting out a piece of her own skin merely underscored her determination. And the night with Jan – you look a bit like your brother, don't you?'

'A lot, actually.'

'Then she wanted to experience a moment with him through you. She toyed with you like a cat playing with a mouse.'

'So, you believe Grall's theory?' Stüter wanted to confirm.

'It all fits.'

The Chief Superintendent rubbed the back of his bald head. 'I'll issue a warrant and set up checkpoints around the town.'

Anita tucked her thumbs under the straps of her bullet-proof vest. Her lips were so tightly pursed her mouth looked like a thin line.

Jan knew that expression all too well. 'There's something on your mind. What is it?'

'This whole time Tamara has been focused on you,' she replied. 'Why would she suddenly stop? What if she finds out Maik is dead? How will she react?'

'But she can't get to me right now,' he said. 'Or to Rabea. At best she—'

Oh no.

# 80

Miriam's phone was playing *I Fought the Law* by The Clash. She reached out her hand, but Tamara was faster. The creepy woman switched off the ringtone and looked at the display.

'Unknown number. Ooh, there's a text as well,' she trilled. 'It's Jan. Wants to know if everything is all right. How sweet. Almost fatherly.'

Something in the stranger's expression and gestures had transformed. She was no longer a human being; she was a predator. The way she kept her insect-like sunglasses fixed on Miriam, the suppleness of her movements.

Miriam's heart was booming. She felt like liquid nitrogen was rushing through her veins, flickering incomprehensibly cold. A high whine pierced her brain. She had to get out of here. It was the only clear thought she could grasp.

She pushed back her chair, supporting herself on the table. Stood up. Instantly her legs gave way. Everything spun. Like a wet sack she slumped back down into her chair. What was wrong with her? Why was she so weak?

The woman with the cotton-wool hair at the neighbouring table glanced over, her arms outstretched. 'Everything all right, child?' she asked.

Nothing was all right. Somebody had to call the fucking police! 'Help!' Miriam wanted to scream, but her tongue wasn't working either; it was a slippery cloth inside her jaw. All that came out of her mouth was some unintelligible babble.

'Looks like an allergic reaction,' said Tamara with false concern. 'My car's just outside – I'll take her straight to hospital.'

Again, Miriam tried to scream, to make the woman aware of her, but all that came out of her mouth was saliva and groans. The café flickered around her like an ancient computer monitor, colours blurring, and all the voices sounded dulled.

Grabbing her under her arms, Tamara pulled her up. Easy with a flyweight like her. Despite her petite frame, Tamara's grip was impossible to escape.

Outside on Wilhelmstrasse, they were lost in the sea of shoppers. Tamara held Miriam close as they slipped through the crowd. A gesture that must have looked affectionate and motherly to unwitting observers.

They headed for the car park at Neumarkt. Tamara fished a car key out of her bag and pressed it. A black SUV opposite Westerwald Bank responded with a flash of its lights.

'No—' gasped Miriam, surprised she could get the word out.

'Oh yes, dear. We're going for a little drive.' Tamara flung open the car door and forced Miriam onto the back seat before getting behind the wheel and immediately activating the central locking.

'Do you want to know why you're feeling so peculiar all of a sudden?' Tamara took off her sunglasses and stared at Miriam. 'I put Rohypnol in your cappuccino while you were picking up my handbag. You probably know it better as roofies. You'll be out of commission for a little while. I've had practice turning drifters like you into tiny, helpless dolls. I used to do it all the time with Jan's brother. Gero. He made his own alphabet out of them.' Tamara leant forwards. 'Is Jan the same way inclined? Is that why he picked you up?'

What was the woman talking about? How could this have happened?

'How—' she stammered faintly.

'You've finally recognised me, eh?' Tamara started the engine and steered the car out of the parking spot. 'Now you're wondering how I could be here. Why I'm suddenly no longer in danger. It's simple. I was never in any danger. I am the danger.'

Miriam's heart raced. She was hot and cold in turns. Her body seemed to recognise the danger while her mind was slipping further away. Tamara evidently didn't care whether she was conscious or not. She continued: 'In Mainz you got away from me. You weren't there when I went to pick you up. In the end I had to make Jan's apartment look as though your druggie friends had broken in. But now, now it was shockingly easy.' Tamara's laugh sounded like a hyena's howl. 'Jan's never been very good at protecting the ones he loves.'

Tamara went on. 'They've probably got Maik by now. I knew that would happen. After Jan's assistant nearly caught us, it was only a question of time. It's just the way Maik wanted it: he's facing Jan once again. The man who stole the alphabet from him.'

Something lying on the passenger seat caught Tamara's attention.

'Speaking of Jan, he's calling again,' she said, reaching for Miriam's phone. 'Time to put him out of his misery.'

# Z

'"Z", the last letter in our alphabet, designated *zed* [...]. As a single sound within the German language, "Z" is limited to High German, excluding borrowings.'

The Grimms' Dictionary

## 81

'"Z". You are going to be our "Z".'

Tamara's voice. For a moment Jan put down the phone and focused on calming his breathing. His fears had been proved right.

'Please tell me you haven't done anything to Miriam,' he replied.

Keep repeating the name of the kidnapping victim. Try to create a personal connection, to exude concern.

'Is it her?' whispered Anita, sitting at the wheel of her Audi.

Jan gave her a quick nod.

They were halfway between Jan's home town and Hachenburg, hurtling down a road that cut like an aisle through the snow-covered pines. When they'd called at the station and learned that Miriam hadn't come back from the town centre, they'd immediately been alarmed. An unintelligible groan came from the mobile. Then Tamara's voice again: 'Did you hear that? It's her. Don't worry, she's fine. She's just a little dazed.'

'Sorry, but that could be anybody,' said Jan. 'I've got to be sure!'

'You're not in any position to make demands, Jan,' she said coldly. 'You're back in Westerwald, hmm? And you have Maik.'

Jan swallowed. Did she know Maik was dead? What would happen if he told her? Would she kill Miriam?

Soon all the major media outlets would be reporting his death. Better she heard it from him than on the news. At least that way he could monitor her response.

'Maik is dead. He was shot during arrest. I tried to stop them.'

Anita stared at him sidelong. Her eyes said clearly that she thought telling Tamara was anything but a good idea.

Silence. Had she hung up?

No. He could still hear her breathing; he heard it quickening.

'Please, Miriam hasn't done anything!'

She ignored him. 'You've got your brother on your conscience. And now his son, too.'

'I—'

'The alphabet will be completed, Jan. Even without Maik.' Were her lips trembling? Jan couldn't say for sure. 'I want you to be at Gero's favourite place in two hours. If he ever really meant anything to you, you'll know where that is. Get there too late, and Miriam will be a letter. Bring the police, and Miriam will be a letter. I only want you, Jan — you're "Z".'

He gripped the phone tighter. 'Tamara, wait! Don't hang up!'

A monotone beep. She'd ended the call. Jan flung the mobile onto the dashboard and buried his face in his hands. 'Fucking shit!'

'Does she have the girl?' asked Stüter from the back seat.

'Yes, and she's using her as leverage. She wants to meet me in two hours. Alone, without police. Otherwise she'll kill Miriam.'

'You can't do that,' said Anita. 'It's a trap.'

Jan rubbed his chin. 'I know. She wants to make me "Z". But what choice do I have?'

First Rabea, now Miriam too. He never should have brought her here. How did Tamara even know about her? Had she been following him for months, even years, watching him? She wanted to take everything of any meaning from him.

'Where does she want to meet, anyway?' asked Anita.

'That's the other problem. I don't know.'

Ichigawa paused.

'She said my brother's favourite place,' he continued. 'But I've no idea where that could be.'

'Then start racking those grey cells,' growled Stüter. 'I've just set a stopwatch going. We have until four twenty. That's another hour and fifty-five minutes.'

'I'm thinking!' Fingers pressed to his temples, he dug deep into his memory.

Gero's favourite place. Where could it be? He and his brother had been close, true, but Gero had never shared all his secrets – a lesson Jan had learned the most painful way of all.

Wolfstein? The village hall in Langenbach, where Gero had had his first kiss? Kirmesplatz in Bochum? How had he even let it get to this point? As hard as he tried to concentrate, questions of guilt were still hammering against his skull and interrupting his thoughts.

'Pull up on the right!' he said to Anita. 'Please!'

'Why?'

'I can't concentrate. Please, just do it!'

She rolled her eyes but did as he asked and pulled up outside a field. Jan leapt out of the Audi, his hand already buried in the inside pocket of his coat. He needed it now, no matter what the others thought.

Fingers shaking, he fumbled the joint out of the plastic baggie and flicked his lighter. But the wind instantly blew out the tiny flame.

'Anita, can you give me a hand?'

Seeing the bag, she groaned. 'Are you serious, right now?'

'It helps me think. Otherwise I can't calm down.'

'I always thought it was a phase,' she said, cupping a hand around his Zippo. 'A stupid little thing you'd eventually grow out of.'

Finally, the joint caught light, and Jan thanked her with a nod. He inhaled the marijuana smoke deep into his lungs. 'Some stupid little things have more staying power than others. But you've never had space in your life for stuff like that.'

'This really isn't the moment to get petty,' she replied, leaning against the rusty gate that opened onto the field. 'We've got to find the girl.'

Stüter walked up to them, eyes wide. 'Are you completely off your trolley? We've got less than two hours to find a young girl and you're getting high!'

'I'm trying to think!' said Jan, justifying himself for the second time. 'Do you think I don't realise how serious this situation is?'

'Then we'd better leave our genius to think in peace,' grunted Stüter, reaching for his phone. 'I'll call the team. I want to have SWAT and a hostage negotiator on standby.'

'Don't do that!' Jan leapt up, almost dropping his joint. 'Nobody can know except us. If we call in back-up, we increase the risk that Tamara will find out and make good on her threat.'

'You actually think the three of us can stop her by ourselves?' persisted Stüter, his bald pate now completely red. 'Do you have any clue how many rules we'd be breaking? Going in alone could cost us our jobs!'

'Then do what you have to!' Jan blew out smoke. 'But I just want you to be aware that you're putting Miriam's life on the line!'

Stüter lowered his eyes remorsefully, his free hand clenched. 'What's your take, Ichigawa?' he asked.

She stood up from the fence. 'I'm in.'

'Okay, fine,' sighed the Chief Superintendent. 'She's got my friend's son on her conscience. Let's play cops and robbers with her.'

Jan rolled the joint between his fingers and shut his eyes, feeling himself become weightless. Cops and robbers. Something in him had shaken loose. He often used to play it with Gero and his friends. But where? In his mind's eye he saw a rock face, vast and steep. Where? His brother, a hunter and nature-lover, had gone there many times. Got drunk there with mates. Taken his girlfriends there. Including Tamara?

'Stüter, I need your help! Where exactly is the Bacher Lay Nature Reserve?'

'Between Bad Marienberg and Fehl-Ritzhausen. You think that could be the place?'

'I'm almost one hundred percent sure.' He stubbed out the glowing end of the joint and put it back into the baggie.

'Strange place to choose for an exchange,' remarked Stüter. 'There'll still be a few people out walking this time of day. Risky for Tamara.'

'For her it's all about the symbolism,' said Jan.

## 82

Still twenty-five minutes.

'I'm on my way now,' said Jan over the headset.

Stüter's reply was prompt. 'Understood. Ichigawa and I are approaching from the south.'

Anita had dropped Jan off by the evangelical church in the heart of Bad Marienberg. From there he'd walked down to Marienquelle, a small grotto with a statue of the Virgin Mary and an oaken balustrade that was the oldest part of the park. It was a tradition to take a short break there, but he had no time for that now.

Anita had insisted Jan be armed, giving him a Walther P99 from the armoury at Hachenburg Police Station. It had cost them half an hour.

Now he felt the pistol, which was in his inside coat pocket, digging into his chest with every step.

He climbed deeper into the woods. Any other time he would have found the snowy treetops and white paths crossed with only a few footprints romantic. But now this winter wonderland was his own personal icy hell.

The path led east, along the half-frozen bed of the Schwarze Nister.

At last he saw a sign that read *Bacher Lay Nature Reserve*. In the silent quarry, the basalt mining had led to grotesque rock formations and steep slopes, home to rare animals and plants. There were countless hiding places, but only one that suited Tamara's flair for the dramatic.

He crossed the Schwarze Nister over a narrow wooden bridge. The walls of rock either side were becoming increasingly bluff, covered with icicles that glinted in the vanishing evening light.

He glanced at his watch. Twelve minutes. Time was running through his fingers like newly fallen snow.

At last he reached a broad clearing, at one end of which was the most imposing basalt wall in the whole reserve. It was parted in the middle by a frozen waterfall, like a blade of pure ice.

Leaving the path, he entered the clearing. As he did so, he noticed a dozen stones in the centre of it. The rectangular stones, approximately the size of a human head, had not got there by natural means. He went closer – and realised they had been arranged in the shape of a "Z".

He swallowed drily. Activating his radio, he said softly, 'I'm here. It's the place I mentioned.'

Had Tamara brought the stones here by herself, or had Maik helped her? It didn't matter anymore. He was here on time – that was the only thing that mattered.

'You made it.' Tamara's voice, echoing off dozens of rock faces. 'Maybe you loved your brother after all.'

Jan looked up. Two silhouettes at the top of the basalt wall, black against the red evening sky. The taller one, Tamara, was gripping Miriam's arm; she was staggering, as though stunned. The Alphabet Killer was holding a gun to Miriam's head.

'Of course I loved him,' he replied, his head craned back.

'Then why did you kill him?' Tamara's voice cracked. 'You never really knew him! I was the only one who understood him! Who loved him for what he was!'

'You were fifteen! Of course you did!' replied Jan. 'He was a paedophile. You were never more than a toy to him. He used you to lure other children in front of the camera.'

'Don't talk about him like that!' she screamed, before softening her voice once more. 'He loved me!'

Jan had to change tack. It didn't matter what he said about his brother; she'd never change her mind. 'Tell me about Sapkowski.'

'I enjoyed going to a therapist like him. Telling him about my fantasies, about my world. About you. He found me fascinating. Maybe that was why I slept with him. But his fascination ended a few days ago, when he realised what was going on here. So, I had to silence him.'

Very good, just keep talking, thought Jan. Every second brought Stüter and Ichigawa closer. He had to make sure her stream of words didn't dry up.

'Why Maik? What did you see in him?'

'Maik – he was so similar to his father, yet so different. This world betrayed him. People who can't read are excluded. So, I helped him create his own alphabet. An alphabet out of everybody who despised and degraded him. Zanetti, one of the authors I knew through a manuscript he sent in. Ziehner wanted me to translate it for him so he could make even more money. Zanetti raped the language, that so-called publisher was actually helping him. Tugba Ekiz got off on helping others. Dr Ehrberger wrote hypocritical religious stuff. Gero's friend, that Timo guy, was supposed to take the fall for that. He got too close to me, poking around like that. What gives them more right to language than Maik?'

Profound paranoia, clearly indicative of a schizophrenic psychosis.

'Maik was the body, I was the spirit. He would have done anything for me. I helped him create his alphabet – like I helped his father.'

'What alphabet? What are you talking about?'

'Your brother told me a lot about you both. You were never on top of anything in your life, while he was always in control. Like the names of the films and photos on his computer, in strict alphabetical order. I still remember them today. Alyosha. Andra. Bogdana. Cedrin. Cosmin – I've been fascinated ever since by sorting the world that way. Putting it in alphabetical order.'

'What about the woman I met in the restaurant? Where's that part of you?' asked Jan, trying one last time to find a trace of sanity.

'She never existed. Losing Gero made one thing clear to me: the only language that matters is the language of death. Everything else – the billions of words spoken every day, the billions of printed pages – is meaningless. The world should speak my language. Learn my alphabet. The alphabet of Gero and Maik.'

'I'm afraid the world hasn't quite deciphered your alphabet.'

'It will, believe me.' Tamara dragged Miriam closer. 'Once you're my "Z". I want you to do it. Like you killed your brother – now you're going to kill yourself. I know you've got a gun. Put it to your head and pull the trigger. Colour the snow around you red.' Her voice was becoming a roar, astonishingly deep for a woman. 'But first: tell me how it happened. And no lies.'

Jan's whole body trembled. He breathed jerkily, panting a Morse code of clouds into the cold. He had to buy time for Ichigawa and Stüter to arrive.

'In the accident report it says I lost control of the car because I was drunk. But maybe I wanted to lose control. I confronted Gero about what he was doing – and all he said was: *Who's going to believe you?* It floored me. The way he simply shrugged it off. We went hurtling into that syca-more, right into the passenger's side. Petrol started leak-ing, and it caught fire. I got away with a leg injury and a slight concussion, and I was able to escape the wreck. But Gero – Gero couldn't get out by himself. He was too badly injured.'

Jan felt like a rhetorical bomb disposal officer. One false word or peculiar emphasis might make Tamara explode. He had to tell her the truth, but he couldn't trigger her rage.

'He begged me. But I simply stood there. I couldn't move. I kept seeing those children's eyes – *I'm your brother! Your brother! Please!* Those were his last words, before the smoke took his voice. I just stood there. I literally just stood there.'

He gasped for breath. He had to concentrate. This was about Miriam. Not about his brother, not about Tamara. Only about Miriam. He had to save her, at least.

Tamara didn't scream or get violent. She became totally calm, which worried Jan far more. 'I was at the sycamore the very next day. They'd already taken the car away. That fucking tree. The endpoint of Gero's life. So, I made it the endpoint of the alphabet too. A "Z". I always knew you must have sensed something. That it wasn't an accident – and that at some point you'd stand in front of that tree and regret it.' She motioned to Jan with the gun. 'Do it or she dies!'

His fingers shaking, he took the P99 out of his inside pocket and removed the holster. He'd known it would come to this. Ichigawa and Stüter would never get here in time to save him, but at least Miriam would be safe.

He pointed the barrel at his temple and took the safety catch off.

'Jan, don't do it! Please!' howled Miriam.

He could see Tamara smack her with the butt of the revolver.

'I've been waiting years for this moment, Jan. Years!' she shouted.

At least he could leave in the certainty that this madness was about to end. Everything in his head was thudding. His veins pulsed.

He dropped to his knees and shut his eyes.

Here in Westerwald he'd been born. Here he was going to die.

He pulled the trigger.

## 83

Click.

Jan opened his eyes. His chest felt tight. Oh God. The gun wasn't loaded. It couldn't be.

'What's going on, Jan?' yelled Tamara.

'Empty. No ammo.' He raised both hands. 'Let's talk, Tamara. I'll do anything you want!'

'Don't try to play games with me! I always knew you were a coward.'

She pointed the gun at him. He held out his arms, waiting for the final shot.

With a scream, Miriam threw her whole bodyweight against Tamara. She staggered and the gun fired, but she didn't lose her balance.

Jan leapt up. 'Miriam, no!'

'We can see them! We're nearly there!' came Ichigawa's tense voice through the radio. 'Too dangerous to shoot. We might hit the girl.'

Tamara and Miriam were locked together, Miriam trying to wrench the gun from Tamara's hand as they kicked and lurched. They swayed back and forth, whirling around – until Tamara stumbled.

For a heartbeat time seemed to stand still. Jan saw the ice and rock underneath Tamara give way.

Saw her grab Miriam's jacket, screaming.

Dragging her over the edge.

The bursting sound of their bodies falling into the thicket at the base of the rock wall made Jan's stomach twist. Instantly he sprinted over.

'There – there you are,' murmured Miriam. She blinked at him dazedly. She was lying on her stomach on top of Tamara's battered body, which had broken her fall like a pillow. All she had was a little blood on her forehead.

Jan breathed a sigh of relief, sensing all the tension drain from his body.

'Can you stand up?' he asked.

'I – I think so.'

He tried to help Miriam to her feet, but she couldn't put any pressure on her right ankle. Even if it was broken, she'd been incredibly lucky. At least he'd been able to save her.

'Sorry this happened,' whispered Miriam, giving him a hug.

He stroked her hair. 'You've got nothing to be sorry about.'

'Up here!' came a yell from the top of the basalt wall. Ichigawa and Stüter were standing at the edge, waving down.

'The kid's got a guardian angel who's doing a bloody good job,' observed the Chief Superintendent.

'You can call for back-up now,' said Jan, and Stüter gave him the thumbs-up.

It was over. It was really over.

## 84

Jan watched the ambulance leaving to take Miriam to hospital in Hachenburg. A broken ankle and a slight concussion – that seemed to be all she'd suffered. And the roofies Tamara had given her probably meant she'd remember little of what had occurred.

As he walked back towards the basalt wall, which was now swarming with police and forensics techs, he kicked away one of the stones that formed the 'Z'.

The alphabet would forever remain unfinished. Tamara's words were still buzzing in his head.

*The only language that matters is the language of death.*

He stuffed his hands into his coat pockets. Death was unavoidable. But everything that happened before it was in the hands of human beings, consisting of letters that could only organise themselves. Tamara had understood death, perhaps, but never life.

Beneath the frozen waterfall, Stüter and Ichigawa were having an animated exchange of words. Even from a distance, Jan could see the deep furrows on Anita's brow.

'He's not disputing that the operation was a success,' she said.

'Who?' asked Jan, stepping up to them, although he thought he already knew the answer.

'The Commander. He made a report to the prosecutor then took out his frustration on me.' She sighed. 'The usual blah-blah. We broke a whole list of official rules. They're very sorry, but they're going to have to start disciplinary proceedings.'

Stüter shrugged. 'They can do what they like! I still say we did the right thing.'

'I don't dispute that,' replied Anita in a dull voice. 'But I'm not exactly looking forward to explaining the whole thing to the press.'

'Why wasn't my P99 loaded?' Jan asked Stüter.

'Think I'm giving someone like you a loaded weapon?' he replied. 'It was only so you'd feel safer. In hindsight it's lucky for you I didn't. Still, sorry. It was stupid of me.'

'Well, Stüter, I suppose I should be grateful you have such a low opinion of me.'

'It's Rolf. My name is Rolf.' Stüter held out his hand.

Jan took it, surprised. 'Jan.'

'Finally burying the hatchet, then,' said Anita. 'I'm holding a press conference with the prosecutor and the Minister for the Interior in an hour. After that it's back to Koblenz. I'll leave you to tidy up here, Herr Stüter.'

'You can call me Rolf too,' he replied.

'As you can probably imagine, I'm not fond of long goodbyes,' said Anita, giving them both a stiff hug and pressing a dry kiss onto Jan's cheek. 'This was one of the most disorganised, appalling and ignominious cases I've ever worked on. But I'm glad I took it.'

'I think you speak for all of us,' said Jan.

'All right. Merry Christmas, then.' She turned to go but threw one last look back at Jan. 'Keep in touch, when you've got time.'

Stüter nudged him after she was gone. 'Something going on there?'

'Between me and Anita?' Jan laughed, amused. 'The only thing going on there is a ceasefire.'

'You've made peace with your local area at last,' said Rolf. 'Maybe you'll even come back from time to time.'

Yes, thought Jan. Maybe he could finally make peace with the past and come back to Westerwald sometime.

Shaking hands once more, they said their goodbyes. With measured steps, he walked back through Bacher Lay, listening as the snow crunched under his boots and the wind rattled in the branches.

He was overcome with the sense of having always belonged here. That this was a place he could call home.

# 85

*21ˢᵗ January*

The University Hospital in Siegen. Jan hadn't been there since December, but he'd kept in touch with Rabea's doctor by phone. Now he was striding down the endless corridors of the Intensive Care Unit.

In the past few weeks he'd had no time to visit. The disciplinary process demanded all his strength, and he was still visiting Kathi in Westerwald regularly to help her come to terms with Maik's death and his true identity. It was therapeutic not just for her but for himself as well. On one of his trips he'd made a detour to see Tugba. Since getting out of hospital she'd been living with her sister but hoped to return to teaching in February. Listening to her talk about her students had reminded Jan that it was all worth it.

Christmas and New Year he'd spent with Miriam. Quiet parties they'd used to catch their breath. Afterwards he'd helped her and the Mainz police to arrest the guy they called Diver, who'd been pursuing her for so long.

He'd also visited Dr Sapkowski's practice in Frankfurt and looked at Tamara's files. Her psychiatrist had evidently learned too much about her life – presumably the reason she'd killed him.

Her apartment was where Tamara had kept the things she'd taken from Gero's widow after his death. A whole library of DVDs and cassettes, sorted alphabetically by the child's name. Children from Eastern Europe and from difficult backgrounds. The first alphabet. Jan still didn't know whether Maik had also been part of Gero's alphabet.

The smell of disinfectant burnt his nose. His trainers squeaked on the linoleum floor. He hated hospitals. Now another right turn. Three doors and he was at Rabea's room.

Today was the first time she'd been capable of conversation, although she was obviously very confused. Her family, who had been with her at the time, had called him straight away.

He knocked at her door without expecting an answer and stepped inside. In her room he sat down on the visitor's chair, next to the table of get-well-soon cards and flowers. He kneaded his hands and lowered his eyes.

Her face was still pale, a little sunken. The ash-blonde hair was neatly combed but dull. At the corners of her mouth he could still see the rebellious twist he'd liked when they first met.

He couldn't help thinking about what had prompted him to give her the job back then. It was the inexplicable, still unsolved disappearance of her sister, Marie, nearly twenty years earlier.

Her sister. His brother.

Both he and Rabea had lost someone to the dark side of human psychology early in life. They were different from the rest of the world, and more similar to each other than outsiders might think.

He reached for her hand, stroking her delicate fingers. 'I couldn't have done it without you,' he whispered.

'Wi – without who?' A breath. Nothing more. Blinking, she opened her eyes, which were sticky with sleep. 'Oh my God!'

He shifted forwards on his chair. 'It's okay, you're safe.'

She swallowed drily. Coughed. Her body doubled up. The ECG spiked.

'Jan, is that you? The alphabet . . . You, you're "Z"!' She tried to sit up.

'Everything's fine.' He squeezed her hand tighter. 'The alphabet will never be finished.'

# Acknowledgements

## A for Acknowledgements

What could be more fitting for a novel like this than to say thank you in alphabetical order? The following, then – from A to Z – are the people who made this book possible by giving me their time, their confidence, their knowledge or simply the space to write in peace for many, many hours.

F for family and friends: Adil, Brigitte, Carissa, the people on the German Writers' Forum, Klaus, Moritz, Renate and Roger.

F for four-legged friend: Felix. I've got another treat for you.

P for Police Station, Montabaur. My thanks go to the press department, and especially to Andreas Bode for his generous help.

U for Ullstein. Here I'd like to thank Heide Kloth, Ingola Lamers, Katrin Fieber and Lara Gross.

**W** for Wortunion. Many thanks to my agent Ilona Jaeger, to Jeannette Wistuba and Patrizia Barth. You gave an eternal doubter back his faith.

And, not least, **W** for Westerwalders: Astrid, Filou, Henrike, Niklas, Simone, Thomas and Tristan.

I have tried to depict Westerwald and the job of profiling as authentically as possible. However, this is still a novel meant for entertainment purposes, so where necessary I have always prioritised dramaturgy over fidelity to the facts. If any errors have crept in, they are mine and mine alone.

Lars Schütz
Düsseldorf, November 2017

Want to read
# NEW BOOKS
before anyone else?

Like getting
# FREE BOOKS?

Enjoy sharing your
# OPINIONS?

Discover

# READERS
# FIRST

Read. Love. Share.

Sign up today to win your first free book:
## readersfirst.co.uk